ANSWERED BONES

NC LEWIS

Copyright © 2022 NC LEWIS

All rights reserved

The characters and events portrayed in this book are fictitious. Any similarity to real persons, living or dead, is coincidental and not intended by the author.

No part of this book may be reproduced, or stored in a retrieval system, or transmitted in any form or by any means, electronic, mechanical, photocopying, recording, or otherwise, without express written permission of the publisher.

CHAPTER 1

Detective Inspector Fenella Sallow walked quickly towards the bar, her gaze fixed on the man with the devil's wisp beard.

The lunchtime crowd filled the Navigator Arms on this crisp Friday in April. A pub for workers who liked their drink strong and their food local. The ancient brick fireplace roared with bright flames as logs crackled and spat. A savoury scent of roast meat, pies, and fried food mixed with the mellow tang of ale.

The man with the devil's wisp beard raised his hands, palms out, back against the bar. No more than five feet tall, he wore black leather trousers and a matching shirt. As he watched the detective approaching, his dark eyes became as wide as his mouth.

Fenella paused. Men with flat caps in jackets with patched elbows sat around bench length tables dipping white bread into brown gravy. Hard faced women in tight headscarves downed glucose stout by the pint. The room cackled with laughter.

She continued to make her way across the bar, Detective Sergeant Robert Dexter a step behind. At a table near the back of the room, Detective Constable

Zack Jones waited. PC Woods and PC Beth Finn stood by the pub door.

They had the man with the devil's wisp cornered.

And, to Fenella's relief, no one in the pub knew they belonged to the Cumbria Constabulary. The Friday lunchtime crowd could get rowdy as they let off steam from a hard week of manual grind. No one wants the police at their end of week party. If her team handled this badly, they would face a raucous squabble with a half-drunken mob.

Softly, softly, catchee monkey.

She scanned the scarred oak bar. A barmaid with bleached black rooted hair in a low-cut top the colour of raisins worked the cash register. The pub landlord chatted to a wizened man in a flat cap who ate pickled onions from a jar. Nice, Fenella thought, and let the breath she'd been holding come out thin and slow between her teeth. That's when the pub door creaked open. A stab of cold air rushed into the room.

"Mick?"

Everyone turned to look at the source of the shout. A nun in a black habit stood in the doorway, hands on hips. She had a long, pale face and wisps of brown hair streaked with grey poked out from her veil. Tucked under her arm was a copy of the *Westmorland News*.

"Mick, you here?" She spoke in a shrill voice, but the accent was clear. American. "Mickey Knowles?"

The call quieted the lunchtime chatter. The

soft spit of logs on the fire made the silence seem even more still. Everyone in the pub turned to watch.

"Anyone seen Micky?" asked the nun to the room. She had an air of fierceness, even brutality, about her in the dimpled light of the pub. "Anyone?"

"Not seen him today, ducky," said a gap-toothed woman in a tight green headscarf, her cane resting at the side of the table. In front of her was a half-eaten plate of steak and kidney pie with beefeater chips. Her thin spindly hand clutched a pint glass of ale. "Who should we say wants him?"

"Let him know Sister Burge wants a word."

"Aye up me ducky." The woman took a long pull from her pint. "I'll spread the word."

The nun took two steps deeper into the pub. Her fierce gaze roamed the room, left hand pointing at the patrons. Her ring finger was missing. Gone. She pulled out a set of prayer beads, hands kneading the string as she continued to scan the bar.

"I expect he'll be here soon," she said. "But I can't wait. He knows what I want and where to find me."

She spun and hurried from the pub.

As the door clattered shut, a blast of cold air spilt into the room and a cheer went up from the crowd.

"Give us a twirl," a man yelled.

"How's about a jig?" bawled the gap-toothed woman in the tight green headscarf, waving her cane.

Fenella turned back to the bar. The devil's wisp stood on the slippery oak counter. He wobbled to get his balance.

"Stop, police," she yelled.

The man didn't. He jumped down on the other side and sprinted through a doorway.

CHAPTER 2

"Hey!"

The landlord moved from the bar towards the doorway where the devil's wisp ran, his face a mask of murderous fury. The crowd began to clap and someone whistled the tune to the World War II song, "Run, Rabbit, Run."

"That's not funny," yelled the landlord. He turned back to the open doorway and ran a hand along the back of his neck, red with aged boil scars. "Come back up here, you drunken fool."

But the devil's wisp had already squeezed through the doorway and disappeared from view.

Fenella clambered over the counter, flashed her warrant card, eyed the darkened doorway and yelled, "Police!"

"What the hell's going on?" the landlord barked.

"Where does that door lead?" Fenella asked.

The landlord stared at the warrant card, and he looked at the cheering crowd and he glanced at the open door where the first few steps dipped away into black.

"I don't want any trouble."

"The doorway, sir?" Fenella spoke with an

urgent tone.

Dexter climbed over the counter to join her.

"I run a respectable establishment," the landlord said. He stared from Fenella to Dexter. "And before you lot ask; I've never seen the bugger before. He's not a local. My regulars can hold their drink. It's the outsiders that cause bother."

"And the door?" Fenella repeated. The first few steps were visible. Steep and down. "Is there an exit?"

The landlord did not answer. He just stared at the doorway, rubbing a hand over the boil scars on his neck.

"It leads to the cellar." The reply came from the woman with bleached black rooted hair in a low-cut top the colour of raisins. "I'm Stacy Bird, Alf's wife." She smiled with a mouth full of teeth which were not her own. "There's nowt in their but casks of ale, a few crates, boxes of crisps and old junk—tables, chairs and the like. We use it as a storeroom. Bloody cold too. No windows or doors. The only way out is the way he went in."

Fenella considered. Her team came to the pub for an end of week lunchtime social. A chance to let their hair down, team build and enjoy a good meal. But as she ordered a second round of food and ale, she saw the man with the devil's wisp beard. For months she'd been chasing leads to find the man. One dead end after another. It was frustrating, and she wondered if he'd simply vanished. Just like her sister, Eve.

Seven years ago, a car crash left Eve in a hospital bed. Her husband, Grant, died. Although she'd suffered injuries, Eve climbed free of the bedsheets, evaded the doctors and nurses, and vanished into the night. No one knew why she left. No one knew where she went. Not a word from Eve until the devil's wisp delivered a note. Penned in blue ink on cream paper. Eve's handwriting.

I'm sorry.

Eve.

And then to see the devil's wisp downing pints at the bar in the Navigator Arms gave Fenella a shock. And by the stunned stare of the devil's wisp before he ran, the feeling was mutual. But now she had him trapped in a windowless cellar.

Softly, softly, catchee monkey.

"Call this one in, Guv?" Dexter asked.

"Let's bring him up here, get his details, have a quiet chat, then decide," Fenella said.

The landlord, Alf Bird, had a different idea. He held up a thick hand. "Now hold on a minute. This pub is private property. You'll need paperwork before you go down there."

"Really?" Fenella said.

Alf folded his arms and stood in front of the cellar door. "Really."

A crowd gathered at the bar. They watched with the attentiveness of theatre-goers at a London West End show.

"For crying out loud, let them look, Alf," said the wizened man in the flat cap, who ate from a jar of pickled onions. "Ain't nowt down there but dust and chicken feathers."

"What you hiding in that cellar, Alf?" asked the gap-toothed woman in the tight green headscarf, pointing her cane at the cellar door.

Alf's hand returned to the boil scars on his neck. "They can't come waltzing in here. It ain't right."

Stacy Bird added, "How'd you like the Old Bill rummaging through your cupboards at home when they feel like it?"

"Yeah, how'd you like it?" Alf echoed with a sneer. He curled his fists and took a step towards Fenella.

"One step closer to the boss and I'll have ya," Dexter growled.

There was something chilling about Alf and Stacy Bird that reminded Fenella of bare-knuckle fighters or soldiers who'd come to enjoy grisly death. She held the large man's gaze. Slowly, he relaxed his fists, flexed his hands, and looked away.

The crowd began to murmur. Someone gave a drunken shout. An agitated slur of curse words at the police intrusion into their Friday unwinding routine. The atmosphere turned hostile as others joined in.

"Shame on you," someone hissed, keeping the language civil.

"You ought to be out catching crooks," another bellowed.

"An Englishman's home is his castle!" yelled a

third.

Fenella ignored the jibes and faced the landlord. "Mr Alf Bird, correct?"

"That's right."

She pointed at the doorway. "And you don't want me to search your cellar?"

"Right again."

"Let 'em take a peep," yelled the gap-toothed woman in the tight green headscarf, enjoying the show. "Suppose that's where you store the fresh food because you serve precious little of it in the bar."

Everyone laughed. The atmosphere changed again, upbeat, light-hearted, but an underlying menace lay just below the surface.

"We know our rights," Mr Bird said. "This pub is private property. No one goes down there without my say-so."

Fenella suspected the cellar stored bootlegged booze and cigarettes. Not her concern, though. She worked for the Port St Giles police station, not the regional crime squad. And there was no way she'd leave the Navigator Arms without the devil's wisp in tow.

"Okay, Mr Bird, we'll be back with paperwork inside the hour. And we will have to close the pub while we wait. I hope that won't be too much of an inconvenience for you." Fenella held his startled gaze. "My team will go stone by stone once we have the order. Might take a day... or two. No knowing what we'll turn up, is there?"

"Now just wait!" Alf Bird bawled. "Can we take

our time and think about this? There ain't no way for the bugger to get out."

"It's happened before," added Stacy Bird. "They don't stay down there for long. Let him sleep it off. Once the cold nips at his balls, he'll come scurrying back up."

Fenella glanced at the bar. The crowd had grown larger. A sea of sharp faces with bleary eyes waiting for her next move. She sensed the tension. The crowd was on the side of the Birds. It was their pub. Their watering hole. Get this wrong and she'd have a riot on her hands.

She walked up to Alf Bird so her face was close to his. In a voice which could be heard throughout the pub, she said, "You've got two choices. One. Step away from that door and let my team through or spend the night in the nick. Which is it to be?"

"Leave him alone, you stinkin' cow," a drunken voice shouted.

Fenella ignored the taunt, didn't even look. "I'll give you three seconds to think about it, Mr Bird. One."

"This ain't right," another voice shouted. The crowd was getting agitated.

"Two," Fenella said, holding Alf Bird's gaze.

"Tell you what," said Alf speaking fast, "I'll go get him. He ain't nowt but a shrimp of a man. A drink for you and your team on the house while you wait? Stacy, pull some pints for our friends in blue."

Which is when a clang rattled up the stairs followed by a deep-throated grunt.

"Sounds like a member of the public is calling for help, Guv," Dexter said.

"Aye, happen you're right," Fenella replied. "We'd best go to investigate. No paperwork required. Step away from the door, Mr Bird."

Alf gawped. "I... er... well... you see..."

Dexter cracked his knuckles. "Step aside, sir."

Alf cursed and rubbed a hand on his neck. But he did not move.

"Let em' through," yelled the gap-toothed woman in the tight green headscarf.

"Sir," Fenella said. "Step away from that door."

Alf Bird swore, rubbed a hand over his boil scarred neck and slowly shuffled from the doorway.

CHAPTER 3

Fenella hated cellars.

She hated them even more when she was off duty and had to chase a perp into one. If she was on duty, she'd have sent a uniformed officer down and hung around at the top until they brought the bugger up.

But when that perp is dressed in black leather, less than five feet in height, might know what happened to her sister, it was a job she'd not let anyone else do.

It was a narrow stairwell with no handrail, just the solid red brick of ancient wall which sloped down into the dark. She eased down the stone steps, breathing in the stink of mould and damp. As she moved, she assessed the situation. Would a cornered devil's wisp put up a fight? Possible. She put that likelihood to low. In her experience, he'd try to flee again rather than let the blows fly. She heard the grunt of Dexter a few paces back and adjusted the chance of a struggle to nil.

She shouted, "This is the police! Show yourself."

Then stopped and listened.

Only the soft breath of Dexter behind and the

fading echo of her voice. She continued down, one hand against the wall. There was the faint smell of the barnyard mingled with the tang of ammonia and damp. It curdled in her nostrils. After a few steps, she once again stopped.

"Step out with your hands where I can see them."

Nothing.

An eerie quiet hung in the damp air. The shadows which faded into the dark added to the spook. And above came the soft drone of voices from the pub. She shook her phone to turn on its torch and slowly made her way to the bottom step.

"You all right down there?" yelled the landlord.

"Aye, stay where you are until we come back up," Fenella replied.

Steadying herself on the uneven floor, she shone the phone torch around the room. Brick walls with a cobbled floor and two broad stone pillars black with grime under a low arched ceiling. Other than that, it looked like a square-shaped room. A vault to store valuables, she thought, or a tomb for the forgotten dead.

And everywhere broken furniture parts. A cracked full-length mirror hung on one wall. It bulged slightly as if poked in the back. Next to it rested an armchair with no seat and a pile of legs from a dining room table. A warped dartboard covered in brown dust leaned against bicycle wheels. From under a pile of army helmets peeped a rusted typewriter.

Dexter said, "Ain't nowt like I expected, Guv. The fuss Mr Bird made, I thought we'd find a smugglers' den." He shone his torch around. "Like his wife said, ain't nowt but junk. Stinks too."

"Aye," Fenella replied, glancing about. "But where is Mr Devil's Wisp hiding?"

They listened. Only a drip from an unseen pipe. It didn't feel right. Too quiet. No movement. The dank air soaked the room with an ice-sharp chill.

"Call it in," she whispered to Dexter. "And stay here to guard the steps while I have a look behind those pillars."

"Righto, Guv," he replied, fingers tapping on his phone.

One devil's wisp.

Two pillars.

Which would it be?

She walked to the nearest pillar, phone tight in her hand, and swept a beam of light to each side of the dark stone.

"This is the police," she shouted and stepped behind the broad bricks. "Show yourself."

Nothing.

A thick darkness cloaked the space, and it took a moment for her eyes to adjust. The only light came from her phone. She swept the bright beam around and realised the room wasn't square, but L-shaped.

More junk. A wooden cabinet, doors wide and inside, a television with a dull green screen bulging like a beer drinker's gut. Against the wall leaned a stout Victorian wardrobe; a dated gothic style unlikely to make a comeback. An iron sink lay on its side next to a stone mortar and pestle. From the thick crust of grime, they had not been used to pound spices for quite some time. No devil's wisp, though.

Fenella stood perfectly still, eyed the second pillar and shone her phone's torch to either side. She started to move, convinced she'd find the devil's wisp crouching in the shadows.

"Show yourself," she said again. "This is the police."

But two things bothered Fenella as she walked on. First, she could not see the door where Dexter waited and in the dull quiet, it seemed as if he wasn't even there. Second, the sound. Just the sharp thud of her footfalls as she edged closer to the stone column.

She stopped to listen for the rasp of breath or the scutter as the devil's wisp changed position. No sound, just a thin drizzle of dust which clung to the still air, carrying with it the faint stench of rot and decay. Again, she was struck by the absolute quietness of the room.

"Step out from behind the pillar," she said. "There's nowhere else to hide."

But the devil's wisp did not step out.

Fenella took a step towards the sturdy brick pillar. A hollow pang thudded in her gut. It pounded like the slow grind of a pestle against mortar—the thrill of anticipation of what came next mixed with fear of the unknown. Always the same battle between curiosity and dread. Always the same result. Her nosiness won.

She moved quickly to one side of the pillar; a beam of light directed to where she thought the devil's wisp was crouched.

"Hands in the air, you're nicked," she yelled.

Except, nowt but cobblestones showed in the beam.

She did a quick three-hundred-and-sixty-degree scan. More junk—an upturned beer crate, glass jugs filled with sludge, and grime-streaked computer parts in a rotted box. No devil's wisp, though.

"He's not here," Fenella yelled, baffled.

Heavy footsteps. Dexter was at her side, scanning his phone's light across the space. The two stood stock-still in the damp dark, astonished and confused. How did the devil's wisp escape from a room from which there was no way out?

CHAPTER 4

"The bugger can't just have vanished, Guv," Dexter said, grizzled face puzzled. "He ain't a ghost."

Fenella puffed out her cheeks and let the air out slowly. "Where the hell has he gone?"

They searched the area, lifting junk and shifting piles of rubbish. Then they walked quickly to the first pillar and continued their hunt.

As Fenella poked at the iron sink, she had the feeling that someone was watching. She turned towards Dexter. He knelt, hands twiddling the knobs on the television. The soft splash of water dripped louder in this part of the cellar. Other than that, the space was as she'd found it minutes before.

It's nowt but the dark playing tricks on your mind, she told herself. Who would be watching? And from where? There was no one else here. Yet, she could not shake the feeling of being watched. Unless...

"That wardrobe," she said, her voice low and slow. "I don't suppose..."

Dexter stood and moved swiftly to the squat wardrobe.

Softly, softly, catchee monkey.

He tugged at the handle.

"Locked," he grunted, then heaved.

The door groaned and came off in his hands; rotted wood splintering in every direction. He stumbled backwards, slipped, and clattered to the ground.

"God Almighty," he yelled.

Not at the fall.

But at the desiccated corpse which tumbled from the wardrobe and clattered on top of him.

CHAPTER 5

Mick Knowles' day went bad fast.

He sat in the galley of his narrowboat, the Gold Kite, moored on the banks of the Port St Giles canal, and tried to enjoy his mug of tea. The curtains were drawn, lights off, so the sun's glow seeped around the edge. But how could he enjoy his Friday afternoon wake-up brew with her always at him?

"What do you think about next June for our wedding?" Jane Ragsdale asked.

"Height of my busy season," Mick replied, lit a cigarette, took a long draw, and then exhaled a spiral of grey smoke through his nose. In front of Mick was an unsliced loaf of bread, a knife, and a slab of cheddar cheese. Breakfast, Jane's way. He didn't eat much bread and wasn't too keen on cheese.

He said, "June won't work."

"This winter then?"

"It'll be cold."

As his gaze wandered from the familiar timber walls, framed print of the Pope, to the worn kettle, Mick found himself reflecting. They had met the previous summer when he worked in a gang which drudged sludge from the canal. Seasonal work. It gave him the winter months to do as he pleased. It was a good life.

Jane peered into a hand mirror and touched her face. "Do you think these wrinkles are getting bigger?"

"No."

"I look like an old hag."

"You've always looked like that."

"They are getting deeper, aren't they?"

"No." Mick flashed a wide smile, showing all his teeth.

Jane's eyes flicked from the mirror. "Don't look at me like that."

"Like what?"

"Like a creature that crawled from a swamp. Like a crocodile." Her gaze went back to the mirror. "I had skin as smooth as Snow White a few years back. Everyone said so. Now look at it. The dwarfs had better skin. I still look good, don't I?"

Mick didn't answer and wondered what about the woman had hooked him in. Her oval face with its pug nose and large innocent eyes? On their second date, Jane announced the landlady had kicked her out. She moved into his narrowboat, having nowhere else to stay and attached herself to his life with limpet force. He didn't notice the wrinkles then. Saw them now.

Jane said, "Ten months since we met, it's like one of those telly romances."

"Ten months isn't long in a relationship," he said, but to him, it felt much longer.

"Long enough for you to propose," she

snapped, her quick temper rising.

Yes, guilty as charged, but on that night he'd downed four pints of stout and as many whisky chasers while Jane watched, sipping from a small glass of red wine. Nowt but a blur remained in his brain cells. But the following morning's memory burned bright—Jane's thin-lipped grin as she asked with sour breath when he'd buy her engagement ring.

He'd tried to tell her it had been a drunken mistake. Jane had simply stared at him coldly, her pebble-grey eyes dots of ice. Mary, Mother of God, his courage failed before he got to the part that she should move out at once and get out of his life for good.

Now she watched him with that look on her face. When they first met, he'd mistakenly taken it as the desire for his physical touch. Not so. Life in that department was about as exciting as a Bishop's Y-fronts now she'd got a bee in her bonnet about wedding bells ringing.

He sighed, drained the dregs from his mug and took another pull on his cigarette. Jane's life seemed to revolve around one devious scheme after another. She'd said her stay would be a night or two; then until she'd found a job. Now, somehow, he had proposed, and they would soon be wed.

Mick tilted the empty mug to his mouth and watched her for a long while. That girlish face, pug nose, large innocent eyes, and smell of weed. Yes, there was a sweetness to her face, but she could be as savage as a pit bull. He had to be careful. She knew his secret.

"Are you excited, Micky?" she asked in her little girl voice.

The voice he'd found so sexy when she first called him Micky. The voice which now pestered him day and night about the wedding. The squeaking, squealing high pitched voice that came to nag him in his dreams.

"Yes, very excited," he said.

"You don't sound it."

Mick didn't reply and thought about getting a dog. He'd been thinking about it for years. But the first time Jane climbed aboard the boat, she'd been pleased there was no dog in sight. She didn't like dogs and said they could do without. He knew different. A hound would be better company, forever grateful, didn't make plans for him, and would do as it was told.

He poured more tea into his mug and added a dash of milk. He didn't take his brew strong or with sugar and liked to drink it in the quiet dark while he smoked. Footsteps crunched on the towpath and mixed with mumbled voices. He picked up the mug and took a sip. Somewhere a dog barked.

"Let's plan for the winter," Jane said. "I've got my hands on a beautiful wedding dress."

"No rush," Mick replied, stubbing out the cigarette. "We've got the rest of our lives stretching out before us."

"You're forty-two, Micky. At your age, you'd be

lucky to catch a broiling hen. You are blessed to have a girl as young as me."

"Mm," Mick replied.

"What does that mean?"

"All I'm saying is that these things don't need rushing."

"Ten months is a long time."

"I know."

"We'll have to ditch this boat and rent a flat in town with large windows and no curtains; lots of sunlight for my plants. I have a friend who has a place going cheap."

"You're winding me up," he said and saw the mug trembling in his hand. He loved his narrowboat, called it the Gold Kite because with gold you can fly anywhere you wish.

"I want to have bairns before I'm thirty-two," Jane snapped. "We can't have a baby if we are living on a boat. It's just not right. Our bairns will have a nice home and garden to play in. Why don't we get wed at the town hall? No need to book a church and it will be quick."

A sudden urge gripped Mick. A violent itch to thrust his mug into her pug nose and squeeze his thick hands around her neck until her face turned purple, veins burst and pebble-grey eyes swelled from their sockets.

"What is it?" Jane asked, voice filled with alarm.

"Nowt. I just got lost in my thoughts."

"You went so quiet. And that look on your

face... it was... horrible."

Mick put the mug down, shot her a crocodile grin, and trudged to the aft door. In that instant, a plan formed and solidified. Heat rose to his cheeks, and he felt suddenly happy.

"Where are you going?" she asked.

"Work."

"Good, we'll need the extra cash when the baby comes, and I have got a little earner I'm working on the side." Jane looked at Mick, smiled and spoke in a little girl's voice. "Micky, it won't be long before we ditch this boat, move into a flat and then save for our dream cottage in the country. You've made my wishes come true."

Mick tore off a hunk of bread and slashed off a slab of cheese with the bread knife. He folded the bread around the cheese and stuffed it into his pocket. He licked his dry lips and climbed up the steps to the aft door. The door handle squeaked as it turned.

"Get some oil for that, will you, Micky? You know I don't like the noise, reminds me of mice."

He turned to stare at her. She went to the kitchen and spooned sugar into a mug from an oversized jar, grinning to herself. She'd grinned at him that way when she said her landlady had kicked her out. And the same grin kissed her lips that groggy morning when she'd asked him about the engagement ring.

He said, "Why the hell do you take so much sugar?"

"What's wrong with having a sweet tooth?"

"It will kill you."

"Don't be daft. Now sod off to work. I've got things to do."

Again Mick licked his lips, flexed his strong hands, turned away and climbed onto the deck. Jane had her plans, and now he had his.

CHAPTER 6

Sloane Kern dropped onto the sofa and leaned back against its plush cushion and fretted.

In front of her, the flames danced in the large gas fireplace. Bamboo chimes played softly in the background. The remains of a delicious meal lay on the table, along with an empty bottle of red wine and another halfway through. As her gaze roamed from the polished oak floor to the watercolour paintings on the wall, she tried to think of the last time she spent lunchtime alone with her boyfriend, Jack Parkes. And on a Friday in his posh Westpond flat, too.

Jack said, "What's wrong, honey?"

"Headache."

"You've been having a lot of those lately."

"I'll be fine in a moment."

"You need to see a doctor."

He curled an arm around her and rested his head on her shoulder. He wore a tweed jacket and a crystal healing bracelet on his wrist. Odd, Sloane thought. Very odd. She said nothing, didn't want to ruin the atmosphere. But he'd been acting strange recently, and she feared he was bored with her and her three kids.

It was exhausting being a single mother, a role she'd never signed up for. Her three girls were always at each other's throats. Jack was kind, but taking on a ragged middle-aged mum and her three stroppy kids required never-ending patience. Was his odd behaviour and this meal his way of saying goodbye?

In a matter of seconds, his breaths became heavy, and he let out a soft snore. Sloane stared at the watercolour paintings on the wall and wished there was a telly. Jack wasn't one for the goggle box and still played vinyl records. A romantic die-hard to the past.

On their second date, he'd gifted her a bottle of perfume. Lust by Lush. She'd never dreamed of wearing such an expensive fragrance with her first husband, Tim. They couldn't afford to splurge on luxuries back then. Once, she'd tried to make her own perfume with the help of her kids. They had used rose petals, distilled water and vodka. It had turned into a soggy mess which smelled about as good as it looked. When Tim came home, he wasn't happy. They had used the last third from his Glen's vodka.

Sloane glanced at her watch. She'd arranged a meeting at two and didn't want to be late. And she needed time to change and squirt on a few puffs of Lust by Lush.

Just a few minutes more peace.

She closed her eyes, felt the warmth of the wine, the heat from the fireplace and tried with increasing anxiety to tell herself things were fine. Everything was under control. There was absolutely no need to fret.

"What's wrong?" Jack said, suddenly sitting up. His forty-eight-year-old body flexed with the firmness of a twenty-year-old weightlifter.

"Nothing."

"Come on, Sloane, I can feel your negative energy." He rubbed the crystal bracelet and then kissed her on the lips. "The Chakra energy's never wrong. What's up, honey?"

"Can we just sit and enjoy each other?"

Jack ran a hand through his thick hair. "Trouble is, you are sitting in this room, but not here with me. The vibrations are all wrong. I felt it as we ate and you had that distant glare. I love you, Sloane. Tell me what's up."

She walked to the table, filled two glasses with wine, and handed one to him, then sat and tipped her glass to her lips, drained a third, then took another glug.

"It's work," she said and finished the drink. "It's so unreliable."

"You are fantastic at your job." He spoke in a soothing tone that always made her feel at ease. "The best anger management counsellor in Port St Giles... no Cumbria!"

She looked at him and knew how lucky she'd been.

"Thank you," she said, swallowing back a sob. She was the strong one. That's what everyone said when she was with Tim. But no one knew how deep that cut went. She didn't let her daughters see her tears. "Business is slow... has been slow for some time."

"Did you put that bowl of red jasper crystals on your desk?"

"Yes."

But she hadn't. They were still on the back seat of her car, where she'd tossed them late last week.

"They haven't helped," she said, feeling a pang of guilt.

"The energy takes time to build. It cannot be rushed."

"I know."

The soft chimes of bamboo filled the room. Jack closed his eyes and let out meditative breaths. At last, eyes open and soft, he said, "Our energy is so aligned it makes me want to weep." He let his eyelids close, and then let out a long yoga breath. "Your business, didn't the government give you a contract?"

"Yes and no. It renews every six months. If they don't renew, too bad."

"Honey, are you trying to say that—"

"I can barely afford the rent on my office. The bills are crushing me, and my client list has shrivelled to a handful of nutcases. I... I don't know what to do. It is dog eat dog these days in the therapy business. We fight tooth and nail over the barrel of fish. That's what therapists call their clients—fish. They croon if they land a fat cod and wail if their net hauls in a minnow. And then there are the arrogant clients. Shrewd lawyers get them anger management training when they should be locked behind bars and the key thrown away."

"Come on honey," Jack said, touching his bracelet. "I've never heard you talk like that. You are always the positive one. Strong. Full of chakra energy."

"I'm sorry." She sighed. "Since the government cutbacks, I've not had any referrals from social services. Not even a minnow. Nothing from the prison service, either. At least the police still send me their defects."

Jack placed his arm around her and kissed her on her cheek. "I want to help."

"That's so kind, but I don't want a loan from you."

"I'm not offering." Jack put his wine glass beside the sofa and got down on one knee, reached into the pocket of his tweed jacket and pulled out a small black box. "I am offering to make you my wife. The girls too. One big family."

Sloane's heart beat faster. She placed her small hand on her cheek and sobbed. She never imagined their meal would lead to a proposal. But the signs were there. The fireplace, wine, Jack in his tweed jacket and now the diamond engagement ring which glittered in the firelight. That's why he'd been acting odd. It all made wonderful sense.

Jack slipped the ring on her finger. She couldn't stop crying. Jack had money, while she had none.

Inside she howled with joy.

CHAPTER 7

Sloane Kern slowly turned her hand, studying the engagement ring as it glittered in the firelight. This was the gateway to her new life. Here with Jack Parkes. Here in Westpond with her three girls. Here where the rich folk lived. It was so perfect she couldn't stop the tears.

"Oh dear," Jack said, his voice sad. "I didn't mean to upset you. I suppose two years is too soon?"

"You didn't," Sloane said, wiping her eyes with the back of her hand and hugging him. "I love you, Jack."

"You'll soon be Mrs Parkes."

"I don't want to change my last name. I want to stay Mrs Kern."

"But that's Tim's surname!"

"I've got used to it."

"I see."

Sloane kissed him lightly on the lips. "I knew you would," she said in her little girl's voice, leaning into his chest. "My Prince Charming always does."

The bamboo chimes grew louder. A resounding clatter and clang. Then they tapered off to a low jangle that sounded like a cat's purr.

"Maybe I've jumped the gun?" Jack eased her

away. "I didn't want to pressure you to take on my name, and I know Bren can be difficult. But don't be too hard on her. She's the oldest and remembers her dad more clearly. I think she still misses him and can understand if she doesn't want me around—"

Bren had just turned sixteen and had picked up an extra shift at Logan's Bakery to help her mum pay the bills. She brought home stale bread, meat pies, and cakes. It helped cut the food bill a little.

"Shush!" Tears streamed down Sloane's cheeks. "Bren needs a father figure in her life. They all do."

This was so exciting. Sloane could barely hold the thought of being Jack's new wife in her mind. She stared at her left hand and liked the way the ring glittered. *Look at the size of those stones!*

"I'm crying because I love you and... I... er..." Sloane's eyes darted to her watch. She had to leave soon, or she'd be late for her meeting and miss her chance. "... I didn't tell you the whole truth."

His eyes grew wide and focused. "Is there someone else?"

"No, not that."

"It's just that I... er..." She searched her handbag, shook two pills into her hand and swallowed without water. "... I've taken on another client."

"That's good, isn't it?"

"A man."

His jaw dropped. "But you only work with women!"

"He was referred to me three weeks ago. I

couldn't refuse. There was nowhere else to place him. I had to help. It's what I do."

The sofa creaked as Jack shifted his position. He stared into her face, eyes soft and filled with understanding. His hand touched his bracelet.

"So, what's the problem?"

Sloane gazed at her new ring. "Something very wrong happened in a counselling session."

"Did he touch you?"

"God no!"

"What's his name?"

Ethics didn't allow her to share confidential patient information. A breach would result in her being struck off. Then again, Jack's face demanded an answer, and she was soon to be his wife. Sloane glanced at the ring. It seemed to glitter brighter.

"His name is Mick Knowles," she said slowly and felt a pang of guilt. "He likes women to call him Micky. I think he'd be better off with a psychiatrist. He has serious issues."

Jack looked concerned. "So, he's one staircase short of the landing?"

"I wouldn't put it like that."

"How would you put it?"

"He has no landing. Mick Knowles is so damaged he frightens me."

CHAPTER 8

"You have arrived," squawked the navigation device.

Detective Sergeant Ria Leigh shook with rage as she pulled the unmarked Ford to the curb. At forty-eight, she was long and lean. No grey streaks in her close-cropped brown hair. Ten years in the regional crime squad, first time on this street.

She let out a slow breath to help control the shaking. After a count of ten, she scanned the semidetached houses. They snaked in an arc along Irt Avenue. A working-class street with green privet hedges and mowed lawns in Whitehaven.

She'd worked her way through her contacts to trace Ray Briggs to this place. Briggs had a string of drug offences going back twenty years. At thirty-four years old, he'd started early.

CCTV had caught him arguing with the doorman at Jabbar's nightclub the previous night. Briggs up to his old tricks. Selling drugs to students out on the razzle. The clubs in Ria's patch of Whitehaven were drug free, and she intended to keep it that way. Civic Officer of the year, awarded by Chief Constable Alfred Rae three years in a row, was the reward for her efforts.

Catching drug dealing perps was like crack. The more you had, the more you craved it, and Ria Leigh needed more of one and less of the other on her patch in Whitehaven. An obsession, that's how she viewed the job. She wasn't sure how it had happened. Or even when. But now that it had, she focused on drug crime like an archer on the bullseye.

No boyfriend these days. No friends outside of the force. Every ounce devoted to the police. Every second thinking about work. Cleaning the streets and winning Civic Officer of the year for the fourth year straight was Ria's goal.

She re-checked her notes on Briggs to confirm the address, then spent a few minutes going over his file. Last offence, sixth months ago. A hefty fine for possession of cannabis outside St Benedict's high school. He'd been collared by a nun—Sister Burge. Ria's body shook with rage. Briggs got off lightly. She knew he dealt in opioids.

Her gaze fixed on the house with the flag of St George draped from the bedroom window. A brass lion's head knocker hung from the faded orange door. The last known address of Ray Briggs. His mum's house. There's no place like home.

Ria wasn't on duty. She'd taken the week off to make plans to move from her flat into a new house. But when your mother chokes to death in her vomit because of a drug overdose, you are never off the job.

A sudden rage consumed her with such force both hands shook. She closed her eyes, listened, and counted to five. *One.* The groan of a car as it rumbled along the road. *Two, three.* Music pounding from a distant window. *Four, Five.* The harsh rasps of her breath.

As she remembered what had happened on the night her mum died, a fresh wave of rage boiled inside her. She'd never hear her mum's voice again. She swallowed a mouthful of water from her reusable stainless-steel bottle, then took two pills and waited five minutes.

Calmer now.

Much calmer.

A slanted blast of sunlight peeked through the dark clouds as she climbed from the car. Cold for April, she thought as she crossed a patch of brown grass and opened the iron gate. A curtain twitched. A fleeting image appeared in the window. An ashen face. Male. Ray Briggs was in the house.

The door opened a crack before Ria's hand pressed the bell.

A voice hissed, "No witnesses. No tinkers. Get lost."

The door slammed shut.

Ria cleared her throat and then pounded the brass lion's head door knocker. On the third whack, the door opened wide.

"I said no hawkers," bawled a short elderly woman with a flat nose and blackened teeth which jutted from her mouth. She smelled of strong drink and held a thick walking stick. Mrs Kay Briggs, Ray's mum. She had form for drug use and dealing. A family tradition. "Now bugger off before I call the—"

"Police," Ria said, as she held out her warrant card.

For several seconds Mrs Briggs stared at the card. Warm air bellowed from the hall. It smelled of fried food.

"Wondered what that stink was," Mrs Briggs said. "Thought the toilets were clogged, but no, it's the stench of the Old Bill."

Ria ignored the barbs. Par for the course. She glanced over Mrs Briggs' shoulder into the hall.

"I'd like a word with your son."

"Ain't here. Don't know where he has gone neither." Mrs Briggs sniffed, voice cracking. "What a thing is life when your own flesh and blood ignore you. I'm here on my own since my Carl died."

Ria knew Mr Carl Briggs was alive, healthy and had put on weight in Low Marsh Prison. She'd checked on that fact before she arrived.

She said, "Can I come in for a quick chat?"

"No." Mrs Briggs half turned as though she were trying to see back into the house. She raised her voice. "The police ain't brought me nowt but luck of the bad kind."

Ria persisted. "So, you haven't seen Ray?"

"I'm saying nowt."

Mrs Briggs moved to shut the door.

Ria angled her foot inside the frame, kept her voice low and hissed, "I'm not leaving without a chat with your son."

"Get yer bleedin' boot from me door!"

"If I do that, guess what? I'll be back with blue

flashing lights and a team of officers. They'll turn this place over while the neighbours watch. Want that, do you?"

Mrs Briggs hesitated. "What the hell do you want my lad for?"

"He's been up to his old tricks. Selling drugs outside nightclubs to teens and students."

"Don't be daft. He's gone clean. Our family don't do drugs no more."

"I see. That clears that up, then, doesn't it?" Ria waited a heartbeat. "If you like, I can come back later with the paperwork and flashing lights but thought it best to do things on the quiet for your sake. I know you like to keep a few of your supplies in your home."

Mrs Briggs' face darkened. She half-turned and bellowed, "Ray, get your arse here right now."

A door squeaked in the dim hallway and a twig thin man appeared. He wore dark jogging pants and a hooded top, both black. He slouched to the front door.

"Speak with her," Mrs Briggs commanded, then disappeared back into the house.

But he didn't speak, just stood there staring through hooded eyes.

Ria said, "What you been up to, Ray?"

He shrugged. "Nowt."

Ria raised her left hand, thumb and forefinger jerking in a plucking motion. "How about a little reminder? Like last night outside of Jabbar's. Does that help?"

He shook his head with gusto. "I stayed in last night to watch the telly. Mum will vouch for me."

"I've got a doorman who says different."

"Case of mistaken identity. Drugs ain't my style. Not no more. Them's for youngsters. My next big birthday I'll turn forty. I'm almost an old man."

"Who said anything about drugs?"

He blinked. "Why else would you be here? I'm clean, didn't do nowt."

"I have CCTV, along with five witnesses who say you tried to sell them drugs. Oh, and your ploy of sending text flares, we've got those on file as well."

Text flares were messages sent by drug dealers to local users. They contained details of what was for sale, the prices, and when and where to buy. Most used burner phones. Ray Briggs sent texts from his mobile. Not the actions of a criminal mastermind.

Ria was still speaking. "How do ten years in Low Marsh Prison suit your style?"

Fear filled his face. "I ain't no big-time crook. Why are you always harassing us small folk who are trying to get ahead?"

"Because that's how we keep the streets clean," Ria replied. She took in his gaunt face and knew he was still a user. "Where are you getting your stuff?"

"Don't know what you are on about."

One thing she'd learned about small fry drug dealers, they kept their supply close. And with his mum a confirmed user and hardened drinker, he'd keep his goods closer than most.

"Turn out your pockets."

He looked surprised, even turning to glance behind him into the hall of the house as though she'd asked someone else. Then he gave a crooked smile and placed his hands in his pockets. "Eh?"

"You heard me."

"This ain't right, I'm—"

"Now!"

He swore, reached into the pocket of his hooded top, and pulled out five clear plastic bags.

"It's only a bit of weed, man. That's all I got. Honest."

Ria tipped them into a large evidence bag, then said, "And the rest."

"You've cleaned me out. Ain't nowt more."

"Want to argue the toss down the nick?"

He grunted, riffled in his pockets, and pulled out three clear bags, each filled with ten white pills.

Ria stared for a moment, taking in their shape and size. oxycodone. The drug that killed her mum. Even now, all these years later, the sight of the pills made her livid. An anger management therapist in Port St Giles helped her control the rage. She sucked in a breath, counted to five and let the air come out from deep down in her lungs.

She said, "Please explain these pills."

"Just a bit of oxy," Ray said, handing over the stash. "Don't do no harm and it helps folk with their pain."

Ria sucked in another sharp breath. "Where'd you get these?"

"Dunno."

"Ray!"

"Port St Giles."

"Name?"

"Dunno her name."

"A woman then?"

"Dunno."

If she were on duty, she'd have her partner pat him down. Rodents like Briggs always kept some back. But she'd got a decent hoard with his fingerprints all over the evidence. Good enough.

Ray was speaking fast, voice high pitched and wobbly, "Like I say, I'm going straight and that gear is the old stock which—"

"Save it for the judge," Ria barked.

The regional crime squad's anti-drug strategy focused on kingpins. If you cut off the head of the beast, it was supposed to die. The problem? It took forever to bag a bigwig while small fry like Ray Briggs clogged up her desk with paperwork. Then when you killed the beast another rose in its place. If you wanted to keep your patch clean, there was only one way. Push the prawns like Ray Briggs out of your area and warn them to stay out. That's how you won Civic Officer of the year three years in a row.

Ria said, "If I catch you selling gear on my patch again, this little lot comes out and down you go." She waved the evidence bags under his nose. "Understand?"

Ray Briggs nodded, face flush with relief.

And with Ray Briggs suitably warned, Ria checked her phone and quickly walked away.

Not standard police protocol.
Civic policing, the Ria Leigh way.

CHAPTER 9

Detective Sergeant Ria Leigh raced from her car, praying she wasn't late.

She'd parked in the only space free in the small carpark next to the Whitehaven Soup Kitchen on Irish Street. Georgian houses with iron railings and cherry trees in full bloom surrounded the car lot. She ran across the black tarmac, skidding to a stop by a stand of trees. A shopping trolly blocked her path.

"Oi, what's the rush?"

An old woman hunched over the trolly. It was filled with plastic bags. Deep lines creased her dirt-smudged face, and she reeked of cheap beer and old sweat. "Why can't you young folk show us oldies a bit of respect?"

Ria glanced at the bags and knew they held rags, crushed cans, glass bottles and scraps of paper. She knew too what Mrs Shedgett wanted.

"Spare a little change," Mrs Shedgett said. "Cause you nearly tipped over me shopping and food ain't no good when it falls on the ground. Just a couple of quid to ease me shock."

With a frustrated breath, Ria said, "Mrs Shedgett, what are you doing here?"

The woman fished around in her pocket, pulled out a pair of glasses, put them on, and tilted her head. "Oh, bugger me!" Broken teeth filled her red lipstick-stained mouth. "I'm not begging, Ria. No, no, no. Them's a contribution I asked for, cos you startled me and I have... er... doctor's bills to pay. All right?"

Ria knew what Mrs Shedgett was up to, but she was in a hurry and didn't have time to make a fuss. She dropped two pound coins into the bony grime-streaked outstretched hand.

"Tar very much," Mrs Shedgett said. "Some gets all funny if they see me begging... er... asking for a contribution outside the soup kitchen. You are all right, Ria."

Ria flashed a smile. "I hope you will join us for lunch."

"Nah, not eaten yet," Mrs Shedgett said. "I've got a couple more quid to beg, then I'll have enough for me after lunch ale. It's chicken curry today, that lines the stomach well for me booze."

One day a month, on her day off, Ria volunteered at the Whitehaven Soup Kitchen. She served meals, washed dishes and mopped floors, just like her mum did before she died. Ria wouldn't let the family tradition go. She loved it unless she arrived late and ended up on dishcloth duty.

And if she didn't get a move on, that is exactly what would happen today.

CHAPTER 10

Inside, the brightly lit hall smelled of spices, disinfectant and unwashed bodies. Servers dished out great dollops of rice, curry and steamed vegetables. One woman served in an African kanga dress and pink sandals. Mumble of voices. Clatter of plates. A sharp shout followed by a bark of laughter. The soup kitchen served more than hunger.

Ria cursed under her breath. She was too late to bag a server spot. She shuffled to a cleaning station, grabbed a cart, bowl and dishcloth and began clearing tables. A thankless task. Scrape the plates; put them in the cart, wipe the table with a soap-filled rag and repeat.

She was thirty minutes into the tedium when she saw Mrs Shedgett shuffle to a table with her bag laden trolly and a plate full of steaming hot curry and rice. The woman was a regular. She'd lived on the streets of Whitehaven for as long as Ria or her mum remembered. No one knew how she became homeless. One rumour said her child died at birth and she spiralled down from there. Ria didn't ask. Mrs Shedgett knew where to get a hot meal and lay her head down to sleep. If she didn't, Ria would have stepped in to help.

Ria pushed the cart full of dirty dishes back to the kitchen and unloaded it. It was another world back here. The sharp stench of the unwashed was replaced by the fragrance of expensive perfumes. Most volunteers were middle-aged women who came from middle-class backgrounds. And they had done well for themselves, wives of lawyers, bankers and executives. In two steps, Ria had travelled across British society. The needy in the food hall. Those with money in the kitchen.

When she first volunteered, the number of highly strung women shocked her. They had enormous homes, posh cars, the works. Yet their lives were full of stressful drama.

"Just like those who have nowt," her mum had said. "Ain't no one can get free from life stresses. It touches everyone. Best we can do is listen and throw out a word or two to see them through."

She missed Mum.

When Ria was four years old, she suffered from nightmares. She remembered the warm arms of her mum rocking her to sleep. Mum would sing Judy Garland's Over the Rainbow in soft midnight tones to chase away her bad dreams.

And Ria remembered the night terrors that jerked her awake, eyes wide and screaming. It always started the same way. Pitch black except for a dot of starlight which shone on a giant spider. The light moved as it slunk across the ceiling. It stopped on the tile above her head.

She couldn't close her eyes to make it go away.

Her hands and feet were too heavy to move. It spun a single thread, descending slowly, long legs twitching.

"Go away," she yelled, but the words came out as dust.

It stopped an inch above her face and hovered, watching.

Ria opened her mouth to scream, but it was filled with cobwebs. The spider's whole body jerked in a primaeval dance.

Slowly, the silk thread extended. Lower and lower, the spider inched until its thin legs hovered just above her wide-open eyes. That's when she'd wake up screaming and find herself in her mum's arms.

Now Ria glanced about. Her mum loved the food hall. She'd sit at the long bench tables and chat with the homeless and unwashed. Not Ria. She liked the kitchen. She loved to hear about the women's middle-class lives, stare at their fancy jewellery and dream about what it would be like to wear a diamond necklace or a glittering ring. And she made a point of getting to know those whose burdens weighed them down. She got their names and gave them her ear and friendship. That she worked for the police, she kept to herself. There is a stigma about law enforcement in the elite.

When Ria returned to the food hall, she sensed something was off. She looked across the room. The low mutter of voices. Bobbing heads. Scrape of fork against plate. Curry infusing the room with an exotic tang. Everything in place. Yet her gut warned of trouble.

A family group—mum and dad and three small children—walked through the entrance and lined up by the food counter. And Mrs Shedgett's plate of food lay on the floor as a thin man in a hoodie tugged at her trolly.

Ria sprinted over and grabbed the man by his arm. "Leave her be."

The gaunt youth swayed on shaky legs. "Just a bit of fun with the old nag. Didn't mean no harm."

Ria guessed twenty years at most, but he looked much older. The lad took more drugs than food, skin wrinkled and drawn. She wagged the index finger of her left hand and then let the finger and thumb come together in a plucking motion.

"This is a safe space," she said, jabbing a flat palm into his chest. "For everyone."

People quarrelled in soup kitchens. Fights broke out. No one paid much attention. They were too busy with their own worries.

Ria glanced around. Not even a sideways look from anyone. She flashed her warrant card and stared at his pockets. Oxy, weed or something else?

The lad moved a step back from the cart. His left hand tugged his ear as his eyes darted to the door. Too far to make a run. And on his shaky legs, he'd not get far.

Ria leaned forwards and hissed, "Don't let me see you in here again, got it?"

Whatever he had in his pockets, it wouldn't be

much. Personal use only. Not worth the paperwork, especially on her day off.

The lad spun on his heels and sped towards the exit.

When Ria picked up the plate from the floor and placed it on her cart, she saw Mrs Shedgett back in the food queue. The old woman chatted with the family and played a game of who can make the funniest face with their youngest child. Their laughter carried across the hall.

After the last meal had been served and the food hall emptied of guests, Ria went to the storeroom to put away her cart. Rows of shelves snaked the length of the room. Tin vegetables along one aisle, packet goods on another, cereal and canned fruit on a third. She put the cart in the cupboard. A moment later came the whisper of a middle-class woman's voice.

"I am so sorry for you, Felicity. My heart squeezes. What do doctors know? Listen, I ignored mine. Jolly good I did, got what I needed from a friend of a friend. The thing is, it is much cheaper if you buy it from Port St Giles, and your silly doctor doesn't need to know."

Ria shrank back into the shadows of the cupboard, listening.

"Are they cheaper than your usual supplier?" asked another woman's voice.

"Very much so," replied the first. "And it's a pleasant drive. I've let my old friend know I won't be using them again. They were rather beastly about it." The voice paused and became so quiet it was barely audible. "My new contact only sells oxy to women like us. Jane Ragsdale is discrete. Come for sups on Sunday while the men are out shooting. We'll pop a few pills, drink a couple of bottles of red wine and get totally blotto."

CHAPTER 11

This is wrong, very wrong.

Mick Knowles kept that thought to himself and grinned. He'd left Jane on his narrowboat. She thought he'd gone in search of work to help pay for the rent on a new flat she had her eye on. Nothing could have been further from Mick's mind.

He ran a hand through his salt and pepper hair, carefully patting it down over his bald spot. Since he turned forty, his hair seemed to be getting thinner on top. Maybe he should shave his head?

She was waiting for him in the disused carpark by the canal.

"Micky!"

The way she called his name reminded him of his gran. That made him feel good, but he knew his mood could flip at any moment. He sucked in his beer gut, his walk turning into a swagger. She brought out the young man in him.

"How do," he said, eyeing her pert breasts and bright eyes.

She said, "I like your smile. Reminds me of a pet crocodile."

"They are dangerous animals."

"That's why I like it."

He stooped to peck her cheek and sniff her fragrance.

"You smell nice."

"Lust by Lush," she said in a saucy voice. "Like it?"

"Aye, happen I do."

"What about the coat?"

She wore a stylish beige coat with big buttons and flat shoes.

"Love it," Mick said. "Makes you look like a Paris model."

The April sun lifted the chill. Slabs of dark clouds hung low in a blue sky. Abandoned warehouses littered this part of town. Crumbling red brick with smashed windows like jagged teeth. Chimney stacks sagged under their weight. Mick hated to see the buildings in such disrepair. They were once tall and proud and shouted prosperity. Now they were bloated and broken, like a liar struggling to keep up with their lies.

They strolled from the carpark along a narrow dirt trail to the towpath. It followed the canal, bounded on one side by the dark water and the other by a fence which held back bushes and trees. During the mornings and evenings, workers and school children crowded the towpath. A scenic cut-through. At two in the afternoon, they were the sole strollers.

Mick felt like he was floating on a cloud. His mood was so good it frightened him. He knew after the high came the low and with it the danger of dark rage. He wouldn't let it happen. Not this time. Not with her. It was a promise he'd made before, and broken every time.

He glanced at her. "How are things with Jack?"

"He's still a vet and still saving the animal kingdom."

"That's good, isn't it?"

"If you like dogs and cats, I suppose it is."

"And you?"

"I can get along with cats. Dogs frighten me."

An urge to grab her neck and squeeze suddenly seized Mick. Casually, he turned around, scanning the crumbled building that abutted the carpark and the stand of trees by the trail.

No one watching.

Good.

She looked at him. "What's to do?"

"How'd you mean?"

"Who are you looking for?"

"No one."

"Don't lie to me."

Easy to read, that's what his gran always said. The old woman read Mick's face better than a large print book. It seemed she read him just as easily. Mick didn't like that. Rage stirred.

He said, "Thought I saw someone watching. Nowt but a shadow. We are alone."

She looked at him and smiled. "Where are we going?"

"It's a surprise."

"Thought you'd take me to your boat. It's nice

and warm."

"Can't. Jane's there."

"You said she'd left. Packed her bags and moved out, that's what you said."

Mick didn't remember, but it sounded true. "Won't be long now before she is gone for good."

"You said she went to Australia to live with her long-lost aunt." She paused, thinking. "Or was it New Zealand?"

"Jane changed her mind," he snapped. "She is always changing her mind. That's why it won't work."

"So, she is still living on the narrowboat?"

"Yes."

"I see."

They walked on in silence. In the distance came the whimper of a dog. Hidden by the leaves of a tall beech tree a Jay screamed. Mick looked up to see a flash of blue, then its bright white rump. From deep in the bushes, a cat yowled. Mick liked to hear the animal sounds as they walked. It reminded him he was part of the animal kingdom, soothed his nerves and gave him time to go over his plan. The jay screamed again.

She turned to Mick and sniffed. "Have you been married before?"

"Almost. A long time ago."

"What happened?"

Mick hated to talk about it. He felt another wave of rage wash over him and kept walking.

"You said no secrets," she said.

He didn't reply.

"Are you going to tell me?"

"She left me," he replied in a tone that made it clear he'd not say any more about it.

"I'm sorry," she said in a small voice. "I didn't mean to pry."

They walked on without speaking. The soft scrunch of their shoes and the distant putter of a narrowboat filled the verbal void. With a slow movement, Mick patted his left jacket pocket and felt the outline of the bread and cheese he'd crammed in before he left the Gold Kite. He squeezed it slightly with his strong fingers. It yielded to his firm grip, and he felt good.

They passed the blackened carcass of an oak tree. Its scorched branches jutted through the iron railings like pointing fingers. Again came the whimper of an unseen dog. Again came the screams of the jay.

She said, "Where are we going?"

"I told you, it's a surprise."

She thought for a moment. "The Navigator Arms!"

He stared at her in shock.

She laughed. "I always know what you're thinking."

"What am I thinking now, then?"

She placed her small hand on her cheek. "How I knew about your surprise."

"Yeah," he drawled, staring at her through narrowed eyes. "How did you know?"

"You work there sometimes when you are not lugging furniture or dredging the canal." She giggled. "Anyway, I can read your face."

"Smart lass," Mick replied, feeling uneasy.

She watched him. "A late lunch by the canal sounds nice. Shame it isn't warmer else we'd sit outside. Is that where you met Jane?"

"No. The Arms is my place."

"A bolt hole?"

"Of sorts."

"Our place now."

Again, he stared at her through narrowed eyes. "Aye."

She giggled. Girlish. "I feel special today."

"Wouldn't take you there if you weren't. Me thinks a lass like you will enjoy their fine ale."

"I like glucose stout best."

"Reckon you can handle three pints?"

"Are you trying to get me drunk so you can have your way with me?"

Mick laughed. "I bet a lass like you can down four pints. I'll keep count."

She wrapped her arm around his.

Despite the coolness of the April day, Mick felt hot. He let his jacket flap wide and inhaled a slow slug of air. Bren Kern had told her mum she had a shift at Logan's Bakery. Instead, she was with him. He felt a pang of guilt and reminded himself she'd done it before. He sucked in another breath and snatched a sideways glance at her figure.

She caught him looking. "Like what you see?"

"You remind me of someone."
"Your almost wife?"
"Aye."
She gazed at his hands.
"What happened?"
"Crippled."
"How?"
"They became that way when I was a child."
"Do they hurt?"
"Sometimes."
"I'm sorry."
"They are very strong when they don't hurt."
"Really?"
"Stronger than they look. Grip of steel."
Bren giggled.
"Tell me about your almost wife?"
"What do you want to know?"
"Did you write her love letters?"
"Nah."
"They are so romantic. Will you write one to me?"

Mick didn't answer, stopped and gazed around.

"What's wrong?" Bren said, watching him closely. "What are you looking for?"

Then Mick saw it. A narrow dirt trail which snaked between the trees. It led to a broken section of railing, and a little farther beyond, hidden from the sight of the towpath and canal, was a dilapidated wood shack. He knew because he'd used the trail and shack before. His secret place to do as he pleased.

"This way," he said, taking her arm and

heading for the dirt trail.

"Where are we going?"

"Trust me."

"Another surprise?" Her voice rose in an excited thrill, then she saw where he was taking her. "No. No, I don't want to go down there. It's too dark."

"Come on." He yanked her arm, almost dragging her off her feet.

"Stop. You are hurting me."

He didn't ease his grip and continued to tug.

"Come on," he said through gritted teeth. "Come on. A surprise."

"I want to go to the Navigator Arms," she pleaded.

"After."

"Promise?"

"Promise."

Mick Knowles hated himself for making promises to women he couldn't keep. He always did, though. Just to keep them quiet. With a bit of luck, sixteen-year-old Bren Kern wouldn't scream until it was too late.

CHAPTER 12

Bren Kern screamed much sooner than Mick expected.

It didn't bother him, though.

Nor Wayne, who stared at Bren through clouded eyes, mouth half-open, tongue hanging out exposing yellowed teeth.

"He don't bite," Mick said, making a soft clicking sound with his tongue. "I call him Wayne. He's a stray and nowt to scream about."

"I don't like dogs," Bren protested. "They have fleas and growl."

Wayne eased forwards, rear end wagging. The scrawny, misshapen, bandy-legged hound was about the size of an overweight cat. It had a lopsided mouth which looked like it was grinning, a potbelly and a stump in place of a tail. If dogs counted their years, he'd pass as a senior citizen.

"He's harmless," Mick said, rubbing the dog's ears and feeding it a handful of bread and cheese. "Hungry too, aren't you, boy?"

Wayne's rump picked up speed as he gobbled down the tasty treat. When the food was gone, he rolled onto his back for Mick to give him a belly rub.

Mick said, "When I found him here, I wanted

to take him back to the boat, but Jane wouldn't have it." He continued to rub Wayne's bloated belly. "I visit him every day and give him some food and a bit of play. Don't have no dog food, so he has to make do with a bit of cheese and bread today."

Bren looked at the dog as though she felt sorry for it but stayed well back. "Come on," she said, "He looks full now and I need a sip of ale."

Mick gazed at the dog for a long while then turned to Bren. "Can you do me a favour?"

"What?"

"I wouldn't ask anyone else."

"What do you want?"

"Take Wayne to Jack's vet surgery for a check-up?" Mick flashed a broad smile. "His back legs don't look right. Seeing as Jack and your mum are an item, he won't charge you. If I go, I'll have to pay, and that sort of money ain't easy these days."

Bren touched her face. "I don't like my freckles."

"Sign of beauty, and those ponytails remind me of…"

"Of who?"

"It doesn't matter. Will you take Wayne to visit Jack?"

"I can't. Jack will ask questions and find out where I found him. Then he'll tell Mum."

Mick nodded as if he understood. Her tone reminded him of Jane. How did he end up with a woman like that? jealous. possessive. Tantrums. God forbid any other woman even look at him. Jane

Ragsdale lived in her own fairyland and was a slice short of a full loaf.

But he wasn't with Jane, he told himself, he was with Bren. Still, the rage came. If he moved fast, his hands would be around her throat. He felt a cold thrill of anticipation, eager to hear the snap of her neck.

CHAPTER 13

"Let's go," Mick Knowles said quickly. "Let's get out of here."

He grabbed Bren's arm and dragged her through the bushes and along the dirt trail that led to the canal. Wayne let out a whimper but did not follow.

They were back on the towpath and on their way to the Navigator Arms when Bren said, "Do you think they'll let me in?"

"Aye," Mick replied.

"But I'm sixteen."

"If anyone asks, say you're twenty-two."

Bren smiled. "This coat is my mum's. I used her perfume too. Saved up for the shoes."

"Nice."

A narrowboat chugged slowly along the canal. A plump dog sat at the rear and watched. The middle-aged woman at the tiller gave Mick a knowing look.

He turned away and reached into his jacket pocket. "I've got the tickets. Tarns Dub Music Festival."

"Oh my God! So we are going?"

"I said so, didn't I?"

"I can't believe it."

"Don't tell your mum. It is our secret."

Bren giggled and wiggled her hips. "Care to dance?"

"On the towpath in broad daylight?"

"Why not?"

Mick saw the middle-aged woman on the narrowboat watching. Her plump dog let go a nasty yap.

"Nay, lass," he said. "That's what discos are for."

"Disco's?" Bren doubled over, laughing. "Even my mum's fancy man don't call it that, and Jack is ancient!"

"Discotheques, then."

Bren laughed even harder. "Oh, Micky!"

They were on a slow curve in the towpath when he said, "We'll find a bench in the back of the pub. I'll order our drinks. Anyone ask you anything, let me answer. How's about steak and kidney pudding with beefeater chips and peas?"

"You sure it's okay, Micky?" She clung to his arm.

"No worries. Anyway, the landlord pays me to do a bit of stuff on the side. He'll not make a fuss." Mick touched his nose and winked. "Alf Bird is kosher. He's married to a battle-axe called Stacy."

Bren let go of his arm. "She'll know I'm underage!"

"They'll turn a blind eye so long as we don't cause any bother. A pint of glucose stout to start, eh?"

"That would be lovely." Bren looked at him with those bright, innocent eyes. "Can you buy me a packet of cigarettes, too?"

They were on the straight and saw the small frosted glass windows and red slate roof of the Navigator Arms.

They stopped.

Police cars filled the carpark. Blue lights flashed. People in uniforms moved about. Figures in white suits climbed from a van and drifted towards the pub door. An ambulance pulled up to the curb. Alf Bird stood at the entrance arguing with a slender woman with shoulder-length grey hair. Mick knew she was a detective. His nerves jangled and his gut flipped in a woozy jerk. Cold sweat dripped down his forehead. His shirt clung in damp clumps to his chest.

He grabbed Bren by the shoulders. "Oh, Jesus, we can't go in there."

"You're hurting me," she squealed.

His grip tightened as he tugged her to the side of the towpath. They watched under the leaf-laden branches of an oak tree; backs pressed against the iron railing.

Two uniformed officers took Alf by his arms. Stacy Bird flew through the pub doorway shouting bloody murder. Three officers surrounded her. She kicked and yelled as they carted her away.

"Go home," Mick hissed, looking into Bren's eyes but not really seeing her.

Bren stared at him, face pale.

"You… you… know, don't you? You know what they've found?"

Mick's gut cramped. He wanted silence so he could think.

"Tell me what's going on," Bren said. "I have a right to know."

A savage urge seized Mick. A sudden desire to place his hands around her throat and squeeze until her words faded to nowt. Squeeze and squeeze, so she no longer wanted to know.

A police siren blasted through the cold air. His grip loosened. Bren tugged and, in a splay-footed gait, scuttled away.

Mick stayed in the shadow of the oak, back pressed hard against the railing, chest heaving as he sucked in short, sharp jabs of the cold air. That's when he noticed the second detective, tall, grizzled, dark, rumpled suit. No tie. The lawman paced the pub doorway like a lion on the prowl.

Mick tried to think. He should have followed Bren.

The woman detective glanced in his direction and placed a hand on her hip. The grizzled male detective followed her gaze and cracked his knuckles.

That's when Mick Knowles ran.

CHAPTER 14

The three o'clock hour struck on the town clock as Fenella met with her team for a briefing. She'd brought a tray of doughnuts from Logan's Bakery—caramel custard, glazed ring, strawberry jam, triple chocolate and twisted iced yum yums. The smell of fresh paint in the refurbished room mingled with the dark roasted aroma of coffee. It gleamed; except for the ancient tea urn which clanked and hissed. An ominous warning of what lay ahead.

Fenella stood at the front by the new whiteboard. At the flip of a switch, it turned into a giant screen. Dexter paced at the back, grizzled face down. Jones tapped into his laptop. PC Beth Finn sat in the front row; her hair was freshly bobbed. At the back of the room, PC Woods stood by the food table. He stacked five doughnuts onto a small paper plate, poured a mug of tea, and waddled to a chair. No one in uniform, if you excluded Dexter's rumpled suit, which needed a good steam and iron.

Fenella said, expression sombre, "We've got our work cut out here. Ideas, anyone?"

She threw out the question, looking for a bite. Nothing else to do but cast out lines this early in the investigation.

"Can't get my head around this one, Guv," Dexter said, pacing. He rubbed a hand across his chin and looked at her with hound dog eyes. "One minute we are chasing a little man in black, the next I'm buried under a corpse."

"Don't forget we were at a social," PC Woods chipped in. He took a large bite from a jam doughnut and munched. "I never got that second pint of ale."

Laughter cascaded around the room. They were chatty, which pleased Fenella no end. Talk led to ideas. The team spirit was positive. They were off to a good start.

When they settled down, she nodded at Jones. He tapped on his keyboard. The lights dimmed. An image of the crime scene filled the whiteboard. A gruesome dungeon of cold cobblestones, hard brick walls, splintered wood, and a fragile corpse in a ragged floral dress.

Fenella kept her back to the team as she took in the details. The colours on the screen seemed more vivid than in her memory. In her mind, the cellar was dark and smelled of damp. She focused on the dress. Sunflowers in faded yellow with stems a dirty green. Then the shoes. Orange flip-flops. Once they got her name, she'd pin a photograph to the board to make her human. It was her way of clinging to hope. No matter how unlikely the path, she'd do her best to beat the odds.

She spoke to herself. "How long was the poor lass locked in that wardrobe?" Then spun, faced the room and propped a hand on her hip. "Do we know anything about the lass?"

"Sod all except she wore a floral dress and flip-flops, Guv." Dexter stopped pacing, and again came the hound dog eyes. "Seems familiar somehow... she might have been a teen?"

Fenella felt uneasy. Dexter's eyes went hound dog when there was something heavy on his mind. Was he back on the bottle? Or had things turned sour with his plans to marry his long-time on and off girlfriend, Priscilla? She made a mental note to prod. They had worked together for years; she'd not let him stew alone in his troubles.

Jones said, "I've made a list of missing local women going back ten years. I reckon we'll get a good match from dental records."

Jones came straight from the National Detective School. Thirty-five, good-looking and with an athlete's build. New to her team and a dishy catch. PC Beth Finn had hooked him but not yet reeled him in. Fenella decided to take her for lunch and probe out all the details. Not that she was nosy. No. She just wanted to know what was going on in their private lives.

PC Beth Finn raised a hand. "Did your interview with Alf Bird throw any light on things?"

Fenella shook her head. "He's run the pub for three years, said that wardrobe was there when he took on the lease. He never bothered to open it." She turned to Dexter. "Follow up with the last owner, and while you're at it, have a chat with the regulars. Lots of old-timers drink at that pub. Long memories."

Dexter gave the thumbs up. He liked his drink, was supposed to be on the wagon, but she suspected he'd down a pint or two as he chatted to the patrons.

Fenella turned back to the team. Most detective inspectors had a one-way conversation. They barked orders and their nervous subordinates listened. Not her way, though. Not what she'd been taught by Detective Inspector Croll. He'd been her mentor when she first signed up. Long retired now, but his lessons lived on. She wanted to encourage more questions. She folded her arms and waited.

PC Woods licked jam doughnut from his fingers. "Are we keeping Mr and Mrs Bird in custody?"

He liked taking long smoke breaks, gorging on free food, and raising his hand for desk duty assignments. And somehow, he'd wheedled his way onto Fenella's team. She didn't complain. Her team was a detective down with no sign of a replacement.

Again Fenella shook her head. "Nah, the couple are hiding something, but I don't think it has to do with the body. We've given them a good ticking off and let them go." She turned to Dexter. "That cellar, did you notice the smell?"

"Like a chicken coop, Guv."

"Aye, that's what I thought."

PC Woods said, "No stash of cigarettes or booze in the cellar, then?"

"Nowt down there you'd want to drink or

smoke," Dexter replied. "Just junk, dust, and damp. Thought I heard the scamper of rats. God knows what they would find to eat down there."

PC Beth Finn said, "Where'd the man with the devil's wisp go?"

They saw the devil's wisp climb on the bar counter and sprint through the door that led to the cellar. They had searched and did not find him.

PC Woods took a bite of doughnut, munched. "Might be a secret room in that cellar, a trap door, and he pressed a button on the wall to open it."

"This ain't Scooby-Doo," Dexter replied. "The Navigator Arms weren't built with secret rooms but to fill factory workers' bellies with ale."

"Then how did the devil's wisp disappear?" PC Woods asked.

Dexter grunted. "He ain't holed up in a secret room and he ain't no ghost neither. Got no idea where the hell he went, though."

The room fell into an uneasy quiet. The tea urn gurgled and hissed. Outside, a police siren railed. They had a body with no name, a devil's wisp who'd vanished, and no clue what happened to either.

CHAPTER 15

The briefing over, the team left to start their weekend. Dexter sang the praises of his long-time girlfriend, Priscilla. She sang in clubs to make a living and had a gig in the village pub in Grange. PC Woods planned to get in a spot of fishing. Jones and PC Beth Finn were quiet. No number of soft prods yielded their plans.

Fenella had never been a fan of staying late after work to finish paperwork. But here she was in her tiny office trying to get the admin work done. She stared at two stacks of unfinished forms, sighed, and let her mind drift. She was back in Ealing, London, with her sister, Eve. Years ago. They were strolling along Madeley Road with TJ, the stray dog Eve found in a shop doorway. He was a small hound of uncertain heritage with an enormous appetite. Cherry blossoms bloomed under a warm sun in a clear sky. Spring.

Eve suddenly stopped and turned to Fenella. "If anything happens to me, you'll take care of my ward —"

TJ yapped at a squirrel. He tugged on the leash trying to make his way to the tree where it climbed.

"No way TJ," Eve said to the dog. Not that

he listened. His tail thumped in a whirlwind as he continued to tug.

"Nothing's going to happen to you," Fenella said.

"Life happens to everyone," Eve replied in a whisper.

"What's with the morbid tone? You've years of bright sun and fun ahead of you."

"We all need a bolt hole."

"Why?" Fenella asked.

But Eve tugged TJ's leash and strode off without a reply.

The blast of a police siren brought Fenella back to the present. Her hand reached for the first stack of forms. How much of this could she shove to next week? Not much she realised after a quick scan. Most of it was late. Superintendent Jeffery would be on her back.

She pushed the stack away and drummed her fingers on the desk. The thump echoed in the emptiness. Was there a link between the devil's wisp and the woman in the wardrobe?

She considered the facts.

Devil's wisp in Navigator Arms.

Summer dress and flip-flops on the body.

Young woman missing for some time.

A knot of tension seized her neck. She swallowed hard, walked to the window and sucked in a breath. A patrol car pulled into a parking space. The officer climbed out and bolted into the station. The town clock struck the half hour. She exhaled.

The link was so simple she wondered how she'd missed it. Was the woman in the wardrobe Eve?

At the team briefing, Dexter had seemed subdued. Those hound dog eyes. Yes! He thought it might be Eve, too. How the hell did she miss that?

She glared through the glass pane without seeing, wishing she could recall her sister's floral dresses or favourite footwear. But a thick veil descended over the seven-year gap. Nowt in the brain cells about her sister's wardrobe. But… Eve's dental records would be a quick check.

The door opened. A thin-faced woman with a beak nose and hawk eyes came in. Mrs Soper, Jeffery's assistant.

"Thought I'd find you here," she said, face filled with deep sadness. "The superintendent would like a word. She has some news."

CHAPTER 16

Fenella went in without knocking and shut the door behind her.

Superintendent Jeffery sat hunched over her vast desk, head down, writing. Fenella walked to a high-backed chair and sat. The warm air smelled of mint and damp. A radiator hissed by the window, clouding the glass. A thin drizzle of dappled light splashed on the gilt-framed photographs on the walls—Jeffery with the top brass. The boss wanted to climb higher on the career ladder and had applied for the deputy position in the regional crime squad and not got the post. She was still licking her sour wounds.

Fenella waited five seconds, then said, "Ma'am?"

Jeffery's head did not move. Her pen worked its way across the notepad.

"Ma'am, you wanted to speak with me?"

The boss looked up, face wolfish. "Ah, Sallow, there you are." Her head dropped, and she continued to write.

Fenella scanned the sea of files strewn about the desk. Jeffery was late with her form filling, too. This pleased Fenella no end. How many weeks behind? She eyed the piles and did a quick calculation. Three. Her forms were only two weeks tardy. She wasn't late. She was one week ahead of the boss.

"I'm ready when you are," Fenella said, relaxing.

Jeffery dropped the pen and leaned back in her chair. "You weren't at my lunch briefing. Why was that?"

"Today, ma'am?" Fenella tried to sound surprised but didn't quite pull it off. She'd not attend another of the boss's monthly Friday lunch briefings. No way.

"My positive psyche briefings build team spirit." Jeffery gave a thin-lipped stare. "I expect you to attend."

It was standing room only at the first meeting, everyone keen to refuel on an inspiring talk. Only three showed for the second. There is only so much one can take of Jefferey's bragging. Fenella heard the boss showed up to an empty room for today's meeting.

Best not let her dwell on that, Fenella thought and changed the subject. "You have news for me?"

Jeffery eased forwards in her chair. "So, where were you?"

"Team building, ma'am."

"Pardon?"

"I took the team for lunch at the Navigator Arms. It's a pub by the canal. Helped a ton with our positive psyche. Thought you'd appreciate that."

Jeffery sniffed. "I'm well aware of that pub, and the corpse you found in the cellar."

"A young woman, ma'am." Fenella wished she had a name and thought about Eve. "In a summer frock with orange flip-flops."

Jeffery waved a dismissive hand. "I've news to share."

"A name for the body?"

"Not that. News about your team. I am the lead officer at this year's Tarns Dub Music Festival."

"An honour," Fenella replied, wondering why it concerned her.

"I knew you'd understand."

"Eh?"

"I've reassigned Detective Constable Jones, PC Woods and PC Beth Finn. They start their Tarns Dub duties on Monday. If policing at this year's festival goes well, my status… our police station's status will be—"

"I need all the help I can get. I'm working on a murder case, ma'am."

"You don't know that."

"We found the lass locked in a wardrobe in the cellar of a pub. I'd say there is a fair chance it wasn't fair play."

Jeffery snorted, picked up a pen and rifled through the stack of papers. "You are dismissed."

A pulse leapt in her neck. She didn't move.

Jeffery looked up. "Did you hear what I said? You are dismissed."

"Ma'am, I need help with this one."

"Dismissed, Sallow."

"But I—"

"I have made my decision."

"I need your support, ma'am. Two detectives won't be enough to make quick progress. I have faith in you. Impress me. Now go. You are dismissed."

Fenella kept her mouth clamped shut and waited for her fury to subside. One. Two. Three seconds. She said, "I suppose I'll have to work the press for leads."

"The press?" Jeffery's head snapped up. A muscle in the side of her neck twitched.

"They'll go wild when this breaks—woman's bones found in pub while officers rave the night at Tarns Dub. It'll be a feeding frenzy."

Jeffery opened her thin-lipped mouth and let it close slowly.

Fenella said, "They'll be out to find fresh angles. It's only natural to ask if we've found the bones of Colleen Rae." She paused and felt warm inside as her boss's face paled. "I'm sure Chief Rae will want an update. Not sure how you'll spin your decision to pull officers from the case."

Chief Inspector Alfred Rae's teenage granddaughter vanished at the hands of a serial killer known as Mr Shred. The police never found her body and Mr Shred was on the run from Low Marsh Prison. It wouldn't take long for the press to find a link, even if there wasn't one.

"Tell you what," Jeffery said, her brows knitted. "Take PC Woods."

"No."

"Pardon?"

"I want Detective Constable Jones."

"I can't do that."

Fenella stood. "I believe I am dismissed, ma'am."

Jeffery rubbed her brows. "Okay, take Jones and keep the case from the press until the Tarns Dub Music Festival is over."

CHAPTER 17

Sloane Kern arrived early for her meeting, anxious for it to go well.

She lay on the sofa in her small office with her feet swung up on the armrests. Friday evenings were her paperwork time, but with so few clients, she'd already finished. So, she lingered in the office, waiting, praying that the person would show.

Later, when it was all over, she'd make dinner for her three girls. Fridays used to be take-out night. They couldn't afford it now. These days it was beans on toast. After she'd washed up the dishes and stacked them away, she'd bathe the youngest. Then a glass or two of wine, a chapter from her latest novel and time to collapse into sleep.

That's if everything went according to plan.

Most nights it felt like a war zone; arguments between her girls; fighting with her teenager, Bren; everyone shouting. When Tim was alive, the girls seemed more peaceful. He understood her and the kids.

He drove a clapped-out furniture truck during the day and delivered pizzas by night. Day and Night, seven days a week, Tim toiled. But they were always short on cash and long on bills. The doctor said his long hours didn't cause the cancer.

When Tim's illness grew worse, he gave up delivering pizzas and stopped driving the van. Sloane found a job, no, a career, to help pay their way. She was a fully certified anger management therapist with her own office and client list.

Tim died six years ago.

Only dry tears now.

And thirty-five wasn't too old to start again. Not these days. Not even with three kids, one a stroppy teenager. That's what Jack had told her on their first date. Yes, it was time to rebuild her life. Jack Parkes was the first brick. She liked the idea of being married to a vet. And Sloane knew that after the marriage, even if they moved to a big house in Westpond, life at home would never be the same.

Exhausted thinking about what lay ahead, she eased off the sofa and went to water the spider plant on her desk. A gift from Tim when she first moved into the grey concrete building. He'd looked around the poky office, kissed her on the lips. "Second floor. Nice view through the window. You'll be able to see when a client is on the way. Going places is my Sloane. Big future for you, my girl."

Sloane wiped a tear from her eye. She'd gone nowhere and spiralled downwards as she dug herself deeper into debt. If it weren't for her keeping two sets of books, the business would be finished. She'd been fiddling the numbers for years, learnt the skill from Tim. Oh, how she still missed him.

The tick of the clock reminded her of the

meeting. They would be here any moment now. She raised her left hand to the light. Shards of sunlight twinkled in the diamond stones of her engagement ring. It was really too much to hope for, but it seemed with Jack Parkes, her dreams were about to come true.

How she wished she could tell him everything.

About the double set of books. About the person she was waiting for. But he'd go woo-woo and talk about crystals and vibrations. There'd be a cleansing ceremony and after he'd want her to confess to the police.

Tugging a dead leaf from the spider plant, she reflected. She'd met Jack at a widow's night at the gym. After years of mourning, she'd decided to get out of her rut. She wanted something between work and kids. The gym seemed a good idea. A place to mingle with adults, nod at the regulars and lose a few pounds.

At first, she flicked Jack's advances away, trying to scare him off by talking about her kids. It didn't work. He adored children and pets. They went for drinks; she discovered he worked as a vet. Successful. And he lived in a flat in posh Westpond. Her big four o was five years away. Who wants to grow old alone?

She didn't go to the gym much these days. Weight had crept onto her thighs. Cakes, loaves of bread and meat pies that her oldest daughter Bren brought home from Logan's Bakery hadn't helped. Sloane patted her plump gut and wished she hadn't sold her wedding dress. She still missed Tim. She'd always miss Tim.

The wall clock tick-tocked. Sloane sighed. Jack was a good find. For her financial peace of mind. For the future of her daughters. She wanted them to get a good education. Jack would pay for college. Even Bren liked him in her own way, and that was saying something.

Maybe when they were wed, Jack would stay in with the kids some nights while she took up landscape painting. She wanted to go back to acting school. She'd enjoyed taking those classes. And she'd make damn sure he plied her with an endless supply of Lust by Lush.

Sloane glanced at her wrist and sniffed. A moment later, a strange anxiety overcame her, a sense that her life was about to fall apart. Maybe the person would not show. She glanced at the clock. They were late.

She shuffled to the window. A view of the green lawn edged with blooming mauve hyacinths and a path beyond which the silent carpark waited. The sun dipped behind a cloud and Sloane glimpsed her reflection in the window. She touched the bags under her eyes and then opened her mouth to examine her teeth. She'd fix them after the marriage. Jack wouldn't mind the bill. She wanted a pearly white smile like the actors on the telly.

A movement caught her eye. A figure in black moving fast. She peered through the glass and saw a nun walking in the shadows towards the building.

She carried a newspaper in her left hand. At the front door, the nun took out a mobile phone and held it to her ear and shouted.

Curious, Sloane tilted the window, so it opened and leaned out to get a better view. A blast of cold air caused her to gasp. It carried with it the nun's words; her accent American.

"Well, hurry. I've been waiting for ten minutes. Yes… got the goods."

Sloane leaned farther out the window. "Do you want to come in?"

The nun glanced up. Wisps of brown hair streaked with grey peeped from her veil. There was a hint of fierceness to her thin lips, brutality in the curve of her brow. Everything about the way she stared told Sloane they had met before. Sloane wasn't religious. She didn't go to church.

"I can come down and let you in if you like," Sloane said, trying to place the woman.

Without answering, the nun turned and hurried away along the path. At the carpark she glanced back, hawk-like gaze on Sloane. Once again came the unnerving sensation that the nun knew her.

Don't be silly, Sloane told herself. How could a nun she'd never met know anything about her?

As she leaned out of the window trying to see which car the nun got in, her mobile phone tinkled with a special tone. She ran with girlish excitement to her desk, picked it up, and listened for a moment.

"Ten minutes?" she said. "Okay, I'll go down and

open the front door so you can come straight up."

CHAPTER 18

Sloane opened her office door before the first knock.

She embraced the woman who stepped through the doorway as though she were a long-lost friend. A deep, grateful embrace where Sloane's Lust by Lush was overpowered by the potent aroma of weed.

Sloane stepped back and took in the girlish face, pug nose, and large, innocent eyes of Jane Ragsdale.

"Take a seat," Sloane said, pointing to the sofa. She sat on her chair behind her desk. "Thank you for coming. I just need to talk."

"Oh yeah," Jane replied, looking nervously around as she settled onto the sofa. "They always want to talk. Okay, I'm listening."

"It's been a bad few weeks," Sloane began. "One of my worst and—"

"Yeah, yeah," Jane cut her off. "You want something from me, right?"

Sloane did but tried to keep calm. The woman seemed twitchier than last month. She'd have to soften the ground before she asked, work the soil and lift the mood. Building relationships of trust was one thing Sloane was good at. Anger management therapists had to do that before they could help. She sensed Jane's tension, and didn't want to spook her, so she kept her tone easy. "I've some good news?"

Jane shifted on the sofa. "Business looking up?"

"No, things in that department are pretty bad." Sloane flashed her ring. "I'm going to re-marry. What do you think?"

Jane stared with wide eyes. "Wow! Bloody big stones."

"Diamonds," Sloane corrected.

"Must make you feel like a princess. Who is Prince Charming?"

"Jack is a vet, loads of money. Lives in Westpond. I reckon he earns more than a doctor. Loves animals. We've not set a date yet. This year, though." Sloane flashed a smug grin. "Did you bring the stuff?"

"Yeah." Jane's gaze fixed on the ring. "I got it with me, but I want payment for last month plus interest."

Sloane blinked. "I need more credit. Can we roll it into this month's and I'll pay you at the start of next month?"

"Sorry, can't do that."

"Look, you know me. I'll pay."

"Can't help you. I've got other clients and only a limited supply."

"I have to have it." Sloane put a hand to her throat. Her pulse pounded in her ears. "I can't live without it."

"Just a little oxy to get mama bear through the month," Jane jeered. "I've got costs."

"I'm good for my word," Sloane protested.

Jane's gaze dropped to the ring. She licked her lips.

"No," Sloane screamed. "No way."

"I get that ring, you get the goods and I'll write off last month's payment, seeing as we are friends."

Sloane's breath locked in her lungs. She had to have the oxy. There was no way she could face the month ahead without it. The kids, the clients, Jack. She'd go spare. Kill someone. She let out a hard breath.

"You've got my wedding dress and now you want my ring!"

"Want the stuff, mama bear?"

Anger bubbled, ready to explode. Sloane would go mental if her rage broke free. No. she told herself, slowing her mind to give her time to think. Not yet. She softened her voice to hide her panic.

"We're friends, Jane. Can't we do a different deal?"

Jane opened her handbag, pulled out a clear plastic bag of pills, and waved it. "That ring or I walk."

Frustration smashed against Sloane's chest. How could she give up Jack's ring? What would she say to him? She stared into Jane Ragsdale's soulless eyes and knew what she must do.

"You can have the ring." Sloane slipped it off

her finger. "I'll give you the cash I owe next month, and you'll give it back, right?"

"Sure," Jane said, grinning like a cat making friends with a mouse. "Let's deal."

"Deal," Sloane replied, boiling with rage as she dropped the ring into Jane's open palm.

Jane stood, gave a wave, and was gone.

Sloane gazed at the bag of pills and let out a relieved sigh. Now her weekend could begin. She picked two out of the bag, studied them for an instant, popped them on her tongue and swallowed hard.

Within ten minutes, her fury at Jane Ragsdale dimmed in her chest but did not go out. It smouldered like hot coals waiting for kindling to ignite.

CHAPTER 19

It was a surprise planned by Nan and Eduardo.

The waiter lit the candles on their table set for four. The Tudor Inn in Grange was an elegant restaurant come pub, with a view of the river Derwent. Fenella expected to spend Saturday night curled up on a sofa with her husband Eduardo. She'd planned on reading a book and nattering to her mum who everyone called Nan.

They sat at a stylish table, polished silverware, little gold bells and candles floating in petal water. A fire roared in an ancient brick wall. A warm, cosy room filled with laughter.

The waiter stepped back from the table. He gazed with satisfaction at the flickering flames and said in a French accent, "For starters, a beetroot and pomegranate salad with goat cheese, pink lady apple, pistachio, baby greens and raspberry vinaigrette with a hint of garlic."

Fenella couldn't hide the grin on her face. Nan had worked on the sly to get tickets to Dexter's long-time girlfriend's gig.

Nan said, "Thought we'd try something fresh. Give me a break from the stove." She smiled at Dexter. "And to support your Priscilla."

Nan and Priscilla were generations apart, but they both shared a love of soul music and cooking. They chatted, sang, and swapped recipes over the phone.

"She'll be on after dessert," Dexter said. "Her set's a real belter."

"Aretha?" Nan asked.

"Of course. Ain't no one can bring it like Aretha Franklin, but my Priscilla ain't half bad." He winked and began to sing. "Now me and Priscilla are together, ain't nowt gonna keep us apart."

"Not a bad voice," Fenella said. "I'm pleased for you."

"Been years in the making, Guv. Lots of on and off struggles, but we are making it work."

"You look happy."

And he did. She'd never seen him so alive. Beaming. At last her matchmaking brain for Dexter would be turned off once and for all. She was happy for him and began to think about a suitable match for Jones.

The waiter returned with a tray balanced on his right hand and a white cloth over the other. Showman-like, he placed the dishes of green salad on each place setting, stepped back and turned to Dexter.

"The chef sends her regards. She is a fan of 1960s and 70s soul and looking forwards to tonight's show." He gave a half bow. "Enjoy your meal."

He walked away with stiff legs, as though they

were in plaster casts. Fenella thought it was over the top. They were in the village of Grange, not the Savoy hotel in London. Still, she lapped it up and wondered if it was a real French accent or put on as part of the show.

It triggered a memory of Eve. It was years ago when Eve first moved to London, and they were both young and carefree.

Snow was falling by the time Fenella left the underground station and walked the short distance to the hospital in the cold dusk light of London. She kept her pace brisk and twice checked the scrap of paper to assure herself of the ward. The lift doors creaked as they opened to the hospital corridor. As she approached the double set of doors to the ward her breathing quickened. She was the older sister. It was her job to look out for Eve.

The staff nurse guided her to a room where Fenella prickled with laughter at the sight. Eve lay on a bed, left leg raised by a mechanical device that looked as though it came from some ancient dungeon. She'd broken her leg on a skateboard, thinking it was a good way to get TJ, her lazy dog, to run.

"Not funny, Fen," Eve said. "TJ needs exercise, you know that."

"I know it, but I also know he doesn't like to do much more than eat and wag his tail for more food. Granted, he'll bark at the postman to work his vocal muscles but that's because he always gives him a dog treat. The details, Eve?"

"Oh Fen, don't make fun of me! Once I'd picked up speed down the slope in the park, TJ just stopped. I came flying off, and well...here I am."

Fenella smiled at the memory. She'd visit her dad's grave on Sunday. Take him a bunch of blue roses and give him an update on Eve. It had been a while.

Eduardo poked at his salad. He didn't like greens and began to sing the opening lines of I say a Little Prayer as he stared at his plate.

"Gawd help us," Nan cried. "Please stop or you'll turn that salad sour."

Eduardo grinned, stood, spun, glared at the plate and continued to sing.

"You crafty sod." Nan laughed. "That's real food. Eat it, you greedy bugger."

Eduardo poked at the dish, forked in a mouthful and slowly chewed. "Umm delicious."

Everyone agreed.

They chatted contentedly through the starter and the main course, Pan-Fried Halibut with pak choi, saffron potatoes, Morecambe bay shrimps and locally harvested hen of the wood's mushrooms. It was delicious. The crisp fried fish paired wonderfully with the soft chewy texture of the mushrooms. And it came with a delicate sauce Nan couldn't identify. She called to the waiter.

He winked. "Chef's special sauce. Je ne sais pas... I've no idea what makes the sauce, but it's sacrément bon or as you say in English, damn good."

Nan announced she'd have a quiet chat with

the chef at the end of the show. If the woman had a secret recipe, she had to have it.

"Tell Priscilla to join me," she said to Dexter. "She'll help me get it out of the bugger."

No one spoke when dessert came—baked Alaska. Browned crisp meringue encasing vanilla ice cream and a traditional Christmas pudding.

"My God, don't go far, I'll have seconds and thirds," Eduardo said to the grinning waiter. "We can't let food like this go to waste. It has to be consumed the moment it is cooked."

"He's a greedy sod," Nan said. "But like he says, hang about a bit until we've finished our firsts."

After the plates were cleared from the table and fresh bottles of red wine uncorked, the lights dimmed.

The opening chords of "Respect" soothed from the live band. Priscilla came on stage, face full of freckles, in a sequin dress that shimmered and glittered. Her hair, the colour of ripe pumpkin, was swept into a beehive which added six inches to her 4' 11".

When she opened her mouth and let the first words fly, the cheering began. She nailed it. And "I Say a Little Prayer" and "Chain of Fools" and "Until You Come Back to Me." She ended the set, not with an Aretha Franklin song, but an oldie from another era —"Bye Bye Blackbird."

Nan, Eduardo, Dexter and Fenella danced in front of the stage. The chef joined. So did the waiter and everyone else. A little Americana in a little village in England.

After the crowd left, while Nan and Priscilla were in the kitchen talking with the Chef, Fenella stepped outside. The sky was clear and the stars shone as bright as diamonds. On the chill air came the warning squark of hens. She wondered if they sensed a fox on the hunt, and craned her eyes to search the shadows, but the birds soon settled down so that the night was silent. A moment of peace in which she reflected. She loved her family time. She loved work. She needed both in her life.

After ten minutes, and beginning to chill, she turned to go back inside. A movement caught her eye. It came from the far side of the carpark underneath a gnarled oak.

"Nice night for it, Guv," Dexter said, moving soundlessly from the tree and across the carpark. "I came out for a breath of fresh air. Nice bit of singing from my Priscilla, eh?"

"Aye, long time since I've seen her on stage," Fenella replied. "Is she going to sing at your wedding?"

"That's the plan, Guv."

"She'll sound even better than tonight, then."

Dexter sighed and looked at her with hound dog eyes. "My Priscilla's been at it for years. Not a sniff of a break in all that time. She reckons life has passed her by. Says forty-eight is too old to break through now, music's a young gal's game. She's giving it up. Don't know how'll she'll cope, it'll be a big loss for her life."

Fenella understood. Priscilla had worked in nightclubs for years. Late nights in smoked-filled rooms overflowing with booze. That she still had a great voice was one of life's miracles. That it'd never be heard by more than a drunken mob, one of life's unfathomable mysteries. She too had felt the cold hand of loss, knew how tight it squeezed, sucking the breath from the living so they were no more than walking dead.

"Life is about coping with loss and moving forwards so as not to get trapped in the past," she said.

In the silence that followed, a cockerel crowed. Only once but a piercing shriek.

Dexter said, "My grandad used to keep chickens. Whenever he heard crowing at night, he'd keep his eyes wide the next day."

"Oh aye, why's that?"

"To make sure it wasn't a black rooster he'd heard. Find one of those birds crowing on your doorstep is a bad omen." He glanced around. "When I hear crowing at night, I still get the shivers. And my gran used to say if you heard a cockerel crowing at midday, someone had died."

"Aye, that's an old one," Fenella replied, remembering that folklore from her childhood.

Dexter raked a hand over his chin and let his voice drop to a whisper. "That body in the wardrobe, Guv. I've been thinking."

"Go on," Fenella said, feeling uneasy.

"Might be Eve."

"I know."

"Have you thought about what you'll say to Nan and Eduardo if it is your sister?"

"Aye, pet. I've thought of nowt else."

CHAPTER 20

Sloane Kern's Sunday was slowly going to hell.

She crouched next to a bench on the damp lawn in the Garden of Remembrance in the Port St Giles cemetery. The bright noon sun did nothing to lift the chill. For once there were no gusts of howling wind from the beach, so the air smelled of freshly dug soil. She wore black gloves to fight off the chill.

Sloane's gaze fixed on the black letters of a brass plaque at the base of a gnarled oak tree.

In loving memory of Tim Kern.
Forever in our thoughts.

She placed her left hand on the plaque but kept her gloves on so as not to get her hands dirty.

"I miss you, Tim."

She'd gone for a cremation to save money and told her girls that's what her dad wanted.

"Ash and dust are better for the environment," she had said as all her girls cried.

But Tim had wanted to be buried in the soft soil of Port St Giles with a view overlooking the sea. He'd asked her on his deathbed. She'd said yes as he slipped away.

Sloane glanced around the quiet memorial grounds. A red squirrel darted down a tree trunk and dug furiously at the soil. A church bell wailed a slow toll. Farther out came the howl of the sea as it crashed against the shore. Sloane leaned closer to the plaque. "I'm sorry, Tim."

During their last year of marriage, she'd asked the doctor for something to help with her nerves. Seeing Tim in so much pain crushed her soul. Every day she was on a knife-edge of worry. The pills worked wonders and gave her a new lease on life. They helped her through Tim's dying. Through the questions from her girls. And through the struggles to keep her therapy business afloat.

After the fourth bottle of pills, the doctor refused to prescribe more. Sloane swung at the woman, knocking her to the floor. Nurses rushed in and yanked Sloane away as she yelled and kicked and swore.

When the dust settled, it was a close call for Sloane. The doctor's surgery did not press charges. Medical centres do not like negative publicity. But Sloane had been warned by a stout-necked policewoman that if it happened again, she'd go down. They took her fingerprints and sent her on her way. The medical centre removed her from their list of patients. If she came back through their doors, they would report her to the therapy ethics board.

Sloane fretted for months that her rage outburst would be leaked to the press, that there would be reporters at her door, and she'd be stripped of her anger management certification. That thought was so terrifying she couldn't sleep for months. How would she earn a living if that happened? Therapy was what she'd been trained for. It was all she knew.

Two weeks after the attack, Sloane heard about Jane Ragsdale and her endless supply of oxy. The week before Tim passed away, she went to the bank for a loan.

"To pay for the burial costs," she had said.

"Of course," the bank manager replied.

The bank loan went to her habit. She didn't know how, but she saved some back for a brass plaque.

The months following Tim's death were a dark endless blur. Her girls were moody, business thin, and the bills kept piling up. Sloane had no siblings, and her parents were dead. If Tim had a family, things might have been different, but Tim grew up in the constant shuffle of foster and care homes. No one wanted him for long—too difficult to handle. Social workers placed him in Whitby House, a care home in Whitehaven and the last resort for children with no chance of adoption. He was six.

The staff tried to make it a home, but what hope can you give a child who knows it isn't wanted? Then Tim found Sloane. They fell in love, married and had three daughters. That was supposed to be their happily ever after.

Now Tim was dead, and his last wish would be forever left unfilled. His bones would never be buried in the soft soil of Port St Giles. They would never rest in peace with a view of the sea. Sloane had broken her promise to the only man she'd ever loved.

With no one to lean on for support, she leaned on oxy. It was her secret friend. It didn't stop the sobs which now came, shaking her body softly.

A slender woman with shoulder-length grey hair strolled along the path. Ten feet from where Sloane crouched, she paused and flashed a friendly smile.

"Got the place to yourself, pet?"

"We both have," Sloane replied, wiping her eyes.

The woman pointed at the plaque. "Dad?"

Sloane swallowed back tears. "Husband."

"Hubby will not want you sat in that damp grass, luv. You'll catch a chill. Why don't you sit on that bench? You can talk to him from there. I think he would like that."

And with that the woman with the shoulder-length grey hair turned and ambled away.

CHAPTER 21

Sloane yanked a tissue from her handbag and cleaned Tim's plaque with soft swipes. Then she walked to the bench and sat.

Yes, the grey-haired woman was right. This was a peaceful spot to remember the man she still loved. In summer, the rose bushes would be out in full bloom and the trees heavy with leaves. She closed her eyes and let her mind drift into happy memories of the past.

"Thought I'd find you here."

Sloane's head jerked. How long had she been asleep? She glanced at her watch. Twenty minutes.

"I must have dozed off," she said weakly.

Jack's lips curved into the sad smile he kept for clients at his vet's office when the news about their pet wasn't good. His eyes were red and swollen.

"Had a nice chat with Tim?"

Sloane nodded and patted the bench for him to sit. "And how is Ester?"

"The vibrations were wonderful," he said. "She is doing well and gave me her blessing to move on with my life. I left three bunches of pink roses for her. One for each of the children we never had. My Ester always loved roses."

"They are beautiful flowers," Sloane said, wishing she had money to buy something for Tim. His plaque looked so small and bare, as though his life wasn't worth living.

The wind whistled in from the beach with the hiss of a boiling kettle and blew dead leaves around the base of the tree. They clumped over the plaque, leaving patches of dulled brass.

Jack followed Sloane's gaze to the base of the tree. "Ester took my surname. Ester Parkes. Has a ring to it, don't you think?"

Sloane shifted her gaze from the plaque to Jack's face. He looked sad.

She said, "What was Ester's maiden name?"

"Padavona."

"Italian?"

"Her mum was born in Padua, a town not far from Venice, but Ester was a local girl." He paused. "I like the name Sloane Parkes, what do you think about that once we are married?"

"I'll think about it," Sloane said and changed the subject. "Ester's mum's still alive, isn't she?"

"Giorgia? Oh yes, that battle-axe will outlive me. There is always something wrong with her, but somehow, she survives. She lives in Grange Hall Care Home."

"That's Westpond, isn't it?"

"Her family is old money," Jack replied. "She's lived in Westpond all her life."

"Posh area of town." Sloane smiled. "When we marry, we won't have to move into her old house, will we?"

"Oh no, honey." He cracked his knuckles. "She sold that place years ago, didn't tell me until the deal was done. Anyway, she won't talk to me these days."

"Why not?"

"She sold some of my things without telling me. I was very upset at the time."

"What did she sell, your old vet's magazines?"

"Water under the bridge, honey."

Sloane thought his ragtag collection of books and magazines was best suited to a library. They cluttered his flat, collecting dust and turning yellow. She made a mental note never to give them away. She didn't want to make the same mistake as Ester's mum.

She said, "So, we'll have to look for our own house in Westpond?"

"If that is what you want, honey."

"A bedroom for each of the girls and a craft room for me. You need a library with lots of shelves. I've always wanted a yoga studio."

Jack looked at her, eyes narrowed. "A house that big will be expensive."

"It's an investment in our future." Again Sloane smiled. "A man of your standing with three new daughters deserves a big house in a posh part of town, and I'd like to hold tea parties. You need a big garden for that, and with you being a vet… well, we need a home that reflects your standing."

Sloane waited, knowing Jack couldn't resist it when she stroked his ego.

He puffed out his chest. "Yes, yes, a house fitting our status is just what we need."

"If you really think so," Sloane replied. "I'd be just as happy if we moved into my flat. I've still got some of Tim's memorabilia, but me and the girls would squeeze you in."

"No, no. Our lives and those of the animal kingdom must be lived with dignity. My work in providing for them is my noble cause, and your work in anger management is my pride and joy. A large house in Westpond it is."

Sloane said, "I'll start to look when I get home."

Jack rubbed his bracelet and sniffed. It sounded like a sob. His eyes glistened. No tears. He wasn't the type to cry in public. He tugged at a loose strand on his jacket and then wrapped his arm around her.

"I still miss Ester," he said, taking a deep breath. "Alas, grief is a solid wall we all must pass through. There is no way around it. How are you and Tim doing?"

"I'm terrified I'll forget what Tim sounded like," Sloane admitted.

She buried her head in his chest, sobbing so hard her throat ached. He held her tight, not speaking, sharing in her grief.

CHAPTER 22

Ten minutes later, Sloane straightened, blew her nose, and pointed at the patch of wet on his jacket. "Look what I've done."

He gave her a handkerchief.

"Sorry, I should have thought of that sooner."

Sloane took it and dabbed at her eyes. "You are such a gentleman."

They sat for several minutes in silence. More people were in the garden now, enjoying an after-lunch stroll.

Jack said, "You loved Tim, didn't you?" His voice came out small and thin. "I mean, you really loved him. You'll never love me that way."

Sloane didn't speak. What could she say?

"I know this is hard to believe," Jack said, voice soft. "Maybe you are the only person who'll know what I mean. I understand, and it is all right. I still love Ester. She holds a spot in my heart that can't be filled… not even by you."

He kissed Sloane on the lips. A long, lingering smooch filled with desire and passion. She yielded to his embrace, but he eased her away.

"Doesn't mean we can't love another person," he said, taking her gloved left hand. "It's just different."

"That's it," Sloane said and cried. Not tears of sadness. Tears of joy. Nothing would be the same without Tim, but there was nothing wrong with different.

Jack shifted so there was a small gap between their bodies. "I came here to apologise to you and Ester." Before Sloane responded, he held up a hand. "I've done something stupid. Something very wrong."

His earnest face made Sloane giggle. Whatever the opposite of rule breaker was, that was Jack. He lived his life by the book. She wondered whether he forgot to pay for his television license or returned a library book late.

"What have you done?" she said, still giggling.

His face became very pale. "I want you to know that I'm sorry."

Suddenly alarmed, Sloane said, "What is it?"

"I… I can't believe I've been so dumb. Dear God, Sloane, can you forgive me?"

"You are frightening me."

His gaze fell to her gloved left hand. "I… er… I gave you Ester's ring."

"What?"

"You have to give it back."

"What!"

"The energy wasn't right. I didn't know how much Ester's ring meant to me."

Sloane tried to speak, but fear closed her throat. Jack didn't notice and leaned his head against her chest.

"I'm sorry... so sorry. Listen, I've booked an appointment with Dobson Jewellery Store tomorrow. You can choose whatever you like. It's just that you can't have my Ester's ring. The vibrations are all wrong. I've never felt them so powerful. It was a silly mistake. I thought I'd moved on, but you never move on, do you?"

"No," Sloane said, finding her voice.

He sat up, stared at her with trusting eyes, and stretched out his hand. His long, thin fingers opened slowly.

"Please give it back to me now. I'll show it to Ester on our way out to put her mind at peace."

CHAPTER 23

It took fifteen seconds for Jack's demand to sink in.

By then total panic raged in Sloane's mind. Her fiancé would explode if he found out she'd pawned his late wife's engagement ring for oxy. But what the hell could she do?

They sat on a wooden bench in the Port St Giles cemetery as people milled about in the Garden of Remembrance. The sun continued to shine in a bright blue sky, although there was a sharp chill in the air. A chill, which Sloane thought was about to get colder.

"Give me Ester's ring, now," Jack said with a sharpness in his voice Sloane had never heard before. "We'll choose your ring tomorrow at Dobson Jewellery Store."

"Ester's ring?" Sloane said.

"As I say, you can choose any ring you want." His voice softened, but he kept his hand outstretched. "If Dobson's doesn't have one you like, we'll visit Hatton Garden in London. We can spend next weekend searching the jewellery quarter until we find exactly the right ring for you."

"That sounds lovely," Sloane said, wondering

how all this had happened, and what to say.

"Ester's ring, please," Jack said and turned so his head was level with her face, hand still outstretched, eyes as sad as a puppy dog.

Sloane's gaze fell to her gloved left hand, but she did not speak. Jack was her meal ticket to a new life. A life free from the stress of never-ending bills. A life where she'd eat fresh cake and French sticks rather than the stale cast-offs from Logan's Bakery. A life where her daughters' educational needs would be met. She wanted to send her two younger daughters to St Giles Academy and get a tutor for her sixteen-year-old, Bren, to prep for university. That cost money. Jack would pay for it without an eye blink. Yes, he was into woo-woo and the power of crystals, and she thought all that stuff was mad. Still, she'd put up with woo-woo if it meant an easier life. But now it was all messed up because of that ring.

Jack was still staring at her, hand outstretched.

Sloane grimaced. If she told him she was addicted to oxy, he'd drop her like a hot potato. Who in their right mind would marry a drug addict who'd pawned their beloved dead wife's engagement ring? Jack might be woo-woo and kind, but he wasn't mad.

Sloane's gaze fixed on the gold letters of Tim's plaque at the base of a gnarled oak tree. She'd lied to her late husband on his death bed. What on earth would she say to Jack?

She heaved an enormous sigh. There was nothing left but the truth, and she spoke it through gritted teeth. "I don't have it."

Silence, apart from the low mumble of voices, the soft hiss of the wind, and blood rushing in Sloane's ears.

Jack flexed his open hand. "What did you say?"

"I don't have the ring," Sloane repeated, removing the glove from her left hand.

He stared for a long while at her bare fingers, then smiled. "Oh, clever girl."

"Eh?"

"That's why I love you."

"Pardon?"

"You sensed it, didn't you? Sensed the ring wasn't right for you. Most women would have snatched it out of my hands, not my Sloane. You felt the negative energy too. Did you know it belonged to my Ester?"

"No, I had no idea," Sloane replied, truthfully. "But, yes, there was something about it that just did not feel right. Strange, that."

Jack nodded. "I fully understand. I sensed it, too, when I gave it to you. It's the crystals in the diamonds. They have power."

"That's why I didn't wear it today," Sloane said quickly. "I left it at home and hope you are not too angry with me."

"No, never," Jack replied. He leaned forwards and wrapped her in his arms. "I'd never be angry with you. Ever."

They embraced for a full five minutes. No words, just the gentle rise and fall of their chests. All the while Sloane's mind raced, coming up with ideas and forming a plan.

When Jack released her from his soft grip, he said, "Why didn't you say it made you feel uncomfortable?"

"It was such a nice gift. I didn't want to upset you."

Jack's eyes glistened, and he dabbed at them with his hand. "I don't deserve a woman like you. I really don't."

Sloane used the handkerchief he'd given her earlier to wipe his eyes and kissed him on the cheeks. "Let's not look at the rings in Dobson Jewellery Store. It would be more fun to have a romantic weekend in London."

"Next weekend?" Jack asked, a renewed brightness in his tone.

"And I can give you Ester's ring before we leave on Friday," Sloane said. "Let's make it into a celebration. For love lost, and new love found."

Sloane held her breath as Jack thought about it for a moment.

He nodded his approval. "I'll take care of everything, including arranging a sitter for the girls."

"You don't have to do that; I have a regular sitter."

His eyes glittered. "Fancy seeing a show while we are in the big city?"

"I've never seen the Mousetrap."

"Done."

"I love you, Jack."

Sloane wrapped her arms around him and felt a wave of relief. It soon turned to fury at Jane Ragsdale. There was no way she'd lose the good life with Jack because of that drug dealing cow. She'd get the ring back before their romantic weekend.

No matter what it took.

CHAPTER 24

It was seven-thirty, Monday morning. Fenella gulped a mouthful of coffee and hoped it would settle her stomach. She moved quickly along a dim hallway and into the oldest part of Port St Giles Cottage Hospital. She carried a travel mug of coffee made by Nan and a little secret.

Thick stone walls blocked out daylight. Bulbs strung on thin wires glowed in the quiet gloom. The hard tiled floor the colour of dried blood sloped down into the bowels of the building. Her footsteps echoed with an ominous thud as she drew closer to the pathologist's studio.

That's what Dr MacKay called his place of work. His studio. She pushed through a set of swing doors and hoped Dr MacKay would give her solid facts to chew on.

The air became thick with the stench of death —Dr MacKay's domain. At the end of the hallway, a light glimmered. The lab where he did his grim work.

Fenella stopped and stared at the door. A dull thud pounded in her chest. It thumped at the slow beat of a funeral drum. She had never felt so alone in the morgue. In there were the blood-stained tools of Dr MacKay's trade; and on a cold steel trolly, the decomposed remains of the woman in the wardrobe. A woman who might be her sister, Eve. She didn't want to pass through those doors. That was her little secret.

Fenella hated herself at that moment and hated herself for her fear. She put the travel mug to her lips and then stopped. *Best keep the stomach clear and the mouth bone dry.*

"Detective Sallow?"

The voice came from behind. She spun.

A middle-aged woman with bone-white hair scraped into a harsh bun stood in a doorway. Mrs Phipps, Dr MacKay's assistant. She'd worked in the lab for ten years.

Mrs Phipps said, "Please come this way."

Fenella hesitated. Most of the time she went straight into the lab and talked to Dr MacKay while he did his work. What was going on?

"This way," Mrs Phipps said again and smiled.

Fenella could not recall the last time she saw Mrs Phipps smile. Not even the hint of a twitch at the edge of her thin lips at the past Christmas parties. All that death, she supposed. Not much to be cheery about. The smile now on Mrs Phipps' face just didn't look right.

Fenella said, "Having a good morning, Mrs Phipps?"

"Quite dreadful. I've been so busy that I'm already looking forward to the weekend. Rushed off my feet, I am. Same for all of us who work down here."

"Then I'd best speak with Dr MacKay while he's on the job. We both know he gets the grumps if he's not poking at dead flesh when he talks."

Still smiling, Mrs Phipps said, "He asked that I show you to the club. He'll speak with you there."

"Lead the way," she said and followed Mrs Phipps through the door.

It led to a large, plush room that smelled of wax and leather. A syringe and vial lay on a round teak drinks table. Two armchairs were on either side of the table. A giant rust-coloured rug covered much of the hardwood floor. Two gilt-edged landscapes of Port St Giles hung on the oak-panelled walls. The barnacled beams of the pier and the abandoned lighthouse in one. A stormy beach with a stooped man in a black coat in the other. A mini bar on wheels leaned against the far wall, its shelves filled with bottles of hard liquor.

Mrs Phipps said, "Take a seat while I let Dr MacKay know you have arrived."

Fenella sat in an armchair and drummed her fingers on the teak table. So he'd been expecting her? But she hadn't called ahead. That meant he had news. She went over a list of questions. Time of death? Cause of death? Any signs of a struggle? Was the body moved? Is it Eve?

"Ah, there you are Fenella," Dr MacKay said.

He wore a tweed jacket with a white shirt and lime bow tie. Not his usual garb of blood-stained scrubs. Fenella's gut churned. Dr MacKay had dressed up for her! And he peered as if she were a specimen in a petri dish.

    Only one question.
    Why?

CHAPTER 25

Dr MacKay hovered in the doorway. The light in the hallway flickered off for a moment. His outline became a dark shadow. The doctor had news and Fenella knew it wasn't good.

She waited.

She was good at the wait.

He shuffled across the room, back arched as though a question mark. After a few steps, he turned to gaze at Fenella, red-rimmed eyes someplace else. Then he continued his slow progress stopping at the mini bar on wheels. He stared at the bottles in silence. Then turned but did not speak.

How long had she known him?

Years.

Her mind went back to when she was a green faced rookie standing in his lab. Dr MacKay had sliced into a corpse with a giant pair of scissors as he talked in an excited voice. When the hacksaw came out, she forced herself not to faint. A close call. The pathologist's tools of the trade still made her queasy, and he still called her by her first name.

"Fenella, I will not ask if you want a drink from my extensive collection of fine malts," Dr MacKay said, flashing his large sharp teeth. "It's not yet eight in the morning and you are on duty."

"I'll have a large one," Fenella replied, filled with a mixture of curiosity and dread at what was to come. "With ice."

Dr MacKay poured, placed the drinks on the table next to the syringe and vial, sat in the armchair, took a long slow sip, and smacked his lips. "You are here about the woman in the wardrobe?"

"Aye."

There was nowt more to say. Dr MacKay had worked in his lab since Fenella joined the force. He knew her old boss, Detective Inspector Croll, and his boss before that. Must be pushing forty years, she guessed. Now she waited, breath on hold, for answers.

"I need your help," Dr MacKay said. "Those twelve-year-olds in Carlisle have buggered it up again. I've no idea how they can let kids who should be in short pants work in a forensic lab. My God, it's no wonder the world is messed up. And don't get me started on Dr Oz. They should send him back to nursery school..."

Dr Oz, the medical director, was in his forties, well regarded and good looking. Fenella took a sip from her glass. It burned down and swirled with Nan's coffee in her empty stomach. *Best not drink much of this. It'll go to my head. Taste's good though.* She took another sip and waited.

"... well, I don't suppose you came here to hear me rant on about this place," he said, cheeks flushed. "Now, where was I? Ah yes. Dexter called me over the weekend and—"

"I see," Fenella said before he'd finished his sentence.

Now everything became clear. The plush furnishings and Dr MacKay in fancy clothes and the invite to the club. Dexter had shared their theory that the body in the wardrobe might be Eve. And the doctor had dressed up in a mark of respect. Old school. Fenella liked that.

But it didn't stop her stomach. It heaved and soured as her heartbeat picked up. Instinct told her what was coming next, and she knew she wouldn't like it.

"Okay. So what have you got for me?"

"I'm afraid it is too early in my examination to confirm it is your sister. There is not enough flesh for fingerprints and the bloody National Health Service has lost Eve's dental records. I spent Sunday on the phone with my man in London, but to no avail."

"Right." She closed her eyes, willed her heart to slow down and lined up her questions. "Are you sure it is a woman?"

"The floral dress and flip-flops helped, but... I had to make sure, checked the pelvis. Female design requires space for the birth canal. You with me?"

"Aye." Fenella tried to block out the indignities of the autopsy table. "I'm with you."

"I like to be thorough, you see," Dr MacKay said. "Took a good long look at the skull as well. Inside and out."

Too much information.

Fenella closed her eyes, saw Dr MacKay with his hacksaw and let them snap open. She didn't need the detail, but he'd not stop now. Not with him in full flow.

"Amazing bit of kit, the skull. Bones are nature's way of telling us about the past. The flesh gets reused, but the bones can last for ages." He paused for breath then snorted. "They called Van Gough a genius, but the real creative work is done here in my studio. I've nothing but sharp steel tools and a body on a trolley as my canvas. My God, Fenella, my work should be on display in the National Gallery in London."

"You never know," Fenella replied wishing he would hurry up.

"I can tell you it's not a male skull," he said, voice edged with excitement. He loved his job. "Smooth as a baby's… well you get my drift. No visible signs of trauma. Except…"

His voice fell away and he stared at her for so long that she felt uncomfortable. Those x-ray beams seemed to strip away her flesh to examine her bone structure. Was he comparing her skeletal features to the woman in the wardrobe?

"Go on," Fenella said. "Except what?"
Dr MacKay's gaze fell to her left hand.
He said, "The ring finger is… missing."
"How do you mean?"
"Gone. Not where it should be."
"A birth defect?"

"Hacked off."

"After death?"

Doctor MacKay didn't answer at first, and when he did, his voice fell to a whisper.

"She might have been alive when it happened. Can't say, yet. And I thought you should know that her tongue is… missing. Yes, it's a muscle and can decompose, but there are signs it too was hacked off. She died six to eight years ago." He paused a moment for his words to sink in. "The labs will confirm, but I'd bet a bottle of Glenmorangie on that."

She said, "Any idea of her age?"

"Twenties to early forties."

That put the body in the wardrobe squarely in the time range when Eve vanished. Same age range too. And the missing finger and tongue. Dear God, what were they dealing with here?

"Okay," she said slowly. "I think I've got a decent place to start. Now, what did you want my help with?"

The door opened. Mrs Phipps came in. She looked at Fenella and she looked at Dr MacKay and she looked at the syringe and vial on the drinks table. She wore latex gloves.

Dr MacKay said, "I can't tell you yet how the person died, but I can tell you whether it is Eve." He smiled, again showing a mouthful of sharp teeth. "A draw of your blood please, Fenella. I have a gal in the labs in Carlisle who'll rush through the DNA tests."

CHAPTER 26

All Mick Knowles wanted was to sleep.

He pulled the sheets over his head and swore. It was eight, Monday morning. He didn't rise till two. The overnight rest he'd scraped together had been fitful. Now he was wide awake.

Outside, children talked in loud voices. They used the canal towpath as a cut-through to school. Their noise wasn't the cause of his lack of sleep. It was the police at the Navigator Arms last Friday lunchtime. Images of blue flashing lights whirled in his dreams. He ran in his restless slumber but couldn't get away from their shimmering beams.

Mick sat up and swore. Once the police got him on the radar, they would fly straight at him like a moth to light and poke around until they found his darkest secrets.

It would not take them long to dig up the truth.

His five years in Low Marsh Prison felt like a lifetime. A lifetime he did not want to relive. There was no way he was going back inside. Not for Alf Bird. Not for Bren Kern. Not for the murder of the woman in the wardrobe.

More voices drifted in from the towpath. This time deep-throated. He peered through the curtains of his narrowboat. A gang of teen boys shuffled along the path. Behind them, a man in a flat cap rode a bike. He rang the bell as he passed the youths.

He had called the pub landlord on his burner phone. "A body in the wardrobe," Alf Bird had said. When Mick asked for more details, he heard Stacy Bird yelling not to talk with him and Alf told him not to call back and hung up.

Mick slumped back onto the bed. Even now, days later, flecks of sweat ran down his forehead. He wiped the dampness away with the bedsheet and forced his mind to use logic. If Alf Bird kept his mouth shut, all would be well. Still, he'd best lie low for a while. Keep out of sight. He said a quick prayer to the Pope and hoped it was enough to keep him from the hot flames of hell. Enough to keep him hidden.

His boat was the best place to hide. No one ever knocked at his door. It was his home. His safe place.

Mick listened to the voices on the towpath and felt a sense of quiet calm. Nothing bad would happen to him if he kept a level head. He peeled back the edge of the curtain and watched as the dark blue uniformed school children passed in small groups. They didn't have a care in the world, and he'd act as if neither did he.

Mick lit a cigarette and took a long draw, then exhaled smoke through his nose. He leaned back on the bed, feeling the stress drain from his body as he looked at the picture of the Pope. It was encased in a solid rosewood frame with sun-proof glass to stop the image from fading. He had moved it from the kitchen to the bedroom to bring him good luck. It gave him a sense of peace. Nothing had changed, not really. Life would go on as it always had.

Having a long drag on the cigarette, he pulled the stained bedsheet up to his shoulders and let his eyelids drift shut. Nicotine infused his lungs.

It was as the relaxation came that his thoughts wandered to his girlfriend Jane Ragsdale. When he first met her, she'd seemed so exciting, a girl to be proud of. She'd watch Star Trek with him on the telly and talk of fairies, magic wands and fire-breathing dragons. But now he wasn't so sure. She wanted a fairy-tale wedding and a cottage in the country with lots of bairns. He wanted to be left alone to live out his life on the boat.

"What does she take me for?" he asked the photo of the Pope. As though he thought it might actually tell him the answer. "A bloody muggins?"

His body juddered in a fit of hacking coughs. Once again, he glanced at the papal image and then stubbed out the cigarette in an empty beer can beside his bed. He was a simple, honest, hard-working man, and he'd go to church if not that he liked to lie in on Sundays. He didn't deserve this. What had he done wrong?

"Jane," he called. "Make me a cup of tea, will you?"

No reply.

"Jane, a cup of tea. I'm parched."

Where was she? He listened. No noise from her

shuffling about. He swore, climbed out of bed, and listened more intently.

No radio.

No hiss of the kettle.

No hacking smoker's cough.

Nope. She was definitely not on the boat.

He glimpsed his reflection on the glass which covered the Pope. He tried to be a good man and Jane wasn't all that bad. Except for her fairy-tale plans. Then he remembered what she'd said about the Gold Kite. Whatever faint impulse he felt to confess his secret desires to a priest faded at the thought of selling his boat.

A flicker of anger flared, and a moment later, a barrage of cursing exploded from his lips. The cow wanted to be his wife but wasn't even there to make him a bloody cup of tea when he woke up after a late night of hard drinking. The Pope was right. Only a muggins like him would put up with a wench like Jane.

Mick flexed his hands, watching the fingers curl, all the while imagining them around Jane's throat. Then he squeezed so the veins in his arms bulged. Laughter echoed across the boat, startling Mick until he realised it came from his own throat.

Something wasn't right in his head. He shouldn't be laughing like that! His anger management therapist, Sloane Kern, said she could help. He thought of her sixteen-year-old daughter, Bren, and wasn't so sure.

His thoughts were interrupted by the tinkle

of a bicycle bell. It sounded familiar, coming from someone he liked to watch. He peeped through the curtains, smiling as a teenage cyclist made her way along the towpath.

Suddenly feeling a lot better, he climbed between the crumpled sheets and screwed his eyes shut, trying once more for sleep. Instead, his mind drifted back to Jane. She'd been on at him about the wedding and wanted to move it to May. He'd agreed to shut her up, thought she meant next May, but when she pointed at the calendar, a gasp caught in his throat.

This May.

Less than four weeks away. He'd never shake wedding bells from her devious mind now. And she knew all his secrets, knew what he had done. Jane had him by the balls and the throat. If he tried to wriggle free, she'd kick him up the arse.

The days were numbered for his narrowboat, the Gold Kite.

A vein pulsed hard in his neck. He placed a palm against his collar to quell it. But it thundered, violent, relentless, and with it, a flame of anger flared into a white-hot fire of rage. There was nothing he could do but let its flames consume him. He sucked in a ragged breath and closed his eyes imagining with increasing joy the sudden snap-snap as he twisted Jane's neck with his hands. For several minutes his lips curved in exquisite delight as the image played repeatedly in his mind. Suddenly, his body shuddered and a sense of calm washed over him.

    Still, Mick Knowles could not sleep.

CHAPTER 27

Mick ambled to the kitchen to put on the kettle for a mug of tea. He sat in the dark quiet of the narrowboat kitchen, sipping from his mug, all the while thinking about Bren.

"You... you... know, don't you? You know what they've found?"

He ran a hand through his salt and pepper hair, pressing it down over his bald spot, wondering what to do.

The narrowboat rocked.

A knock at the door.

Mick froze.

Another knock. Louder.

Who the hell is that?

Not kids out for a prank, they would knock and run. He sawed his jaw back and forth. Mick never locked the door when he was at home. Did Jane set the lock when she left?

A hard thud, followed by the rapid beat of fists. A moment later came a familiar high-pitched squeak. The handle on the rear door slowly turned.

What the hell!

Definitely not kids playing a prank. Not Jane, either. He didn't hear her calling his name. She always did that when she came home.

The squeaking stopped.

Locked.

At least Jane got one thing right, but the lazy cow should have told him where she was going and made him a pot of tea before she left.

Silently, Mick picked up his mobile phone. He jabbed at an app. It connected to the hidden camera he'd installed on the aft of the boat. An image flickered onto the screen. A woman, long and lean, in her forties with close-cropped brown hair. She tugged the door handle.

Detective Sergeant Ria Leigh. He would recognise her anywhere. It had been more than five years since their paths crossed. Ria Leigh was the officer who sent him down. What was she doing on his boat?

He watched with a shocked grimace as she kicked the door, pounded her fists one more time, and then skulked off the boat and out of the camera's view. Mick eased to the window, lifted the curtain at the lower edge and watched until she rounded a bend on the towpath.

He went back to the kettle and poured another mug of tea. The clock was ticking. The police were closer than he thought. How long until she came back?

Mick left the steaming mug on the table, walked slowly to the bedroom and packed a black bag—clothes, hipflask, gloves, mask, and his surgical instrument kit.

On the aft of the boat, he secured the door, leapt onto the towpath and ran.

CHAPTER 28

The first signs of trouble came after Ria Leigh had been standing by the railings of the Port St Giles canal for ten minutes.

A mist rolled in from the sea. White swirls danced on the towpath as it thickened into fog. The last few children hurried to school, mere dark shadows scurrying away.

Ria had put two and two together and hoped she'd come up with four. Ray Briggs, the small-time drug dealer she collared in Whitehaven, blurted out his supplier was a woman in Port St Giles. Then, one of the Whitehaven Soup Kitchen ladies mentioned a new contact for her oxy—Jane Ragsdale.

Ria had been at this game long enough not to be carried away with coincidences. Most of the time, they went nowhere, but sometimes they paid off. As always, though, she followed each lead to see where it led and had tracked Jane Ragsdale to the Gold Kite, a narrowboat owned by Mick Knowles.

She remembered Knowles.

She put him away.

A crack of thunder boomed through the mist; a harbinger of a bad storm to come. Ria glanced skyward but saw only a sheet of swirling white. No rain yet but it was on the way.

Her plan was simple—warn Jane Ragsdale off her patch. If she got lucky, there might be a nice stash of drugs on Jane. A bag or box packed full of oxy with Jane's fingerprints all over it. It wasn't a wild hope. She'd had that sort of luck before when she uncovered a massive hoard on a dealer she thought was small fry. When she got home, she found the worst terror she would ever know. Her mum lifeless on the bathroom floor. An overdose killed her mum that night, but the oxy did her in years before. It was frightening what addiction did. Her mum could only think of her next hit. The funeral was a haze of pain.

Blinking back tears, Ria pulled out her camera and adjusted the focus on the Gold Kite. The key was to watch without being seen. Her lips twisted into a grin at the sound of the rapid-fire clicks. Of course, there was nothing but blur because of the fog so she crept closer to get a better view. Then she watched and waited. Anyone leaving the boat or going on board would be caught in her camera's eye.

Her focus was so intense she didn't hear the sharp tap-tap and slow shuffle of feet.

"You're all right there, me ducky?"

Ria spun.

A stooped woman in a tight green headscarf leaned on a cane. There was a whiff of stale ale and she stood way too close for Ria's liking.

"Me names Mrs Edna Brown, in case you want to know. I walk this path most days. Never seen you in these parts before, me ducky. What you doing?"

Even before she answered, Ria should have known trouble was coming. "A day visit to the canal," Ria said. "I'm on a working vacation."

"There's nowt but derelict buildings and potholed car parks in this part of town, me ducky. No one comes to Port St Giles to visit the canal." She pointed her cane at the Gold Kite. "Looks to me like you were watching that narrowboat and hiding here so you wouldn't be seen. What you up to?"

"I'm a historian." Ria pointed in the vague direction of the brick warehouses. "I study old buildings and that includes that narrowboat."

"Oh aye, me ducky." Edna didn't look convinced. "Can't say I've heard of that before. You sure that is what you are doing?"

"Our heritage is vanishing," Ria replied, speaking a touch too fast. "Within ten years, there will be little left of the town's industrial past. We cannot let our history slip away. I'm here to see that we remember the glory of it all."

Edna snorted. "Ever work in one of those factories? My grandad did twenty years in the canning plant. It were a hell hole, me ducky. He'd come back stinking of five-day-old fish and no amount of soap lifted the pong. Lost his ring finger, he did. Mangled in the machines. The next day he went back to work. If you weren't on the job, you didn't get paid." Again she snorted, voice rising to a shout. "If it were up to me, I'd blow those old buildings to kingdom come, put up something new and tear out the tongue of anyone who says different."

And with that Mrs Edna Brown turned and shuffled away into the deepening swirls of mist.

CHAPTER 29

The first drops of rain had begun to fall when Ria saw a figure step onto the aft of the boat. She scrambled to focus her camera, but the figure jumped onto the towpath and hurried away into the mist before she lined up her shot. Man or woman? Ria couldn't tell.

What to do now?

Her head told her to follow the person. Her gut told her to stay put. She went with her gut, checked her watch, then focused on the aft door of the Gold Kite and knew what she must do.

She reached into her pocket and put on a pair of gloves, then glanced either way along the towpath. She couldn't see far because of the mist.

Good.

Ria heaved an enormous sigh and tried to quell the rising excitement in the pit of her stomach. A chance to poke around the Gold Kite lay before her. What would she find when she got inside?

Breaking and entering was a criminal offence. If she were caught, she'd lose her job. But there was no better way to collect evidence and get leverage to keep her patch clean. That's how she'd won Civic Officer of the year three times in a row. That's how she'd win her fourth. She'd done it before and never got caught, not even close. Why should the Gold Kite be any different?

A fresh wave of dopamine washed over Ria.

Yes, I can do this.

She'd be in and out in ten minutes.

Not a second more.

CHAPTER 30

Ria had no idea what she'd find inside the Gold Kite. And even less idea that in the next ten minutes, her life was going to change forever.

The mist which earlier swirled in patches of white cotton wool had now become a thick rolling fog. It dimmed all sound except the soft pitta patter of the rain which fell in a constant drumbeat.

It wouldn't take long to search the narrowboat, and she figured whoever just left, wouldn't be back anytime soon. Still, she glanced at her watch. *Ten minutes max.*

She neared the Gold Kite and looked both ways along the towpath but couldn't see more than twenty feet. With one final look around Ria crept aboard the boat. It rocked gently as she approached the aft door.

Ria fished around in her handbag and pulled out a pair of shoe protectors. It took the balance of a gymnast to slip them onto her wet shoes.

Taking a long look at the door lock she again reached into her handbag, pulled out a small toolkit, inserted two slim tools into the lock, and felt for the pins. The lock popped and the door eased open. The stench of stale cigarettes, body odour and weed seeped out.

Ria slipped inside and closed the door. It shut with a hard click. Then she climbed down five steps and stood in the galley. There was an electric hob and oven along one wall. On the other wall was a sink full of dirty dishes, a mini-fridge and a countertop with large china jars and an electric kettle. Ria placed a hand against the kettle. Still warm.

Beyond the kitchen was a diner with two benches and a table, then a living room with a flatscreen television followed by a toilet and a shower no bigger than a phone booth. At the front of the boat, the doors to the bedroom were closed.

She walked to the dining area, noted the full mug on the bench table and wondered where to start. Four ashtrays overflowing with cigarette butts clustered around the mug. There were magazines and dirty clothes scattered on the floor. Used fast food containers and crushed beer cans were strewn in every corner.

Ria headed for the bedroom, eased open the door, and took a step back as a blast of stale sweaty air rushed out. A picture of the Pope hung on the wall, and a double bed, unmade, took up most of the space. The sheets needed a good soak and wash. More beer cans and fast-food boxes clustered like a snowdrift against one wall.

Ria puffed out a sharp breath and then opened the wardrobe. Women's clothes hung on a rack, blouses, skirts, jeans, even a wedding dress. On the bottom shelf, scattered in a pile were men's shirts, jeans and underwear. She poked around, but didn't see anything much, closed the wardrobe and glanced at her watch. Five minutes gone.

Her gaze went back to the photo of the Pope, and half expecting to see a secret safe, she moved the image to one side. Nothing but white walls stained with cigarette smoke. Ria concluded the framed image hadn't hung on the wall for long and went back to the galley.

A boom of thunder shuddered through the boat. It rocked. Rain pelted against the windows. Ria twitched the curtains at the edge and peered through the glass. The fog had thinned, but no one walked on the towpath. Her wristwatch told her she'd been inside the boat for eight minutes.

"Ten minutes max," she said to the empty room. "Not a second longer."

Ria went to the stove and opened the oven. Dirty dishes tumbled out. She slammed it shut, gasping at the stink. As she stooped to pick up the plates, she let out a grunt of surprise. Amongst the dirty dishes was a black notebook. A quick flick through confirmed it contained names, addresses and telephone numbers. On the first page, printed in large blue ink was the name:

Jane Ragsdale.

Now Ria took her time, working slowly through each page until she came to a name she recognised—Ray Briggs. She looked up and let out a guffaw. So, Jane Ragsdale was his supplier.

Another blast of thunder shook the boat and pelted rain hard and fast against the window. Ria turned back to the notebook and scanned each new page, her excitement mounting at the long list of people Jane Ragsdale supplied. Slowly, with no rush, she took it all in. Suddenly she stopped, mouth wide, and jabbed a finger at the page—Sloane Kern. That was her anger management therapist!

Ria stared at the details to make sure she'd got it right. *Yes, that's Sloane Kern's office.* She had no idea her therapist needed pills to get through the day.

Interesting.

That nugget of information would come in useful. She tapped the page and considered. This was the sort of breakthrough that could change her life. Once again, she thought about Civic Officer of the year and for the first time that day made plans to build an extension on her new house so that she had a private office from which to do her research. Thrilled at that thought, Ria reached for her phone and took a photograph of each page. When she finished, she dropped the notebook into her handbag.

Nailed it!

It was more than Ria could have wished for, and she had to control herself from once again laughing out loud. Who'd have thought an oven filled with dirty dishes was a hiding place for a drug dealer's contact list?

She was about to head for the stairs that led to the aft door when her eyes fell to the china jars next to the kettle. Their labels read, Coffee, Tea and Sugar. The sugar jar was the largest. Ria thought its size was odd. It looked more like a flour bin than something you'd store sugar in.

She picked it up and turned it in her hands. The jar had a twist-off bottom. It was not until she'd twisted it completely off that Ria let out a gasp. Clear plastic bags, each filled with white tablets—oxy.

"Well, well, well, what have we got here, then?"

Ria counted the tablets and she counted the bags. Forty tablets per bag and twenty bags. Eight hundred tablets, way too much for personal use. She let out a long whistle. A judge would find this very interesting.

With a glance at her watch, Ria realised she was out of time. She used her mobile phone to snap a photo of the jar and its contents, then tipped the plastic bags of pills into her handbag. No time for evidence bags.

She was about to twist the jar back together when she noticed another clear bag, smaller. It was stuck to the bottom of the jar with black tape. She tugged at it and stared wide mouthed. It contained a ring with huge glittering rocks. An engagement ring. Ria held it up to the light and let out another low whistle.

"What are you doing here, my sweet?"

In the silence that followed, the rain seemed to beat down with added wrath.

This was more than Ria hoped for, more than she expected. She took the ring out of the bag and slipped it on her latex gloved finger. *Perfect fit.* The ring went into her pocket. Not that she had marriage on her mind now, not after the break up with her last boyfriend Tom. She sighed. They said success came at a price. Ria knew that only too well.

Who did the ring belong to? It was clear it had been pawned for drugs. Once she got off the Gold Kite, she'd do a bit of digging. If it was real, it'd be worth thousands.

As she made her way to the door, she heard another rumble of thunder. It pounded like a fist on the aft door. The boat rocked.

Ria froze.

Bang, bang, bang.

"Police! Open up."

CHAPTER 31

Ria Leigh had never been a fan of narrowboats. They were cramped with low ceilings and, well, narrow. If she wanted to live in a tube she'd have trained as an astronaut. If fact, she'd spent her years as an adult trying her best to avoid the canal with its stagnate water and pungent smells. The Gold Kite stunk of the swamp, ashtrays and the sewer. Narrowboats were not her thing.

And now she was trapped on one with a police officer pounding on the door.

Her heart rapped hard against her chest as her gaze darted around for a place to hide. Only one problem, the Gold Kite was less than ten feet wide and only forty-two feet long.

"This is the police!" The officer's voice came from just outside the aft door. "Come out on deck. Now."

Ria remained absolutely still. Her only response to the officer's call was to shift her eyes to the door handle. Her mind worked feverishly for the slightest crevice by which to escape.

Nothing.

There was no place for her to go.

Through the constant rap of rain, Ria heard a

familiar voice from just outside the aft door.

"I saw her hanging about, me ducky. She said she were a historian, but I watched her good. She had her eye on this boat, and what with the thieving we've had recently, I thought I'd let you know."

"Well done, Edna," the officer replied. "We'll have it sorted in a jiffy."

For a couple of seconds Ria stared open-mouthed at the door. The gap-toothed woman in the tight green headscarf had gone to get the police!

Shit.

Her whole body went stiff. She did not know how to explain her presence on the boat. As she thought about what this would mean for her career, she glanced down and saw the packets of illegal pills. What would she say? How could she explain her handbag overflowing with eight-hundred oxy tablets?

A fist pounded on the door. Much louder. Urgent.

"I'm PC Jon Phoebe. Mr Knowles, are you home?" There was a pause. "Miss Ragsdale, if you are there, can you open the door?"

Ria had to get the pills out of her handbag and back into the sugar jar, fast. But the slightest sound would alert the police officer to her presence. There seemed to be no good choice. Move and the officer would know she was inside. Don't move and get caught with oxy.

"Try the door handle, me ducky. Micky never locks it when he is at home, though I've told him often enough."

A second later a high-pitched squeal caused Ria's eyes to go wide. The door handle turned.

Time slowed to a crawl.

The hard slush of rain on the roof of the boat rattled with a nerve-abrading beat. Ria sucked in a shallow breath. A pungent mash-up of stale cigarettes, acrid sweat and rancid fried grease. The stench churned into a foul taste on her dry tongue; tart, fetid, week-old milk gone sour. Even the colours in the dim room became more vivid. Sharp pinpricks of dread prickled her skin.

There was no way out.

The door handle continued to turn slowly.

The best she could do now was damage control. She stooped to rip off her shoe protectors and then tore the latex gloves from her hands. There was no way she'd be able to explain those items. Next, she hid her handbag under a pile of sweaty clothes.

As the door handle squealed, Ria waited, but her mind now raced over all manner of explanations which all came up short. This was it, then. Trapped like a rat in a snare.

Then came a sharp thud followed by a low-pitched grunt.

"It's locked," PC Phoebe said.

"Kick it in, me ducky. Like they do on the telly."

"Um."

"Go on, them boots you have on are big enough. Give it the boot, ducky, and let's have a poke about inside. I've always wanted to have a good look around this boat."

"Can't do that, Edna," PC Phoebe replied. "There are no signs of a break-in, and the door is locked."

"But I saw that woman hanging about and know she was up to no good."

"Whoever you saw has gone about her lawful business. Come on, let's get out of this rain. How about I treat you to a cup of tea and an iced bun while I take your statement?"

Ria waited a full ten minutes before she eased off the Gold Kite and hurried away into the rain and thinning swirls of fog.

CHAPTER 32

It was a little after seven-thirty in the evening and the rain and fog had gone, leaving glorious vibrant views of sand and sea. Glittering shades of orange and gold scattered off the low clouds. The pleasant surroundings gave no hint of the disturbing news about to land at Fenella's door.

She was twenty minutes into her jog and making good pace on the moist sands of the beach near her cottage on Cleaton Bluff. The soft slap of waves against the shore mingled with the salt sea tang. She scanned the flotsam and jetsam as she followed the gentle curve of the beach. Every once in a while, she'd see strands of netting, bottles or shreds of plastic bags. That meant a quick stop to pick them up and toss them in her backpack. She didn't mind. It gave her a breather and helped keep the beach clean.

Jogging in a slow arc, she doubled back on herself. Sunset was a little after eight and she wanted to be home before dark. Nan would have a hot cup of cocoa ready, and she liked to hear about Eduardo's day. He worked from home, drew comics for a living and always had something interesting to say. Fenella loved that about him and loved the five children they had raised.

But this evening, she needed time to think. About the man with the devil's wisp beard. About the woman in the wardrobe. About Eve. And she could not think about any of it at home.

No way.

That was her golden rule. She kept police work out of her house. Life as a detective could be crazy and the hours just as bad. She'd seen others take work files home and fuss over unsolved cases while their family drifted from them. The spouse and kids did their own thing, while the detective pondered dark crimes. Year in Year out.

Then divorce came as a sudden tear in the fabric of life, and the detective turned to the bottle or pills or worked even harder on the job. It happened to a lot of police officers and their families. Sooner or later, if you obsessed over the job, it did you in.

Fenella loved her family.

She loved her job.

That's why she never broke her golden rule.

Ever.

Her legs picked up the pace. She'd put on a few pounds around her waist but didn't think it showed. Still, the extra weight seemed to slow her progress as she pounded on through the sand.

Her lungs worked hard as her mind drifted to the past. Seven years ago. The cold icy night of the car crash near the village of St Bees. The night which took Eve's husband, Grant. The night Eve vanished from her hospital bed. The night when everything changed.

Nan still cried and there was nothing Fenella could do about it. The police search drew a blank. No one knew what happened to her sister. Seven years on and they were still healing. Still asking questions. And Fenella was still looking for Eve.

She was the only one.

Eve's case fell into the unsolved file, and inch by inch had fallen off the police radar. There were thousands of missing person cases where the truth had not been found. No one searched for the long-term missing. No one knew where they went.

Friday's discovery of the body in the wardrobe seemed an age away on this Monday evening. They had kept the press away, so far. Fenella exhaled a long breath. If it was her sister, at least her family would find some peace. But with the tongue torn out and the ring finger missing, Fenella knew she'd not rest until she'd found the killer.

"I'll not let the bugger who did this to you get away."

She gasped in quick breaths of the cold sea air and glanced at the sun low on the horizon. A flock of black-headed gulls screamed at the edge of the shore. She jogged from the firm sand of the shoreline to the deep soft pockets further inland.

Jogging on this part of the beach required more work. Puffing hard, it was much slower, but she had enough time to get home before dark. The screaming gulls stayed close to the shore.

As she passed an outcrop of rocks, her mobile phone rang. She did not recognise the ring tone, and for a short while let it ring to voice mail. It stopped and three seconds later began again. She pulled it from her pocket and gazed at the screen. A private number.

Curious, she slowed to a walk, again glanced at the screen and noted the time, seven-forty-six, then answered. "Fenella Sallow."

"Is that Inspector Sallow?"

Not a voice Fenella recognised. Raspy. A woman? Or a high-pitched man? Something about the shrill tone made her instantly alert.

"Aye, how can I help you?"

"That woman in the wardrobe." There was a long pause. "I know who she is."

"Who's calling, please?"

"There will be more now that you have found her."

"What are you on about, pet?"

"Never disturb the dead."

CHAPTER 33

Fenella took a sip from the paper cup and scowled as though she knew the hell the day was about to bring.

It was all you can eat Tuesday, 8.00 a.m. in the Port St Giles police station canteen. It heaved with a large crowd as officers gorged on the breakfast fry-up. A few added large cups of the Cumbria Constabulary bitter coffee brew. Not Fenella. Too early for fatty foods, and the initial high from a blend of sugar and caffeine wasn't worth the inevitable low. Not today. Not with her mind whirring at full tilt.

She sat at a table in the canteen with Dexter and Detective Constable Jones. The air in the warm room was heavy with the smells of fried food, clang of plates and chatter of voices. She wanted to discuss the woman in the wardrobe and the mysterious call to her mobile phone but held her tongue while they ate. Or rather, while Dexter gobbled his down. He never took long. *Best have his belly full and mind focused before I begin.*

"Can't beat an English breakfast, Guv." Dexter wiped a piece of fried bread around his plate. "Black pudding, beans, eggs nice and soft, fried tomatoes, bacon with three slices of fried bread. It'll keep me going for hours."

"And you've eaten enough for four." Fenella wondered how he'd stay awake. She needed him alert and bright now her team was down to three. She nodded at Jones. "Not having any?"

Jones sipped from a cup of hot water. "Late night, boss. Downed one too many." He gulped hard as if not trying to throw up. "Don't think I could eat that lot, not in my state."

"Don't talk daft, lad," Dexter said. "Quickest way to come back from too much booze is to fill up on a greasy fry-up. Didn't they teach you that in detective school?" His lips curved into a devilish grin. "Here, have a slice of me fried bread and dab it in that egg yolk. It'll do you the world of good."

"No, no," Jones gasped, raising a hand. He lacked the beer hardened gut of Dexter. "I can't face it."

"Come on lad, it's all runny and greenish-yellow. Have a dip with me grease-soaked fried bread and get it down ya."

Jones clasped a hand to his mouth, stood and hurried towards the toilets. Dexter chortled and waved the fried bread at Jones who'd broken out into a trot.

It was a full ten minutes before Jones returned on unsteady legs to their table. Fenella took a quick sip from her cup. A late-night booze session was odd for Jones. He wasn't much of a drinker. This was the first time he'd been out of sorts on the job.

She'd let it pass and watch for signs that it might be a problem. *Not that unusual for the police, look at Dexter. Recovering alcoholic. Badly at times.*

She pushed that thought out of her head and something else clicked in her mind. Fenella called it her detective switch. Nan and Eduardo called it her nosy gene. Was Jones with a woman last night? Her matchmaking brain clicked over the possible lasses. Not PC Beth Finn. That lass wasn't one to knock back booze on a Monday night. She barely drank more than a glass of red wine on the weekends. Some other lass, she thought, wondering if Jones and PC Beth Finn were no longer an item. She'd find out even though it was none of her business. They had made that clear in the management training class.

The instructor had said, "Management must not poke into the private lives of their team."

Fenella agreed, but in this case, it didn't apply. No one on her team had a private life because they blabbed it all to her, and she had to listen, didn't she? That was her duty as their manager.

She pointed at Jones. "Don't keep us guessing, pet. What's the name of the lass you boozed the night away with?"

"It wasn't a woman," Jones replied. "It was Dr MacKay. He invited me to his studio for a demonstration. I think he got the worst of it. He knocked back two for each one I drank."

Fenella had heard rumours that the doctor lived in his studio. She'd seen his club with her own eyes and now wondered if there was a bedroom and fancy kitchen as the rumours suggested.

She said, "You met him in his studio at night?"

"He says that's when he does his best work. I didn't want to go but lost a bet." Jones took a sip of hot water from his cup and looked like he was about to throw up. "Damn near drank half a bottle of whisky. The only good thing about it was that it dulled my eyes."

Dexter was laughing. "Next time have a big plate of greasy food beforehand, lines the stomach so you can enjoy his good booze. That's what I do but Dr MacKay don't invite me no more."

Fenella was laughing too. Light-hearted banter lifts the spirit even in the grimmest of times, and Jones was a good sport. She liked that.

Dexter stuffed the last of his fried bread into his mouth and chewed thoughtfully. "Any news on your DNA test results, Guv?"

She'd not said a word about the DNA test but wasn't surprised Dexter knew. He had his ear so close to the ground that Fenella wondered whether he slept.

"A few more days is my best guess." She changed the subject. "Found out anything about Alf and Stacy Bird?"

"Did a bit of digging, Guv. Family, friends. Nowt much has come up. The only thing I've found is that they entered poultry shows a few years back. Won ribbons for their Old English Game chickens. Beautiful birds, those. My grandad had a few, never did the poultry shows, though."

"Nothing unusual with their finances, either," Jones added.

Jones liked to work with bank accounts and computers. Quite a talent. That pleased Fenella. Still, she sensed that Alf and Stacy Bird were up to no good. They had interviewed the landlord of the Navigator Arms and his wife separately at the station. They both had a wary look and a tense attitude that comes from having something to hide. Was it relevant to the woman in the wardrobe?

She said, "Keep working the soil, see what comes up."

"I'll have a quiet chat with a few more of the regulars, Guv," Dexter said. "Might catch a whiff of what Alf and Stacy Bird are about. By the way, I've tracked down the previous landlord, a Mr Ken Finch." He fished around in his pocket, pulled out his notebook, and studied it for several seconds. "Mr Finch lives on Fleetwood Lane."

"Let's the two of us pay him a visit," Fenella said, thinking she didn't want to be trapped in the office all day. She looked at Jones. "Any joy tracing the call to my mobile phone?"

"All we have is the wireless provider's name," Jones replied.

She expected no other answer. It didn't stop her from feeling a deep sense of frustration. She wanted the name of the person who called her. How did they know about the woman in the wardrobe? Were they the killer?

Jones said, "I've put in a request for a warrant

to the Superintendent. Once she signs off, we'll have access to the phone company's records."

It had been months now since Superintendent Jeffery ordered all warrants to go through her desk. Carlisle wanted lower numbers so they looked good to the politicians in London. All the political parties were riding a wave of public outrage at the ease and number of warrants issued. The police were under the magnifying glass. But Jeffery was late with her paperwork and things piled up unless you gave them a swift kick.

Fenella decided to add a chat with the boss to her list. If it needed a kick to jolly things along, she was game for the task. Still speaking to Jones she said, "How is that list of missing women coming along?"

"I've narrowed the timeframe to the past eight years and come up with ten names, boss." He handed her a printout and then lowered his voice. "It includes your sister, Eve."

"Good work," Fenella said, wishing it wasn't so. "We're getting closer to finding out her name, and that's progress in my book."

Another wave of officers flowed into the canteen and lined up by the counter to fill their plates. Len Moreland, the duty sergeant, strolled to the front of the queue. No one seemed to mind. They knew he had to be quick. He waved at Fenella and then carried his tray from the hall.

Dexter rattled the change in his pocket. He did that when he had big news.

"There was a talent spotter in the crowd on Saturday night, Guv. He liked my Priscilla's set and invited her to sing at the Tarns Dub Music Festival. Only a backing singer, though. I've got free tickets, so both of you can come along." He handed out four tickets, two each. "Bring a partner with you. This is her big chance."

"Fingers crossed," Fenella said, wondering whether she'd go with Nan or Eduardo. She decided on Nan then flashed an innocent smile at Jones. "Who are you going to bring with you?"

Jones didn't get to answer, for at that moment they saw Len Moreland, the duty sergeant, running towards them.

CHAPTER 34

Duty Sergeant Len Moreland slammed to a stop at their table. From the look on his face, he brought news. And it wasn't good.

"Got one for you, ma'am," he said and rubbed his hands. "A body's been pulled out of the canal near the Navigator Arms. Thought you might want to take a look seeing as what you found inside that pub."

That was not what Fenella expected. Not at all. She stood and headed for the door. They took her Morris Minor, Dexter at the wheel with Jones in the back, and saw the flashing lights two streets shy of the canal. Dexter parked next to a fire truck. Its lights pulsated in slow ponderous flares.

They ditched the car and walked towards the activity. Jones moved in jerky steps as though his stomach were a bowl of sour soup he didn't want to spill. Figures in white suits climbed from a van and set out along a dirt trail. A constable stretched blue and white tape between two trees to hold back a small crowd—kids on their way to school, workers in grubby overalls, and dog walkers. They all used the trail as a cut-through to the canal towpath. Standing apart from the crowd, a nun watched, newspaper folded under her arm.

Fenella recognised the constable by the police tape, PC Jon Phoebe. She'd worked with him before. A good cop.

"Morning, ma'am," he said. "Follow the trail, take a right at the towpath."

A stooped woman in a tight green headscarf appeared at the back of the crowd. She used her cane to prod and poke her way to the front where she nodded at PC Phoebe.

"What's going on, me ducky?"

"Stay back, Edna," PC Phoebe said, lowering the tape for Fenella, Dexter and Jones. "This is official police business."

"Aye, me ducky. I'll not cross that line." Edna leaned in on a cane. "But this towpath is used by schoolchildren. We wants to know the details of what happened so we can stay safe, ducky."

There was a murmur of agreement from the crowd and several people clapped.

PC Phoebe said, "I can't say a word, Edna. It's more than my job is worth. Why don't you go home and have a nice cuppa to warm you up? I'm sure you'll read all about it in the newspaper."

Fenella grimaced. The last thing she wanted was the press on her heels. Once you set them off, they would not stop digging. She wanted to keep them away for as long as possible. They would only poke about and cause more problems. She spun and scanned the crowd to see if any looked like they might be from the news media. She noticed the nun in the black habit. No one from the press. They continued on their way as PC Phoebe argued with Edna.

It felt colder on this side of the tape. That much closer to the water, Fenella supposed. Or maybe it was the grim business of death which flowed through every crime scene. Techs in white suits, police photographers, firefighters and ambulance crew. And the small white tent which shrouded the corpse from prying eyes.

That was where she had to go next. Beyond those thin white walls lay a once-live human. Her heart fluttered with the rapid beat of a hummingbird's wings. Always the same sense of nervous energy as she approached the heart of a crime scene. Always the same sense of loss for a life cut down too soon. And that was another of her little secrets. She'd been a detective for donkey's years, but never got used to death.

"Guv," Dexter said, touching her arm and pointing.

Through the trees the frosted glass windows and red slate roof of the Navigator Arms were visible.

"Aye," she said. "I see it. A body in a wardrobe and now a body in the canal, what are the chances, eh?"

"Could be a coincidence," Jones said, staring at the ancient pub. "The random hand of fate, boss."

Fenella didn't mind the random hand of fate when it brought good luck. When it brought dead bodies, she wasn't so keen. She said, "Jones, once we've had a look at what's inside that tent, go back and have a word with the crowd. Then knock up Alf Bird and see if he or his wife saw anything."

"I can start on that now if you like, boss," Jones replied.

He didn't want to go in the crime scene tent, either. Fenella didn't blame him. Not with all the alcohol running around his system and making him feel queasy.

She said, "Detective Constable Jones, I would like your observations on the crime scene."

"Yes boss," Jones replied through clenched teeth.

That'll teach him, she thought. Next time he won't be so keen to booze the night away.

The door to the crime scene tent opened and a woman in a white crime tech suit and mask hurried towards them wheeling a large black crime-scene suitcase behind her. She took off her mask—Lisa Levon. She headed the crime scene techs and had a figure like a Paris model and the glittering smile of a Hollywood star. Nearly forty and gorgeous.

"Two girls on their way to school found the body," Lisa said. "Teens."

"Jones, get the details and have a chat with them when we are done here." Fenella turned back to Lisa. "Do we have the victim's name?"

"Can't help you on that one." Lisa shook her head. "No identification on the body. Nothing on time of death, yet, although Doctor MacKay is inside."

Fenella stared in shock. From what she understood, Doctor MacKay had a skinful of booze last night; twice as much as Jones, and Jones still looked as though he was about to throw up. What was he doing at the crime scene? And how the hell did he get there before them?

She said, "No handbag?"

Lisa's brow crinkled. "She must have left it at the hospital."

"What makes you think that?"

"When we pulled her from the canal she was wearing a medical gown. Nothing else."

CHAPTER 35

Fenella approached the crime scene tent. Dexter and Jones were at her side. She'd spent years as a detective; tracking killers and dealing with gruesome crimes. It made no difference to the slow churn in her gut. You never knew what you'd find when you entered those soft white walls.

She suited up, stepped through the flap of the crime scene tent and felt the first chill through her body. The phone call on the beach played out in her head as she breathed in the cold moist air.

Never disturb the dead.

Her heart feared a link. Her head told her not to jump to the worst-case conclusion. How could a call from a nutter while she jogged on the beach be related to a death in the canal?

Best wait and see what we've got.

To the untrained eye, it looked like chaos. White suits were busy at work. They took photographs and collected evidence. At the centre, Dr MacKay crouched over the body.

He eased to his feet as Fenella approached, and she got her first clear view of the woman—girlish face bloated and pale with vacant eyes which stared at the heavens; lips blushed with a bluish tinge. Her mouth was partly open. She wore a beige medical gown.

Dr MacKay turned. "Ah, Fenella, thought I might see you, and you've brought your team."

"What have we got?" Fenella asked, not taking her eyes from the woman's face. She didn't like what she was seeing and sensed there was more to come she wouldn't like.

Dr MacKay said, "Death in mysterious circumstances at the very least. But it is too early to know for sure what happened."

"Don't give me that," Fenella replied. The man wasn't one to hold back on his ideas, especially when it came to death. "I want to know everything you are thinking, including the wild stuff."

Dr MacKay chuckled. It always surprised Fenella that he could laugh in the face of death. He'd been like that from the very first day she'd met him. Laughing and joking as he sliced and diced and examined. He kept his finger on the pulse, built a network from the cleaner to high-flying politicians, and seemed to know everyone in town. Was that the secret of how he'd kept his job for what she figured was close to forty years?

Damn good at his job, too. She'd not met another pathologist with his passion. Nor one who'd freely speculate on the cause of death and bet a bottle of Glenmorangie to back up his view. There was no knowing what he'd say. She liked that about him.

"I'll do my best not to disappoint," he said, the

smile still in his voice. "First, I feel I should inform you that I know the victim."

"Go on," Fenella said, trying to hide her shock. "Are you going to explain?"

"You've met the wife?"

His wife was as thin as a wisp, wore African kanga dresses with pink sandals and drove an ancient Volkswagen minibus with black windows to keep folk from seeing what went on inside.

Dr MacKay was speaking. "She likes to drag me to social events. Springs them on me on the day so I can't object." He looked at Dexter. "Women! You know what I mean?"

Dexter gave a sly nod but did not speak. Fenella gave him the evil eye.

"Now here's the thing," Dr MacKay said. "My wife likes her hobbies, always trying something new. Says it keeps her mind active. Not me. I like what I do and it's all that I do. She is a volunteer at the Whitehaven Soup Kitchen. It's on Irish Street. She's been serving food there for six months. Know the place, do you?"

"Aye, I've heard of it," Fenella replied. She ran a group that cooked meals for police officers whose spouses fell ill. A few of her helpers also volunteered at the soup kitchens in nearby towns. "Keep going."

Dr MacKay said, "Lots of middle-class women like to help serve the food. The mothering instinct, I suppose." He looked at Dexter. "Don't you agree?"

Dexter kept his face straight.

"Well," Dr MacKay said, glancing around. "One

thing led to another and about a month ago my wife received an invitation from one of her fellow soup kitchen helpers to a rather posh do in the village of Grange. She dragged yours truly along with her. Lots of French wine and smelly cheese. Nothing but an excuse to get blotto, if you ask me. I didn't resist. When in Rome..."

He paused for a moment as the crime scene photographer took a volley of photos.

He continued. "Most of the women at the event were middle-aged and well-to-do." He pointed at the corpse. "Not this lass. She was much younger and appeared... a little rough around the gills. Out of place, if you get my drift. Well, I asked myself what was a young lass of her background doing at a well-to-do dinner in Grange?"

"And what was the answer?" This was Dexter.

Dr MacKay shrugged. "That remains a mystery. But I do recall her name." He paused for a moment, clearly thinking. "Ragsdale... Jane Ragsdale."

CHAPTER 36

The name rang no bells with Fenella but she felt a wave of relief. Now she had a name, she could build a picture of the person, get photographs and ask questions that brought Jane Ragsdale to life. The next step was to get a clear picture of what had happened to the lass. She gazed at the body not seeing a corpse but a person.

"What happened Jane, luv?"

"Name rings a bell, Guv." Dexter leaned closer to the body, eyes on her face. "Don't look like the lass I have in mind, though. Must have been five or six years ago. A Miss Jane Ragsdale got into a fight with her landlady over late rent. Uniform responded, and you'd have thought that would be that. But I got dragged into it."

"Why?" This was Dr MacKay.

"Jane was on my list of contacts. When a person on your list gets into difficulties, you try to help them out. But Jane was a strange one."

This was the first time Fenella had heard Dexter talk about Jane Ragsdale. He kept his list of contacts secret from her prying eyes. The chance to peel back the curtain and take a peek was irresistible.

She said, "How do you mean, strange?"

"Turns out she was a slice short of a full loaf," Dexter replied. "Jane got it into her head that the landlady, Mrs Edna Brown, agreed to pay her rent to stay in the flat."

It was early and despite the coffee, what he said made no sense to Fenella.

"Eh?" she said. "How'd you mean pay *her* money?"

"After Jane moved in, she said she was a fairy-tale princess awaiting her handsome knight who'd help her find her lost magic wand." Dexter glanced around, lowering his voice. "She said once the knight showed up and the wand was found, she'd grant the landlady three wishes. But the landlady would have to pay her money each month until then. Jane complained to me that after two months in the flat, Mrs Edna Brown hadn't paid her a penny. Granted, the landlady's place wasn't the Ritz, but her claim was a bit... out there."

"Now let me get this straight," Fenella said, speaking slowly. "Are you telling us Jane Ragsdale expected the landlady to pay her money to live in the landlady's flat?"

"That about sums it up real nice," Dexter replied, eyes still on the corpse. "I smoothed things over and Jane moved out of Mrs Brown's lodgings that night. Later, I did a bit of digging and heard that the lass was away with the fairies most of the time— high on weed and oxy."

"I'll run a test, see if she had any in her blood

at the time of death," Dr MacKay said. "Might be gangland revenge."

"This ain't New York City, Doc," Dexter replied. "Anyway, I dropped Jane from my list, unreliable. She faded into the shadows and fell off my radar." He shook his head and again stared hard at Jane's face. "Why don't I recognise her?"

Dr MacKay said. "I once examined a woman from the village of Dent who'd looked older than my great-grandmother. So many wrinkles. Turns out she was only thirty-seven. That one was a drug-induced drowning in the River Dee, nothing to do with gangland crime." He looked at the corpse and shook his head. "If you knew Jane Ragsdale from five years back, it is no surprise you didn't recognise her today. When a person hits the drugs hard, they age in dog's years. Opiate addiction wreaks havoc on the skin."

His words were lost in the swell of relief which continued to wash over Fenella. They had made a major step forward. Now they would run a background check on Jane Ragsdale—friends, family, known associates. That would scare up a list of names.

The next step was to get a clear picture of what had happened to the lass. She nodded at Dr MacKay to go on. He cleared his throat and there was something about the way his eyes slowly moved back to the corpse that set Fenella on edge.

"Time of death is within the past twelve hours," Dr MacKay said. "I'd say sometime after dark... oh, let's say around 11 p.m. or midnight. It appears she has been operated on."

Fenella's blood froze. Dr MacKay stooped and tilted the victim's head with gloved hands so they could see more clearly into her mouth.

"No tongue," he said. "Recently removed."

Fenella felt her heart pound faster. It was terrifying to imagine what had happened. She couldn't stare at the gaping mouth for more than a few moments. Jones, who'd been quiet the entire time, made a glugging sound and rushed from the tent.

"Soft sod," muttered Dexter, a tremor in his voice. "I'll make a copper out of him yet."

"What are we dealing with here?" Fenella said softly, searching Dr MacKay's eyes and not liking what she saw.

"I'm not the detective," he said. "But there may be a link to the body in the wardrobe. Please take a close look..." His voice trailed off, and he eased the body so they could see the hands. "... her ring finger is missing, also recently removed."

A hard swallowing sound came from Dexter as though he were forcing his breakfast back into his stomach. They had entered a land where nightmares lurk and truth hid deep in the shadows.

"Can't believe what I'm seeing, Doc," he said, voice as dry as toast. "I mean, what type of maniac hacks out a woman's tongue and saws off her ring finger?"

"I'd say she was alive when they were

removed," Dr MacKay replied. "But she died before she hit the water." He shook his head. "Such a pity Jones had to run else I'd have bet him a bottle of Glenmorangie on that. The labs will confirm." He heaved an enormous sigh. "Please come closer and take a look at this."

Fenella didn't want to get closer, nor she sensed did Dexter. But curiosity got the better of her and she noticed Dexter leaned in close too.

Dr MacKay lifted the medical gown to expose the naked torso.

"A freshly stitched incision," he said. "Not the hand of a Harley Street plastic surgeon. Too untidy for that."

They stood very quietly for a long moment, staring at the stitches.

Fenella felt a sudden knot of tension form in her neck. She tilted her head from side to side and kept up her façade of calm strength. Inside, the wild horses of dread stampeded. She thought of the woman in the wardrobe and Eve and this poor lass who'd been tossed into the canal and her eyes filled with tears. She couldn't speak at the horror of it all.

Dexter touched her arm. "What are you saying, Doc?"

Dr MacKay stared down at the body for a long while, then in a slow measured tone said, "I'd say the person who did this was..." He paused and ran a gloved hand over the stitches. "Umm... quite possibly... a rusty surgeon out for revenge. Yes, I like that theory. A bottle of Glenmorangie, anyone?"

CHAPTER 37

Mick Knowles crouched low in the damp dust, rubbed his gloved hands and seethed.

It's all gone wrong!

Because it seemed the police had found Jane Ragsdale's body floating in the canal.

Did anyone see me run?

He crept on all fours, then slumped against the bare brick wall on the second floor of an abandoned warehouse which overlooked the canal. The stench of human waste flooded his nostrils. The homeless used this graffiti-stained place as a toilet. In front of him, smashed panes of glass let in a stream of cold air which chilled his damp clothes and froze him to his core. His chest heaved so hard he felt a soreness in his sides.

He listened for the sound of footsteps, watched for movement in the shadows, every sense on high alert. The howl of the wind as it whipped up the stench of rot and decay. A harsh rattle of rusted chains from the beams overhead. From the shattered window a police siren screeched above the low mumble of voices.

They had dragged his girlfriend's corpse from the canal. It wouldn't be long before the police put two and two together and came looking for him. He'd be locked up for years. It wasn't his fault he lost his temper. Why should he go down again because of rage?

Mick panted hard and tried to slow his breath. What he needed was a sign. A light to show the way out of this mess. He thought of the picture of the Pope on the wall of his boat and hoped God would send him one soon. While he waited, he wondered if he should have run farther. Left town. Lie low in Carlisle or disappear into the ghettos of London.

No!

Not yet.

He had to see Jane lifeless on a stretcher to close her off in his mind. He didn't know why that was key for him, all he knew was that he had to watch, and this place gave him a bird's-eye view of the scene. Just like when he was a small boy and he'd hide under his mum's bed to watch. He had a photographic memory for details. Never forgot what he saw.

But he didn't remember much before he was seven.

Because of the beatings.

What did he remember? His mother. He recalled her face but would not let that image into his mind. She smelled of sweet lemon scents and was lying in bed with a newborn in her arms. His baby sister. His mum turned to him and spoke a name. It was the baby's name. A nice name to do with the farm, but he didn't remember what his baby sister was called.

Then it was Sunday, and he was in the kitchen with the wide windows that overlooked the vegetable plot with potatoes growing from the humped soil and the aga oven which hissed. And there were the smells. Savoury roasted meats mingled with onions and gravy. A smell he'd never forget. He asked his mum what it was. She told him they would have chick-chick for dinner, one of gran's Old English Game birds, a black-breasted cockerel called Rocky.

"Wrung its neck with my own hands," his mum had said with pride. "Squeezed until it clicked."

"Poor chick-chick," he remembered saying. "Who will I play with now?"

"Snap," she said. "Snap. Snap. Snap. Chick-chick smells good to you?"

But he'd smelled roast chicken before, and it didn't smell like that.

"Not chick-chick," he said. "Not Rocky."

His mum slapped him across his face with the back of her right hand. Her wedding ring caught his nose. It started to bleed.

"You eat it all when it is cooked," she said. "Don't you dare leave a scrap. Chew hard on the bones. Crush them between your teeth. Rocky make you big and strong."

Mick wished with all his heart his mum had let him see Rocky lifeless on the butcher's board. Plucked clean of feathers, as pale as the dawn. Why hadn't she allowed him that? Why didn't she let him see Rocky after his bird friend's life had faded to dark?

In his next memory, he was hiding in the coal chute, peeping through a grate into the kitchen. His mum put a roasting pan in the oven and left the room. Micky opened the grate, climbed out the chute and was alone in the kitchen. He tiptoed to the oven and opened the heavy door to look inside. A waft of hot moist air caught him by surprise. He squinted through the heat at the roasting pan. His eyes grew wide at the chicken. He never saw his baby sister again.

Breathing fast he flexed his hand, then let his body relax. He didn't want those images, wanted memories of Santa Claus and opening gifts on Christmas day. Didn't want to recall the face of his mum; wanted to see his gran.

For a moment he thought about Bren Kern and began to breathe even harder.

You... you... know, don't you? You know what they've found?

She was only a teen. So young. He made a silent vow to leave town after he'd visited his gran and set his gaze on the innocent face of Bren Kern for the very last time.

Time. He didn't have much. Easier after dark. Lie low here until then. He took out his mobile phone and smashed it with his boots. No chance of tracking him. Panting, he reached into his other pocket for his burner phone. He'd keep that, but only for use in an emergency.

He reached into his pocket and pulled out a pen and a slip of pink paper. Slowly, in his best hand, he began to write. A shuffling sound came from behind. He turned, expecting to see a homeless person. Instead, two pigeons saw him and flew. He stuffed the pen and paper back into his pocket, letting out a curse as he did so. It could wait until later.

Mick listened once more for the sound of footsteps and scanned for a flicker of motion.

Nothing.

He held his breath, eased to a window, and peeped out.

He hadn't realised there would be so many police.

A dozen vehicles parked in an arc a hundred yards from where he watched—patrol cars, a fire truck with lights still flashing, an ambulance next to a blue Morris Minor, and a white van.

For a while, he watched the small crowd of locals. They gathered in front of the police tape where a lone constable stood guard. A gust blew through the window and rattled the chains on the beams. Mick shivered. His clothes stunk of swamp. *Canal water is a bugger to wash out.*

He was staring at the ancient blue Morris Minor and wondering if joy riders had dumped it when he heard an excited hum. Suddenly, the cold seemed more intense. Outside, the sun burst through a wall of low clouds, shining shards of jagged light onto the crowd.

And then he saw them.

They picked their way through the patches of grass and gravel. Two paramedics. Heads drooped. They carried a black body bag on a thin stretcher. The crowd parted to let them through.

Then he saw the slender detective with shoulder-length grey hair. At her side, the grizzled man in the rumpled suit he'd seen prowling outside the Navigator Arms. They got in the Morris Minor. Those detectives would be a problem.

He moved away from the window. It wouldn't be long before they were on his tail. That meant he had less time than he'd have liked.

How far can you run before you are caught?

At the scream of a siren, he turned back to the window. Near the entrance to the building, a figure in black looked up. He recognised Sister Burge. Could she see him watching her?

She carried a newspaper and raised it to shield her eyes. She appeared to look straight at him. His breath caught in his ribs. He wasn't expecting this. For a long while, she stood very still and stared.

Welcome to the Last Chance Saloon.

A sign from God to turn himself in? He closed his eyes and saw the smiling face of the Pope inside the glass and rosewood frame that hung on the cabin wall of the Gold Kite.

"It wasn't my fault Jane died," he whispered. "I couldn't save her. Only God can now."

He opened his eyes, glanced through the window and was about to call out to Sister Burge when she turned and hurried away.

And with that, Mick Knowles scurried back into the shadows, determined the police would not get him.

CHAPTER 38

Ria Leigh knew she should have gone home. She should have gone back to her flat to think about what to do about the black diary, bags of oxy and that diamond ring. In short, she needed to figure out what to do next.

But she'd spent the night hidden in the bushes by the canal watching the Gold Kite. Now, at nine in the morning, she sat in her car parked in a side street near the canal. Her stomach churned with anxiety as her damp clothes slowly dried. The engine hummed softly, whooshing warm air into the cabin. It condensed on the glass to cloud out the view. Ria didn't notice. Her eyes were closed, total focus on the police radio which played low through the speaker.

She'd been listening for hours and learned they had hauled a woman's body from the canal and Port St Giles detectives had visited the scene. Another team of crime scene techs were on the way, along with three divers to search the canal.

Waste of time and money, Ria thought. No other body lay in those murky waters. Only one woman died last night. And that lass got what she deserved.

Ria lowered the driver's side window. A stream of cold air flowed into the car as the dispatcher's voice continued to crackle over the car speaker.

"They've found her body, so what?" she said to the empty car.

Ria felt like a ghost. She was off duty, and no one knew she was there. No one knew she'd been aboard the Gold Kite, moored a few hundred yards from where they had hauled out the body. No one knew what she'd found. The diary, drugs and ring were her secrets. And that's the way she liked it. That's how she hauled in the drug dealing prawns, kept her patch of Whitehaven clean, and would win Civic Officer of the year for the fourth year straight.

Again, Ria spoke out loud. "Go home and get some sleep." She glanced at her ring finger and liked the way it glistened. "When you wake up refreshed, nothing will have changed. Nothing. Life will go on as it must."

She wiped the windscreen with a flat hand and shifted the car into first when she suddenly remembered the gloves and shoe protectors. She had hidden them under a pile of clothes and forgot to take them with her in the rush to leave the Gold Kite. Her shoe prints would be on the floor and fingerprints on the door handle.

Ria cursed.

She put the gear stick to neutral, closed the window and cranked up the heater, but a chill sweat stung her eyes. What else had she missed?

The engine rolled over in a soft hum. That

woman in the green headscarf! She had a good look at Ria and called a police officer to the boat. Ria pounded her fists into the dashboard until she felt a stitch in her side. Now, she must play a different game. Do what it took to tilt things back in her favour. She had done it before, called heads and won. She'd do it again now. Place her bet and toss the coin. There was no guarantee it would land head's side up. That was part of the thrill.

She who dares wins.

Now Ria Leigh knew what she must do.

CHAPTER 39

When Sloane Kern took an early lunch, the question was already running around her head.

She tried to think of the exact words, get their order precise, and say it so it didn't make her sound sly. She went over it, backwards and forwards, never getting it quite right, and that just left her feeling frustrated. What would Jack think when she asked?

She rolled to her feet and walked to the bright prints of cats and dogs that hung on the wall in the back room of Jack's veterinary clinic. Two armchairs, a mock coal fireplace fired by gas and a desk by the window made up the furniture of the small room. This was the place Jack retreated to when he needed a break from dealing with clients. Neither his receptionist nor assistant were allowed in this space, only Jack and now Sloane.

Before leaving her office, she called to see if he was free for a bite to eat. He sounded so excited and said he'd be ready when she came. She'd brought prawn sandwiches and two cans of pineapple pop from Marks and Spencer, knowing that's what he preferred. She'd get him to eat and drink, then as the food digested and his mood mellowed ask her question.

As she stared at a photo of a tabby kitten with its head dipped in a bowl of food, she felt her impatience growing. Why was Jack taking so long? She knew the answer of course. He was with a client. The man never stopped working and she supposed that was why he was so rich.

Sloane swore.

This was supposed to be their lunchtime, and she had her question to ask. But when she arrived, she found the receptionist and assistant had gone for lunch leaving Jack to hold the fort. A last-minute visitor had showed up with a small puppy which whimpered. Jack had gone into action; said he wouldn't be long and ushered Sloane into his private room. Healing pets was Jack's life's work.

Would it be like this when they were married? Jack rushing off to save animals at all hours of the day and night, while she sat around and waited. No way! She'd lived that life with Tim. She'd insist Jack work regular hours. He didn't need to slave day and night to make ends meet.

For a long while, Sloane had barely managed to juggle the balls of business and family, paying bills late, taking on dodgy clients. But now her life was on the turn, so she felt more able to let her hair down. Once they were married, she'd ease herself off oxy and be free of that curse. No one would know about that past. Her secret. She sighed. It would be good to be herself again. With Jack paying the bills she'd take art lessons, or maybe a photography class. Hell, why not both?

One step at a time. First, she had to ask Jack for a big favour. Yes, it was a calculated risk. If it backfired, she'd be in hot water. But Jack loved her blindly, and love made you agree to do strange things.

Her gaze drifted to a watercolour of a corgi, fur puffed up, mouth open so it looked as though it were grinning. Its dark eyes seemed to see right through her. She shuddered and wondered if Jack would insist they had a pet to complete the family. She didn't like dogs or cats or any animals unless they were from the farm and roasted or grilled or fried and served on a plate—beef, pork, lamb or goat. Same with her girls. Pets weren't their thing. Jack had no pets either, and she supposed his practice was enough.

She turned away from those dreadful piercing eyes of the corgi and decided. When Dr Doolittle came home, he'd have to leave his playthings at work. They wouldn't take in pets; she'd make that clear on day one in their new house.

She walked to the desk, looked at the drawer and listened. The door to the office was shut but she made out the low rumble of Jack's voice. With a soft tug, she pulled at the drawer handle. It slid open on silent rails. She rifled through the files and papers, taking her time to work through each drawer until she found what she was looking for—Jack's private planner.

She flipped it open then ran a finger over his jottings, stopped at the previous night and smiled at his neat handwriting:

Nothing much planned. Night in with a book. Miss Sloane.

A shout caused her to drop the planner and spin. It came from the front office.

Thank God the door is shut.

She hadn't been caught snooping. Relief washed over her as she shoved the planner back and closed the drawer.

More raised voices. Jack sounded angry.

Sloane tried to make out the words. With the door closed, the voices were muffled. Jack's deep voice and a higher-pitched tone. A woman?

Sloane squirmed for a moment knowing what she was about to do was wrong. If she found Jack eavesdropping on her private conversations, she'd tear a strip out of his hide. But he wouldn't mind if she did it. He loved her. She drew a breath, gathered her resolve, tiptoed to the door and eased it open a crack.

CHAPTER 40

The din of the animals in the kennels splashed into the room along with the soft clang of bamboo chimes. Sloane peered through the slit to see Jack standing behind a desk shaking his fist. In front of him sat a solidly built woman of about fifty with black hair tied back in a harsh bun. A small brown puppy whimpered in a cage by her side. Its huge eyes stared at Jack.

"I'm sorry, but I can't do that," Jack said in a loud shout.

"You're a vet, aren't you?" The woman spoke with a strong local accent. "You know how to do these things nice and quick."

"There is nothing wrong with Max. He is a healthy pup and should live a long and hearty life."

"I'm willing to pay," the woman said. "How much do it cost?"

"I won't do it." Jack kneaded the crystal beads on his bracelet with the dexterity of a catholic priest. "The answer is no."

"Look, it's not like I'm asking you to break the law. I don't want him no more. Put the bugger to sleep."

"I'm sorry, but killing a puppy because it barks

is not what I do. I fix animals, not break them."

"Then I'll do it myself with a rock."

"You'll do no such thing!"

"Sod you," the woman said, getting to her feet. "You keep the bleedin' hound. Let its howls keep you up all soddin' night."

And with that, the woman stomped out of the office. The door slammed shut.

Jack placed his head in his hands and sobbed. He looked all alone and desperate. The crystals on his bracelet caught a flash of light scattering it like broken glass.

For the first time, Sloane saw a real glimpse of the man she would marry and felt a deep sense of unease. Max, the whining puppy, was now one of his children—an abandoned orphan who needed his help. Jack's kennels were full and ironically, he led a life so busy saving pets that there was no room in his own life for them. Yet, he wanted a family more than anything else in the world. Did he expect his wife to tend to the animals he couldn't keep in his kennels?

Sloane was thinking about this when Jack turned. If he was surprised to see her peeping through the doorway, it didn't show on his face.

"Sorry to keep you waiting," he said. "Difficult client."

"I heard." Now Sloane had visions of him bringing home crates of stray cats and dogs and hoped it was a one-off. "Is it often like this?"

"Some days are better than others." He raked his hand over his chin. "I've got the owner's address and will report this to the police. We'll give them a statement."

"You can't," Sloane said. The last thing she wanted was to get involved with the police. Not after last night. Anyway, the woman was gone and the dog was safe. "What if it is a fake address?"

"I don't think she is that smart."

"But you can't speak to the police."

"Why not?"

"She didn't actually do anything," Sloane replied, thinking fast. "Just hot words and she left the dog with you. I think that was her plan from the start."

"But you heard what she said?"

"I... I'm not sure. What can the police do?"

"They'll keep an eye out."

Sloane changed the subject. "Come and eat. You need a break."

Max whimpered.

"I think he likes you," Jack said, looking at the puppy and smiling. "The girls will love him."

Oh no, Sloane thought. He's not dumping that hound on me. No way.

She said, "I've brought you a prawn sandwich and a can of pineapple pop."

"You'll take Max, won't you? Just until we can find him a forever home."

"Let's eat, I feel light-headed," Sloane said, knowing how Jack would react.

He was at her side, hand on her elbow and steering her back into his private office. A smile welled inside which Sloane kept from her lips. She had him like a puppet on a string. No way would she have that flea-bitten dog in her home. Yes, she felt sorry for Max, but if there was no room in the kennels for him, Jack would have to put the thing down or ask his assistant to do it.

They sat in the armchairs and Sloane watched as Jack began on his sandwich and sipped his pop. She could tell he was in a black mood. She didn't have his love of animals and wondered if she'd feel the same if she were a vet and folk asked her to kill their pets. If only his heart were a little harder, he would have taken Max's owner's cash. But he had to be Dr Doolittle; and though she tried to care, there was always something to buy if you had the money.

"Good?" she asked as he took another birdlike bite at the sandwich.

"Umm delicious."

"I thought of you when I bought it," she said and thought about her question while she waited for him to finish.

Endlessly, the moments stretched out as Jack pecked at the food. When at last he swallowed the last bite, she said, "What did you do last night?"

"The usual. Read a bit of my book, *Jane Eyre*. It's my go-to when I'm alone. Oh... and I had a glass of wine and a slice of cheese." He drained the can of pop and placed it on the floor. "I can feel your negative energy, what's wrong?"

"Nothing. I'm fine," Sloane said, still uncertain of how to form the question. "It's just... that last night... I missed you."

He smiled. Her sly words of praise always lifted Jack's mood. They were her mallet which got an instant response when she tapped them on his knee.

So far, so good.

Jack said, "This weekend after we choose your ring, we'll set a date for the honeymoon. How about Paris or would you prefer exotic Thailand?"

From the next room came the sharp yap of Max. The wail of a police siren drifted in from the street. Sloane's mind swelled with a sudden panic. What if Jack said no?

Trying to ignore the fear that flooded her thoughts, she said, "And I wondered if... if anyone asked where I was, you'd tell them I was with you."

"I take it you are not talking about Paris?"

"Paris?"

"It doesn't matter." He stared at her, looking worried. "Weren't you at home last night?"

"I had to go out."

"Where?"

It was dark when Sloane arrived at the canal. Even darker inside the Gold Kite.

She said, "Just out."

He watched her as though waiting for more. When she didn't speak, he kneaded the bracelet and said curtly, "I see."

"It's not what you think."

"What do I think?"

"Oh, I don't know. I just need you to say I was with you last night, that's all. No big deal."

Jack's eyes narrowed. And for the first time, she thought she saw a glimpse of something other than blind love in his gaze. Could he see through her? Did he sense the truth?

Sloane felt sick but somehow managed a smile. Her cute one.

"I wish I was already your wife so that I could look at you every morning. I love you, Jack, and so do our girls."

He beamed. "I get it. It's a surprise for me. That's why you sneaked out last night, eh?"

"That's right. A surprise."

Jack folded his arms looking pleased with himself. A second later he blinked and a wary expression crossed his face.

"Who would want to know where you were last night?"

"Probably no one. But if they do, you'll say I was with you, right?"

"It depends."

"On what?"

He did not answer for some time. Sloane tugged at a lock of hair.

"On who is doing the asking," he said at last.

"Suppose it was the police?"

"You mean you want me to lie to the police!"

"No. No. But if it was the police, you'd stand by me, right?"

"I don't like to lie, and certainly not to the police. Why don't you tell me what is going on? Are you in some sort of trouble?"

Sloane felt a shard of pure terror stab at her brain. Her alibi was dwindling by the second. Jack was mister straight and narrow. He followed the rules and did things by the book. She held his hand and looked deep into his eyes.

"I love you, Jack," she whispered. "For us. Please do it for us."

Jack bit his lip, then let out a long sigh.

"Well, I... suppose... but if the police ask, you'll tell me what this is all about, surprise or not?"

"I promise," Sloane replied.

"Well... if you take Max home you've got a deal."

"He's such a cute pup," Sloane said, knowing she'd bring it back after a day or two and claim the kids had allergies. She squeezed his hand. "Our girls will love him. Max will be our family pet. Our baby."

Jack puffed out his chest, reminding Sloane of a cockerel.

"You were with me last night and that is that," he crowed. "I'll shout it from the rooftops and to the police and anyone else who asks. I'll stand by you, honey. Whatever life throws at us, we'll face it together."

As he took her in his arms Sloane grinned. When Jack gave his word, he kept it.

CHAPTER 41

The following morning the call Fenella dreaded came through.

She had finished her scrambled eggs and was having a second cup of tea when her mobile phone rang—Dexter. At this early hour, a call meant he was on his way. What Fenella didn't yet know was what he'd have to say.

Nan stood by the sink as the phone rang. "It's just 5 a.m., dear," she said, as she dried out a pan and carried it back to the stove. "Tell Dexter I'm making waffles and eggs. New York style. I'll put on a pot of coffee. A man needs to eat before he goes to work."

"Women too," Fenella said, phone in hand.

"Some women need to watch their figure," Nan replied, wagging a finger. "If you're not careful, you'll end up looking like your hubby's twin. That man of yours is a lazy sod, does nowt but eat, fiddle with pencils, and sleep."

Eduardo hadn't yet stirred. Artists, Fenella had learned, either rise at the crack of dawn or slumber until the late afternoon. Dexter had told her that most days he crept out of his flat with a slice of toast and eased the door closed. His Priscilla did not get up before two in the afternoon. Club singers work late and rise late. At least she brought home small blue packets of peanuts which she swiped from the bar when no one was looking. They came in useful on days when he didn't have time for lunch.

Nan was still speaking. "I suppose when the fat sod rises from bed, I'll have to make him one of my special fry-ups. I bought some of that extra thick smokehouse bacon he likes, but he'll have to make do with wholemeal bread and goat's milk butter." She glanced at the window with the reddening skies of dawn. "Red sky at night, shepherd's delight. Red sky in the morning, shepherd's warning."

The phone continued to ring. Fenella glanced anxiously at the screen and let her eyes close for a heartbeat. There was her sister Eve in her flimsy summer dress, flip-flops and cheeky grin. She tried to make out the pattern on the dress and the colour of the flip-flops, but everything was in black and white except Eve's face. When her eyes opened, she saw Nan watching.

"What are you thinking about?" Nan asked, looking at her with concern.

"Nowt."

"Then pick up that bleedin' phone. I'm sure he has police things to discuss, else he wouldn't call so early."

Fenella placed the phone to her ear and held her breath. This was it then. Now all she could do was wait.

"News, Guv," Dexter said, in a voice so gruff he sounded as though he'd been up all night smoking cigars. "Big news from Dr MacKay. I'll be at your door in five."

CHAPTER 42

"It's bad," Dr MacKay said. "And what I'm about to tell you will make it worse."

Fenella sat at the desk in his office deep in the bowels of the Port St Giles Cottage hospital. Her left hand clutched a mug of coffee, her fourth of the day. Dexter gulped a mouthful from his cup. Dark stubble clung to his chin, which seemed to match his crumpled suit and deep scowl.

It wasn't yet six a.m., yet the chemicals used to mask the stench of death hung as dense as a midnight fog in the room. Manmade scents or the scents made by the dead, Fenella didn't know which was worse. They both pointed to the same thing. A thing most folk did not wish to think about as they sipped their morning brew.

"I'm not one to beat about the bush," Dr MacKay said, bearing large sharp teeth in his version of a sad smile. "So let's begin with the woman in the canal. I've more work to do on the corpse, but as I said yesterday, I have got a pretty good idea of what happened. It wasn't a drowning. Did we bet a bottle of Glenmorangie on that?"

"No," Fenella replied. "Jones left the crime scene tent before you got the chance to squeeze a bet out of him."

"Pity," Dr MacKay replied. "I thought perhaps you had taken—"

"No," Fenella snapped. He'd not suck her into a bet that he'd already won. You had to watch Dr MacKay on that score. She thought for a moment. "You said around 11 p.m. or midnight for the time of death, any change?"

"No change in my estimate, but the labs will confirm. But let's not quibble over an hour or two."

"Might be important," Fenella said.

"I'll have all the details nailed down in my report, including the brand of stitches. Alas, that won't be for a few days."

His reports were always jam-packed full of useful information which could spin their investigation in new directions. Fenella couldn't wait a few days, though. Not with that mysterious phone call about not disturbing the dead and two mutilated bodies on her plate. The quicker they shut this down, the better.

A timid knock came from the door. It opened slowly and a short plump man in a grey porter's jacket trotted into the room. He stopped and bowed at the detectives. There was something of the wild boar about the man. His two front teeth hung like tusks from his ill-fitted mouth—Smyth. Fenella had seen him only a handful of times over the years, and every time he smelled of mothballs. She'd never heard him speak.

"News?" Dr MacKay said, staring at Smyth.

Smyth reached into his pocket, pulled out a small sheet of pink paper, and holding it in both hands approached the desk. He gave a slight bow and handed the sheet to Dr MacKay, who studied it for a moment, licked his lips then said, "I'll take the crab bites and lime pine nut salad. Peach cobbler for afters. Noon in the club, if you don't mind."

Smyth let out an approving grunt and withdrew from the room.

"Lunch?" Fenella asked.

Nan had packed cold mutton sandwiches with an apple from their neighbour, Mr Bray's orchard. His fruit was usually sour and hard to chew. Good for the waistline, though.

Dr MacKay said, "A little treat for me to look forward to."

"I've nowt but a packet of peanuts for my lunch," Dexter said. He pulled out a small crumpled blue bag from his jacket. "Not sure how long they've been in here, either."

Fenella wondered if they had a sell-by date. Probably smudged off. "Best keep those for when you get stranded on a deserted island."

"Must be nice to have staff bring you fine grub," Dexter muttered. "Real nice. Crab bites and lime pine nut salad sounds better than stale peanuts. Suppose you'll wash it down with a shot or two of fine whiskey, Doc?"

"It's going to be a long day," Dr MacKay said. "A pleasant lunch gives me the boost to go on."

"Aye, a decent lunch fuels us all," added Fenella,

wondering whether to ask Nan to whip up crab bites and lime pine nut salad for their lunch on Sunday.

Dexter stuffed the peanuts back into his pocket. They had not see the light of day for a long while. Probably a good thing, Fenella thought. She'd share her mutton sandwiches with him. Nan packed enough for a small army. And he could have the apple. A bit of green would be good for him.

She said, "You've got more news?"

Dr MacKay slowly rose from his desk, plodded to the coffee pot, and returned, filling each of their mugs. "Your DNA bloodwork came through," he said and looked at his wristwatch. "Three hours ago, and I wanted to discuss the results."

"Oh aye," Fenella said, heart picking up speed. She was the older sister. She took a shallow breath. It was her job to look out for Eve. "What have you found out?"

Dr MacKay coughed but did not speak. Dexter's breathing became laboured. Fenella willed her heart to slow and wished she could turn back the clock seven years to the night of the car crash where her sister's husband died and Eve disappeared from the Port St Giles Cottage hospital. She had felt sick to her stomach ever since the phone call from Dexter announcing that Dr MacKay had big news. Now, she sat in the bowels of the Port St Giles Cottage hospital awaiting results which could shatter her life, and that of her mum, Nan, and her husband Eduardo.

She took a massive breath and flipped the switch in her mind to full-on detective mode.

Whether the lass in the wardrobe was her sister was no longer relevant. What happened, and who did it, became her sole focus.

"Go on," she said. "I'm ready."

The room seemed to go silent as if it too waited in anticipation of the news. Dexter leaned forwards so his arms rested on the desk. It suddenly felt as if someone had turned up the radiators. Fenella steeled herself and shifted in her chair.

Doctor MacKay did his doctor thing, lips twisting into that sad, large tooth-bearing smile. "It appears there is no match between your blood sample and the DNA we took from the corpse. The woman in the wardrobe is not your sister Eve."

Fenella's eyes blurred with relief and then shame. It wasn't her sister! But the woman they had found was someone's daughter, sister, or mother, and that thought jerked her to full tears.

Doctor MacKay reached out and took her hands. "Fenella!"

He always called her by her first name, even when she was a rookie constable and bright green behind the ears. Fenella liked that. No airs and graces. No pomp and ceremony. Still, the tears came. She'd work this case as if it were her sister. That was her secret promise to the lass in the wardrobe. Putting away the bugger that did this was all that mattered.

Dr MacKay said, "I've always said you'd have made a great pathologist because you care. Now me, I'm good for nothing else but what I do." He paused and again flashed that big-toothed smile. "I had the results triple checked before I called you over."

Fenella sniffed, not yet able to speak. It suddenly felt as though she'd been plunged into a cold tank of water with the lights off. There was nowt to see but dark and choking swirls as you held your breath and tried to clamber out. They had a body but little else to go on. She'd not let the cold water get the better of her. She was good at her job. Exceptional. There was no way she'd let the death of this lass get away from her.

Dexter cleared his throat. "Gawd almighty Doc, I had me heart in me mouth. Not Eve, eh?"

He jerked to his feet, pumped a fist, and laughed long and hard from his gut. Then he squeezed his eyes shut and turned away from the desk, gasping in quick breaths. When he turned back, his eyes were red and swollen.

"I thought it were Eve," he said. "She used to wear those floral dresses and fancy flip-flops." His voice fell away to a murmur. "Any chance of a name for our lass in the wardrobe, Doc?"

Dr MacKay leaned back in his chair and folded his arms. "Well, my friends, it appears I've struck a seam of gold. I've found a match in the dental records. The woman in the wardrobe is a Miss Pam Wells."

"Are you sure?" Fenella leaned forward.

It was one of the names on the list compiled by Jones. She fixed on Dr MacKay, not because she doubted his word, but because his solemn face quelled the flutter of joy and shame which still flitted in her gut.

Dr MacKay said, "Need you ask?"

"Just thought I'd check."

"Well don't."

"We have to be sure."

Dr MacKay let out a chuckle. "Ah, our Fenella is back. I'll run some additional tests to confirm and let you know if anything changes. It won't. Nor will my view that the person who killed Pam Wells is the same person who did in Jane Ragsdale."

Fenella valued his opinion, and even though his ideas were often way out there, he was more often right than wrong.

She said, "Any other thoughts?"

Dr MacKay frowned. "It might be some kinky killing ritual. Read about a woman in Richmond who'd do men in with her silk stockings then chopped off their privates with a bread knife. But that's the type of thing they do in London, never expected to see it up here. I fear we are dealing with a serial killer with a passion for women's body parts. Any takers for a bottle of Glenmorangie on that?"

CHAPTER 43

It was Wednesday lunchtime when things went from bad to worse for Sloane Kern.

She turned the key in the front door of her flat, still trying to forget all that had happened at the canal late Tuesday night. What she had done was wrong. Very wrong. But thinking about it would not put it right. What she needed was peace and quiet in a space that was not her bleak office. A meal at home and a catch-up chat with her daughter Bren would ease the dark thoughts racing around her head.

As she opened the door, there came a wild yapping. Max, the abandoned puppy, wanted to go out for a walk. The small dog danced around her legs, wagging its tail at hyper-speed. Sloane seethed. She didn't have time to walk the bloody hound. Where was Bren?

She dropped her keys on the hallway table, ignored Max, and trudged along the threadbare carpet to the kitchen. A cup of tea to calm her nerves, then she'd deal with the dog. She hesitated. Better yet, have Bren walk the pup while she rustled up a bite to eat.

"Bren, I'm home."

No reply.

Max whined.

"Bren, take Max out. He wants to go potty."

Max ran to the front door and continued to whine.

Sloane walked to the kettle, filled it from the tap, and flipped the switch. Bren didn't start work at Logan's Bakery until two. Where was she?

"Bren!"

When there came no answer, a sourness began its slow churn in Sloane's gut. It had brewed ever since Tuesday night and now felt like an acid-filled stew. Breathe, she told herself. Breathe. Take your time. One thing at a time. First, Bren. Second, tea. Third, Max. *And don't think about what you did last night. Jack has got your back. No one will ever know.*

She knocked lightly on Bren's bedroom door, shared with her other two sisters, and walked in. Chaos everywhere. Clothes were in piles on the floor, blankets scattered across the beds and the curtains were drawn tight. The air was thick with the smell of sweat and perfume and moisturising cream. But no Bren.

"Bren!" she called, this time with an edge to her voice. "Bren, get up. You've got work."

Max yapped from the front door; a yowl as sharp as the screams of a newborn who just won't settle. Then he scurried into the kid's bedroom and yapped some more.

"Stop it!" Sloane yelled at the puppy and swung her foot but missed. "Bloody thing."

She went back to the kitchen and added a tea

bag to her mug, a teaspoon of sugar, and hot water. As it brewed, she ran over the last conversation she'd had with her daughter. *Yes... yes, she starts at Logan's Bakery at two today.* She added a splash of milk and walked to the living room.

Bren lay curled up on the sofa, duvet over her head, mobile phone and keys scattered on the coffee table. On school days she'd taken to using the living room to grab extra sleep while Sloane got the other girls ready for the school run.

"Bren, it's after twelve. Get up."

Not even a twitch.

She put her mug down on the coffee table next to Bren's keys and phone. How was it the young could sleep like that? If only a little of it rubbed off on her. She'd tossed and turned and barely got a wink. Life was so unfair.

"Bren! Come on, get up. Max needs to go outside."

At the call of his name, Max trotted into the room and in the far corner crouched to go potty.

"Shit!" Sloane barked.

And that is exactly what came next from Max. A thin brown watery goo with a revolting sour tang. He knew he'd done wrong, for he scurried from the room avoiding her furious eyes.

After Sloane cleaned up the mess, she went to the bathroom, washed her hands with sweet-scented rose soap and dried them on the towel. For a while, she stared at her face in the medicine cabinet mirror. Tufts of grey hair and wrinkled lines stared back. Stepping back, she scowled. The past few days had aged her as much as the last few weeks of Tim's life.

She opened the cabinet door, shook out two pills from a bottle, poured a glass of water, and swallowed. It took less than ten minutes for the first effects of the oxy to wash over her. Then a sort of happy bliss where the sharp edges of life seemed more rounded.

Sloane went back to the living room, picked up her mug of tea, now lukewarm, and slumped into an armchair, watching the wall clock and Bren. No harm, she now supposed, in the lass getting up a little late. Young people needed their sleep, didn't they?

She sipped her tea and decided to wake Bren when the clock chimed the one o'clock hour. That would give her daughter time to get ready for her shift and still give them a few moments to chat. Until then, with Max hiding somewhere, all was quiet bliss.

"Ten more minutes in the land of snooze young lady, then I'm waking you up."

Sloane let her eyelids drift down as, for the first time in what seemed like days, her mind stilled.

It was the high-pitched buzz with its urgent clamour that shook her from a pleasant dream. Sloane squinted at the coffee table. Not her phone. Bren's mobile. Probably a friend from Logan's Bakery.

Sloane picked up the phone.

I'm sorry for what I did. Missed you these past few days.

It felt wrong to read a private text message, but Sloane stared at the screen and wondered who it came from. Not a girlfriend of Bren's, she thought, but a young man. Bren hadn't talked about dating anyone. Still, as her mum, she ought to know. She didn't want her daughter mixing with the wrong sort, not now the wedding bells with Jack were on the horizon. She had big plans for Bren. University for a start, a good career and meeting a wealthy, educated man. A doctor or vet would do the trick. Her Bren would go far.

Another buzz.

Need to talk. Let's meet up for some more wild fun. Details to follow, once things sorted.

Sloane froze. What type of fun? No name came up with the number. She glanced at Bren. No sign of movement. Her daughter wasn't much for drink, but she'd smelled cigarettes on her clothes a few times. Bren denied smoking and said she didn't hang around with people like that. Had she lied? Was she doing drugs?

Again the phone buzzed. Sloane stared at the screen, mouth dropping wide in stone-cold horror.

Free ale on me... Micky Knowles.

CHAPTER 44

Sloane Kern stared at the name at the bottom of the text message on her daughter's phone, unable to believe it.

If this was what it looked like, she'd opened one hell of a can with nothing but nasty worms ready to jump out. Mick Knowles was her only male client. What the hell was he doing texting her precious daughter?

Sloane considered. Should she ignore the message and keep an extra eye on Bren or confront her head on?

It took another two heartbeats for her to realise things were not that simple. Micky Knowles was a client in her private anger management business. He was a complex puzzle. Anger management was a piece of the sky. Maybe two pieces. But those two pieces helped pay the bills. Well, at least until she became Jack's wife.

Her breath slowed. She had to be certain and didn't want to accuse her daughter of something that might be innocent. Maybe it was a different Micky Knowles?

Yes, it was best to wait and watch, she told herself. Bills don't pay themselves. It would be a few months until she had full access to Jack's wallet. Then his money would put everything right. Still, she felt uneasy. Bren was her first daughter, the apple of her late husband Tim's eye. "Protect my girls like a mother bear," he had said on his deathbed.

Sloane's instinct told her there was no other Mick Knowles. The text had come from her anger management client. What had that evil man been doing to her innocent child? He must know she was Bren's mum. She thought about that for a moment and quietly recalled his asking about her family. She'd been careful not to tell him anything and steered the conversation back to his rage. He must have dug into her private life. Followed her even. A silent fury ignited hot guilt for plunging her child into danger for the sake of a business she hated and bills that never stopped. She placed her face in her hands and then massaged her temples as something quietly snapped in her heart.

What could she do? The police? No way. They would start prodding and poking and asking questions that she knew would lead to what she did last night. If they found out the truth she'd end up in jail.

Anyway, what would she tell the police if she called them? That her teenage daughter received a text message from an older man? They would hang up or charge her for wasting their time.

Her breathing picked up as a cold clarity gripped her thoughts. If she could read all the text messages, she'd have a better idea of what was going on. No need for the police. She'd deal with this herself. With one eye on Bren, sleeping soundly, she tried to unlock the phone.

Bingo!

Bren was never very smart about her passwords. Sloane tapped on the text messages icon, heart hammering against her chest, and began to read greedily.

"Mum, what are you doing with my phone?"

How the hell do kids do that? One minute they are sound asleep, snoring. The next, wide awake, bright-eyed and alert. Bren kicked off the duvet, rolled off the sofa and snatched back the phone.

"That's private," she said,

Suddenly, Sloane sensed a storm coming. A very bad one. "I know about Micky Knowles," Sloane said, voice soft but stern.

Bren stared at her mum with a look of hatred in her eyes. "That's none of your business."

"Yes, it is. You are my daughter."

"I don't need this. I've got work soon. I've never been late and this won't be the first time, either."

"You'll listen to me, young lady. I want to know what you two have been up to."

"Don't shout at me."

"Answer my question."

"You sound like you've come straight out of a Victorian novel. Next, you'll be asking if my chastity belt is intact."

"Is it?"

"I don't have one."

"You didn't answer my question."

"Mum!"

"This is no joking matter, young lady. Mr Knowles is a client."

"That's why he said I shouldn't tell you. He knew you'd be upset because I'm your daughter." Bren sniffed. "Mum, you'll like him once you get to know him. I told him about you and Jack, and he was very happy. Micky says he loves me... and I love him."

"He's forty-two, honey. You are only sixteen."

"I'm not a child."

Max barked. High-pitched and furious. He wanted to go potty again.

"Bren, look at me," Sloane said, holding Bren's hands. "Micky Knowles is a very dangerous man."

"Why can't you be happy for me?"

"You don't understand, honey."

"I know how I feel, and I know how Micky feels. He told me his first love was taken from him." She snatched her hands away. "It has taken him years to heal and now he has found me. He says I even look a bit like her. He calls me his special one."

Bren had no idea what she'd fallen in love with. And even less idea of the latent violence which simmered below the surface of the placid face of Micky Knowles. Sloane had caught a glimpse, and it terrified her.

"Listen to me," Sloane said in a shrill. "The man has an unstable mind. He's some sort of freak, a pervert who should be locked up inside the madhouse."

"Stop it," Bren said. "I won't listen to your lies. Micky has a kind heart. He's a good man, just misunderstood."

Terror tore through Sloane. She had to make her child hear. "I... I think he might have killed his girlfriend years ago. A woman called Pam."

"No way," Bren said in a voice that told her mum she believed her. She looked panicked. "Micky wouldn't hurt a—"

It was against ethical guidelines to reveal the contents of an anger management session. Sloane was way beyond that now. Her gut churned hot and sour, all mental control over what she said gone.

"—and he's talked about sacrificing young virgins in my sessions. We explored his ideas. I thought it was an urge, not an actual plan. Now, though..."

"Mum!" Bren began to cry. "Oh God, Mum!"

"Darling, I... I think he might have been talking about you."

CHAPTER 45

It was a little after one as Fenella and her team mixed a late lunch with a catch-up briefing. Across the room, the tea urn hissed and from the hallway, through the open door, a bark of laughter spilt in.

"Nice bit of mutton," Dexter said, chewing on one of the sandwiches from the stack Fenella had shared. "Can't beat a cold cut when you are on the go." He turned to Jones. "Have another sandwich lad and that apple too. It'll put hairs on your chest."

Jones nibbled at the edge of the thick wedged bread, then pulled the meat out from between the slices, sniffed and chewed.

"Cutting back on the carbs," he said, "Protein and fat will keep me lean."

He was big on exercise and eating healthy. It showed in his athletic build.

Dexter frowned. "They teach you that in detective school?"

"If I overload on bread, I'll fall asleep in the afternoon."

"Nowt wrong with solid food, lad." Dexter took another bite, followed by a swig of tea. "Give it here. I'll take them slices if you don't want them."

They ate the rest of the sandwiches in silence.

Jones picked out the lamb from the bread and Dexter hoovered up the empty slices. By the time they came to the apple, Fenella's stomach bulged. She'd had enough of the lamb with its thick meaty taste and greasy texture.

"You have that apple, lad," Dexter said. "It'll keep you lean."

Jones took a large bite and chewed and chewed. It was as his face screwed into a tight ball that Fenella burst out in laughter.

She said, "Mr Bray's apples are best enjoyed a small bite at a time or stewed in a pot with a load of sugar."

"Right you are, boss," Jones replied, spiting the remains into a handkerchief. "I think a half-starved horse would turn its nose up at that thing. I've tasted sweeter crab apples."

"Always did say apples ain't no good unless they are used for cider," Dexter muttered.

Fenella poured a second cup of tea and they began discussing the case. "So," she said after they had brought Jones up to speed on their early morning meeting with Dr MacKay. "Pam Wells and Jane Ragsdale. What else have we got?"

"I've pulled the record on Miss Wells," Dexter said, handing out photocopies of the file. "She went missing at the end of May, eight years ago. Her dad, Mr Bruce Wells, filed the report, but he died a while back. No other relatives. No sightings of Pam over the years. The trail went cold. Now we know why."

They read the report in silence. Less than four

pages—name, date of birth and brief notes about Pam supplied by her late dad.

"Riveting reading," Fenella said, as Jones tapped on his laptop. "Four pages of nothing to sum up her life. What was the lass like? Who were her friends?"

"Aye, Guv," Dexter said, reaching into his jacket pocket and shaking a blue packet of peanuts into his mouth. He chewed for a moment. "You'd think it was a report for some factory widget for all it tells us. Shame her dad ain't here no more. He'd have given us more colour for sure."

"How'd he die?" Fenella asked.

"Old age, boss," Jones replied as Dexter shook out more peanuts and munched. "He passed on three years back."

"Three years ago," Fenella echoed, wondering about the hell of going to the grave with your child still missing. She had five and it would break her heart to lose one. Then there was her sister Eve. Her heart squeezed. If they got to the bottom of this, she'd stop by Bruce Wells' grave and let him know what happened. She didn't know why, but visiting the graves of the dead always made her feel better.

She continued. "And all that time his daughter's body lay in a wardrobe in the cellar of the Navigator Arms. We've not yet spoken with the previous landlord, Ken Finch. About time we jollied that along. Let's visit him this afternoon."

Jones stopped typing, let out a satisfied yelp, and punched his fist in the air. His laptop toppled, but he grabbed it before it fell to the floor.

"What you got, lad?" Dexter asked.

"The social media page of Mr Bruce Wells." Jones got up, pressed a button on the wall, and his laptop screen filled the whiteboard. "Take a look at this. Mr Wells set up a page dedicated to finding his daughter. It hasn't been updated since he died, but the links still work."

Dexter stood and jabbed a finger at a block of text on the whiteboard. "Do you see that, Guv?"

"Aye, I do," Fenella replied and read out loud. "Her boyfriend at the time she disappeared was a Mr Mick Knowles, commonly known as Micky. A medical student at the Port St Giles Cottage hospital. They were to be wed. He was devastated when she disappeared and dropped out of medical school as a result of his loss. He said he'd never stop looking for her, and neither will I. He lost his wife to be and I lost my daughter."

She stopped. They stared at the photographs on the screen. An older man, Mr Bruce Wells, had his arm around his daughter. She had a young face with freckles and two ponytails and wore a dark blue uniform which reminded Fenella of high school. Off to one side stood a slack-jowled man in medical scrubs with a crocodile smile.

"That must be Mick Knowles," Dexter said, pointing at the screen. "Don't like the shifty look in his eyes."

Fenella said, "Let's track down Mr Knowles and have a quiet word, shall we?" She turned to Jones.

"Find out as much as you can about the man. Must have a brain cell or two being a medic. What's he been doing with himself since he dropped out of medical school?"

"Will do, boss," Jones replied, fingers already dancing across the keyboard of his laptop.

"Micky Knowles," Dexter said. "The name rings a bell... I think he's got form. Aye... grievous bodily harm, Guv. He is a nasty bit of work. Like's em young and schoolgirlish."

Fenella folded her arms, leaned back in her chair and knew they were on to something big. She watched Jones as he pressed the button on the wall and the whiteboard screen went blank.

The question forming in her mind caused a knot of tension in her neck. Someone had killed Pam Wells and removed her tongue and ring finger. The same for Jane Ragsdale. Mick Knowles would know how to wield a surgical blade and most murders were committed by those close to the victim. Then there was the freshly stitched incision in the torso of Jane Ragsdale. "... a rusty surgeon out for revenge," Dr MacKay had said.

Jones was at the keyboard again and looked up as if anticipating her next question.

"Five years in Low Marsh Prison, boss. He's out now and living on a narrowboat—Gold Kite. It's moored here in Port St Giles." He pressed a few more keys. "Not too far from the Navigator Arms."

Dexter cracked his knuckles. He only did that when they were on to something. "Should we bring him in, Guv?"

"Aye, I think he'll be more forthcoming in the comfort of an interview room," Fenella replied.

They had made a major step forward, had their sights on a suspect, and were ready to tighten the net. Fenella wondered if she wanted another cup of tea and decided her bladder wouldn't thank her.

She said, "Now we need a link to Jane Ragsdale."

Someone knocked on the door. A woman in her late forties, long and lean with close-cropped brown hair, stepped into the room.

"I'm Detective Sergeant Ria Leigh," she said, "Regional crime squad. Superintendent Jeffery said you'd be in here."

CHAPTER 46

Ria Leigh was taking a big chance.

But she had to get back aboard the Gold Kite to get her shoe protectors and gloves. Now they had found Jane Ragsdale, breaking in was out of the question.

She smiled inwardly as the three Port St Giles detectives eyed her. She'd done her homework and knew all about Detective Inspector Fenella Sallow. A hotshot with an amazing record who'd shown no interest in climbing the Cumbria police totem pole.

Next, Detective Sergeant Robert Dexter, the same rank as her. The man had an interesting record. Fistfights, drunken brawls and the George Cross. A copper who got the job done.

Finally, Detective Zack Jones. In great shape who'd joined the team straight from the National Detective School. Top of his class in financial forensics with a bachelor's degree in history of art from Cambridge, and studied photography at the Royal Academy. Parents from Trinidad and proud. A good looker, too. Ria wondered if he was dating anyone then snapped her mind back on track.

What did she have here? Nothing but a small team of yokel cops and a green behind the ears, if tasty, rooky. Ria wanted to laugh. It would be easy to get what she wanted. It always was.

"Hello pet," Fenella said, taking Ria in. "Are you Civic Officer of the year three times in a row, Ria Leigh?"

"At your service, ma'am." Ria beamed. They might be a bunch of yokels, but they recognised greatness when they saw it. "Did I hear you ask about Jane Ragsdale?"

She kept her voice friendly as she explained. First, she had Jane Ragsdale under surveillance. Second, Miss Ragsdale was suspected of supplying drugs to small-time dealers in Whitehaven. Third, their respective leaders had agreed for her to work with their team.

"Why?" asked Dexter bluntly.

"Because Jane Ragsdale's boyfriend is a Mr Mick Knowles," Ria replied. "And he is a person of interest in both our investigations."

CHAPTER 47

Fenella felt a wave of relief.

She'd fretted at the size of her team. Two murders and four detectives were stretching things thin. And with superintendent Jeffery focused on the Tarns Dub Music Festival that wasn't going to change any time soon. But with Ria Leigh joining their team, her mood lifted.

"Well, fancy that," she said to herself. An ace from the regional crime squad. Civic Officer three times in a row, no less. It'd be good for Jones to see how things worked at Regional. Not that she wanted him to leave her team, just to get a handle on best practice. Then she'd pepper him with questions to get out his thoughts. She couldn't help but smile.

She said, "Detective Sergeant Leigh—"

"Please call me Ria."

"Ria, you've had the Gold Kite under surveillance?"

"That's right."

"What can you tell us about Mr Knowles' daily routine?"

"As regular as clockwork, that one. Rises sometime after two in the afternoon. Leaves the boat around four. Most days he goes for a drink in the Navigator Arms."

"Doesn't he work?" This was Jones.

"Seasonal. Summer months mainly. He lives the life of Riley for the rest of the year. Not too difficult on a narrowboat, as the cost of living is low."

Fenella glanced at her watch. One thirty. "He'll be in the land of nod now then?"

"Most likely." Ria held her breath, praying for what came next.

"Why don't you and Dexter bring him in? Let's call it a joint operation. Then get forensics to go over the boat."

Perfect, Ria thought, stifling a laugh. She'd be aboard that boat and sneak those gloves and shoe protectors out of the place within the hour. Then there would be nothing to link her to Jane Ragsdale. After a week or so she'd ditch this lot and go back to keeping her patch of Whitehaven clean.

Easy.

Fenella said, "Jones, you come with me."

"Where are you going, Guv?" Dexter asked.

"To have a word with a retired pub landlord."

CHAPTER 48

There were times when Fenella thought she shouldn't rely so much on her gut. She'd left Ria and Dexter to haul in Mick Knowles while she swanned off to speak with a retired pub landlord.

Something nagged at the back of her mind that she could not put into words and her gut thought a chat with Mr Ken Finch might loosen her brain cells. Anyway, it wouldn't take three detectives to search a narrowboat and she didn't want to hang about on deck waiting.

She parked her Morris Minor on Fleetwood Lane and turned to Jones. "Which one?"

"Scuffed black door," he replied, eyeing the squat brown brick house with slit-sized windows. "Reminds me of a wild west jailhouse. I wonder if Mr Finch wears a ten-gallon hat."

"Or packs a six-shooter," Fenella added, not totally in jest. "Why don't you wait here, pet? Two detectives showing up on his doorstep might frighten him."

"Okay, boss," Jones replied, looking a bit put out.

"I want you to keep an eye out," Fenella said. "Have a walk around the back, see if anyone leaves when I knock."

"Righto."

"Then come back and wait for me in the car."

"Got it, boss. A bit nippy today."

Fenella walked up the garden gate under low clouds which darkened the day to almost dusk. The damp air smelled of the sea. It brought with it a frigid wind. Joggers used this part of town as a cut-through to the beach, although none were out in this chill.

Closer up, the house reminded her more of a chicken coop than a jailhouse, with slit-like windows covered by net curtains with yellow aged spots. They had not been changed in recent times and looked so brittle they might disintegrate in a cold wash. No sign of a twitch, though. Ken Finch wasn't watching.

A narrow cobblestone alley ran along one side of the house along which Jones strode. Fenella waited until his footsteps faded, then pressed the doorbell.

Nothing.

She flipped the door knocker. Probably having a post-lunch nap. That meant either he'd be jollied by food or in a foul mood from being woken from sleep. She suspected he'd be on the jolly side. You had to have a positive outlook to be a pub landlord. Round and fat with a deep voice and a beard, she added to complete her mental picture.

Another round with the door knocker.

Eventually, the scutter of footsteps on bare

wood floors. They were almost birdlike in the way they scurried. The door opened to a cock hen of a man with a beaked nose and haggard jowls. He was about five feet four inches and she wondered how he'd made it as a pub landlord. A faded red dressing gown clung to his small frame and, on his feet, pink flip-flops slapped lightly on the floorboards as he shifted from foot to foot.

"Yes?"

"Detective Inspector Sallow. Are you Mr Ken Finch?"

He looked at her with surprise. Fenella had seen that look when she first became a detective. Not too many women detectives back then. Times change. No one is shocked by a woman detective these days. But since she'd let her hair go grey, she once again experienced that look. She liked that. A trendsetter.

Mr Finch said, "What is all of this about?"

"The Navigator Arms."

"I see, then yes, I'm Ken Finch. You'd best come in."

Fenella followed him along a dim hallway into the front room. It had plum floral wallpaper and smelled of lemon. On the wall were pictures of prize cockerels and on the mantlepiece ribbons and trophies glistened. The window overlooked the garden.

She walked to the curtains. Through the yellowed netting, she spotted her Morris Minor with Jones already back inside. *The bugger wants to keep warm*. A thought confirmed by the plume of white exhaust smoke.

"See you are keen on cockerels?" Fenella said, studying the trophies and pictures. "They are beautiful birds. Noisy at sunrise, though."

Mr Finch's chest swelled with pride as his eyes travelled across the pictures and settled on the trophies.

"Aye, nowt like an Old English Game chicken." He pointed to a bird who strutted as though on the dance floor. "See that. It's a black-breasted red. A real champion that bird."

"We had one of those when I was a lass," Fenella said. "He swaggered about the place like a king. We called him Fonzie."

"That sounds about right," Mr Finch replied, grinning.

Since Fonzie, Fenella had developed a soft spot for Old English Game birds. They were intelligent, individual, emotional, nurtured their young in a warm, cuddly bundle of love, and were nosey. She studied the picture.

"Our Fonzie had huge combs and wattles on its head. Giant earlobes too."

"Aye, well mine are competing birds. You can't enter a poultry show unless they are cut off. Instant disqualification. Fancy a drop of tea?"

"That'd be champion," Fenella replied. "It'll warm me up a real treat."

He came back several minutes later with a Brown Betty teapot in a tea cosy to keep it warm,

China cups with matching saucers, a pot containing sugar lumps and a plate of custard creams. He placed them on a coffee table and poured.

"Milk?"

"Aye," Fenella replied. It felt like she was having afternoon tea with the vicar, not a quick chat with a retired pub landlord. "That would be lovely."

"Sugar?"

"One lump will do."

Mr Finch spooned it with silver tongs into her cup, handed her a matching teaspoon and watched as she stirred.

After she'd sipped and nodded in appreciation, he said, "What is all of this about?"

"You'll have heard about the lass in the wardrobe?" Fenella hesitated for a moment and watched him closely. "The one we found in the cellar of the Navigator Arms."

"Aye, Alf Bird told me about it. Screaming bloody murder, he was. The bugger said I put it there."

"And did you?"

A bloom came to his jowls and his beaked nose seemed to glow with indignation. "What do you take me for?"

"I have to ask. It's part of the job."

He shook his head. "I didn't put her there."

"Do you know who did?"

Mr Finch didn't reply for a moment and stared at the net curtains as he sipped his tea.

"No," he said at last. "I've no idea."

Fenella sensed there was more on his mind than he was letting on and was once again struck by his diminutive size. Like a bleedin bantam hen, she thought, and just as tetchy.

She said, "I suppose Mr Bird told you about the man who ran into his cellar."

"No... er... not a word."

An obvious lie.

"A short man dressed all in black with leather trousers?"

"Alf never mentioned that." He avoided eye contact. "What about him?"

"Don't suppose he rings any bells?"

"Doesn't sound like a regular."

"Devil's wisp beard, the colour of carrots. Shorter than you. You'd remember if you'd seen him before."

"I'd ask Alf Bird or Stacy."

"Aye, pet. I did." Fenella paused, picked up her cup and sipped. Mr Finch had no height to him at all and the man with the devil's wisp was less than five feet tall. "Do you have a brother, Mr Finch?"

"I'm a single child."

"Cousins?"

"I grew up in an orphanage. I have no relatives that I know of."

"A male friend around your height?"

"What are you trying to say?"

"I have to ask."

"My friends are all taller than me. I was born with a birth defect that affected my height. Other than that, I'm a normal red-blooded man."

Fenella changed the subject. "We have the name of the woman in the wardrobe. Did you know a Miss Pam Wells?"

"You found Pam?" His voice rose in high-pitched shock. A blush bloom crept up his neck and settled in blood-red pools in his cheeks. "In that wardrobe?"

"Aye, luv. Tell me about her."

His eyes welled. "I... I can't believe it... I mean, her old man was a regular at the pub—Bruce Wells. A real solid bloke. Peaceful, too. He used to bring Pam with him to the pub when she were nowt but a nipper. I got a high chair and some toys so the lass could play. My God! I can't believe it. Bruce's wife died, and he didn't remarry. You sure it is Pam?"

Outside, a motorcycle rumbled along the street. Its edgy roar caused Ken Finch to flinch. He got up and walked to the window.

"Damn kids are always racing up and down the street and you lot do nowt about it."

Fenella reached into her handbag and pulled out a notebook.

"I'll make a note and have a word with uniform if you like."

He nodded and sat back down. The blush was very thick around his neck, and it was clear he was still in shock.

He said, "Pam Wells and Micky Knowles were sweethearts, but I guess you know that. Her dad took a real shine to Micky. Most folk thought it was because Micky was in medical school and a good prospect for Pam."

Fenella took a custard cream, nibbled then said, "What did you think of the lad?"

"He did a few odd jobs for me. Was always good with his hands and physical stuff." He picked up a custard cream, split it in two and dunked it into his tea. "He'd come with me to the poultry shows. The lad enjoyed it. Not your typical student type."

Another motorcycle puttered along the street.

"The buggers use it as a race track when they should be in school," Mr Finch said, once again flinching at the sharp splutter.

"Aye, I see what you mean," Fenella replied. "Tell me about the wardrobe."

"Aye well, I had no idea Pam's body was in the thing."

"How did the wardrobe get in the pub cellar?"

Mr Finch sat up straight as if he'd just realised something. He began to sweat, then cleared his throat, but did not speak.

"Go on," Fenella said quietly. "Or we can finish our chat down the station."

"I swear I didn't know anything about it until just now."

"I'm listening, luv."

"Micky Knowles rented the cellar for his furniture removal business. On the side and cash only if you get my drift."

CHAPTER 49

Clouds hung low under a dull sky when Ria and Dexter sidled onboard the Gold Kite their footfalls as soft as alley cats. Two constables stood guard on shore in case Mick Knowles ran. A small crowd gathered to watch on the towpath.

Ria cursed under her breath. The last thing she needed was a show. All she wanted was to get on board, grab what she'd left behind on her first visit, and leave. No harm done.

But word had somehow spread and more people were arriving to watch. Several held pints of ale and she assumed they came from the Navigator Arms. Dexter knocked on the aft door as the crowd murmured contentedly at the show.

"Police, open up," he yelled.

After the second knock with no answer, they put on gloves and shoe protectors. Dexter picked the lock with surprising speed and clambered through the doorway. The crowd cheered, several clinking their pints of ale. But less than thirty seconds later, he came back on deck, shaking his head.

"Ain't no one here, Ria. Looks like our Micky has done a runner. Guess we ought to call in the techs to sweep the place."

"Mind if we take a look around first?" Ria suggested. She knew that's what he wanted to do. She'd read him well.

"Don't suppose there is any harm," Dexter replied, heading back inside.

It was darker than Ria remembered, and it took several moments for her eyes to adjust. Not so her nose, which sucked in the sweaty grease-laden air so thick and sour it made her want to retch.

She stood in the galley with Dexter a few paces in front. He placed his hands on his hips, surveying the chaos. Beer cans, ashtrays, clothes scattered in random piles, everything dark and grimy.

"Never seen nowt like it," he said. "The filth must be six inches deep."

"Not what you'd call house-proud is Micky," Ria said, eyeing the pile of clothes where she hid the shoe protectors and gloves. "Don't think his girl, Jane Ragsdale, was much into housekeeping, either. No time, I suppose, not with all that drug dealing."

"Crafty buggers, these drug dealers," Dexter said slowly looking around. "Real crafty."

He went to the fridge, opened the door and poked about. Then he spun on his heels and yanked at the oven door. A pile of dirty plates tumbled out.

Ria eyed the pile of clothes near the bench table where she'd hidden the shoe protectors and gloves. Yes, that was the pile, although it was hard to tell in all the mess.

She said, "Why don't you search the bedroom while I look about here?"

Dexter grunted but didn't move. His arm raised slowly and his finger unfurled into a point.

"That don't look right."

Ria followed his gaze. He pointed at the kitchen counter. A chill ran down her spine. Before she spoke, Dexter had the sugar jar in his hand and was twisting off the bottom.

"Nice hiding place for things you don't want found," he said, as the jar split in two in his hands. "Wouldn't surprise me if..." He peered into the bottom, tipped it upside down, and then ran his hand around the inside. Nothing.

"Try the bedroom," Ria urged. "I'll look around in here."

"Aye, happen you're right," he said and turned his gaze to the pile of clothes by the bench table. He stepped forward. The long narrowboat rocked and creaked at the weight shift.

Ria stared, alarmed, wondering if he was about to search through the clothes. The man had a nose for a hiding place. It wouldn't take long for him to find what she wanted to keep forever hidden. How would she explain his find?

Dexter took another step. Then another, until he stood next to the pile of clothes. He glanced down, sniffed then took a quick step, then one more, and disappeared into the bedroom. The Gold Kite rocked, rolled, and then shuddered into stillness once more.

Ria moved quickly to the bench table and looked at the pile of clothes. With speed, she riffled through the items. The gloves and shoe protectors weren't there. She squatted in front of the pile and randomly felt about—socks, trousers, hoodie, skirt. Nothing.

"You okay down there?"

The question came from the constable at the aft door. He climbed down the steps into the galley, shoe protectors on, hands gloved, peering into the gloom.

"We are doing a quick sweep through," Ria explained. "I'd be grateful if you stayed on deck and guarded the aft door. The more of us inside, the higher the chance of contamination, and you know how antsy the forensic techs get about that."

"Righto, ma'am," he said, retreating up the stairs.

Ria groped wildly at the clothes and then shook out each item. Her breathing became heavy.

No gloves.

No shoe protectors.

Nothing.

Bloody hell.

A clang from the bedroom echoed in the cabin. Dexter wouldn't be much longer. When he came out, it would be game over. The techs would sweep the boat and find what Ria desperately looked for.

Searching again, on the edge of panic, Ria found a single glove entwined in soiled male underpants. Then another glove close by, and finally, scrunched in a tight ball, her shoe protectors. She stuffed them in her pocket as Dexter returned to the cabin.

"Find anything?" he asked.

"Nothing. What about you?"

"Nowt worth ought."

"Best leave it to the techs, then," Ria said, getting to her feet.

"It's just that I saw you put something into your pocket," Dexter said, stepping closer. "What you got?"

Ria froze. How the hell could she explain taking evidence from a crime scene? That was a criminal offence—career ending. Then they would dig like rabbits uncovering Jane Ragsdale's notebook, her stash of oxy and that ring.

Dexter slowly raised his arm and pointed. Then his lips creased into a curve and he burst out laughing. "Should have seen your face, Ria. Wish I had my camera." He doubled over, barely able to control himself. "I likes me a good laugh cause this job will drag you down if you don't crack a smile."

"Very funny," Ria said, slowly realising he'd accused her in jest. "Might use that one myself one of these days. Yes, very funny. Ha, ha-ha."

CHAPTER 50

This wasn't the first time Mick Knowles ran.

And every time his first port of call was the same—Grange Hall Care Home, a grand Victorian mansion converted into a care home, on the outskirts of Port St Giles. Its elderly residents were well to do, retired doctors, lawyers and business tycoons.

The sky was low and black with wads of thick clouds scudding in from the sea pulling frigid air as they went. Mick stood outside the imposing stone brick walls at ten to eight that night brooding.

It didn't matter to Mick that they had banned him. The head nurse had told him not to come back. His temper and violent outburst frightened the residents.

Tonight he had to speak with his gran, and nothing would stop him. Everyone called her Deb in here. But to him, it was always gran. Then he'd deal with Bren Kern. He got a pain in the pit of his stomach just thinking about what he must do as he glanced at the welcome sign.

VISITING HOURS: 10 A.M. TO 4 P.M.

He stared at the sign and reflected. Apart from his gran, only one person had really loved him. Pam

Wells. And he loved her so hard she died. Then there was his latest, Bren Kern. Yes, she was smitten by him. His lips twisted into a crocodile smile. He hadn't lost his touch.

From close by came the sharp clamour of a cockerel crowing. *Once. Twice.* Micky shivered. Grandad Bob told him a bird crowing twice in the night led to bad luck. Three times and death was certain.

Once again he looked at the welcome sign, then skilfully scaled the stone wall, crouched low to the ground on the other side and carefully patted his salt and pepper hair, smoothing it over his bald patch. He was in the grounds now. The main building next, then the stairs to his gran's room. He'd take them three at a time. It'll be easy, he told himself.

His gran had lived in Grange Hall for years, thanks to the kindness of her last employer. She'd worked as their housekeeper for twenty years, and was a school teacher for twenty years before that. Rather than give her a gold watch for her retirement, the rich family gave her a permanent place to stay for the rest of her life.

Mick half stood and leaned against the wall grateful he'd landed on the soft soil of a rose bed. For a while, he gazed up at the mansion where the residents lived—men and women with money who could buy anything they wanted. He swallowed hard and took deep breaths to control his fury. The urge to wrap his hands around a slim throat and squeeze seized him. It came at him at random times. He didn't know why.

In the distance, he heard a cockerel crowing. He exhaled, and let his eyes travel to the second floor. After another sharp breath, he began to count the windows lighted and dark.

One, light.

Two, dark.

Three, light.

"Hey, what the hell do you think you are playing at?"

A thin old man in pyjamas strode across the lawn, a walking stick in his right hand. He pointed the stick at Mick.

"I said, what the devil do you think you are playing at?"

Mick grimaced exposing a set of crocodile teeth, breath trapped in his lungs. There was no time to turn around and climb back over. No place to run, either.

Two orderlies in maroon scrubs appeared and hurried over. Several paces back, a short plump nurse tried to keep up. Mick recognised her—the head nurse. He cursed under his breath as he eased back into the shadows.

"Now, Mr Kuck, you know you are not allowed to wander the grounds at night," the nurse said.

"I want to pick a rose for my Val," the man in pyjamas said.

"Your Val has been gone these past twenty years," the nurse replied softly. "Tell you what, we can pick a rose for her in the morning from the flower shop. I'll have someone run you over to the town cemetery so you can give it to your Val."

The orderlies took the man by his arms and steered him back towards the building. He didn't protest but said, "A spook is hiding in the rose bushes."

"There always is," said the nurse. "Would you like a cup of cocoa before lights out?"

Mick didn't move until he heard the click of the door. Only when he was sure it was all clear did he heave a huge sigh. Then he crawled out of the shadow on all fours, close to the ground like a dog on the prowl.

With a clear view of the main house, he continued his count of the second-floor windows.

Four, dark.
Five, dark.
Six, light.

The sixth window was his gran's room, and she was still up. Good. Lights went out at nine. That did not give him long. He wondered if her bedside alarm button was still out of order.

With one last look at the main entrance, he scurried across the lawn, slipped into a side door and was outside his gran's room in less than thirty seconds, willing the rage not to explode again.

CHAPTER 51

Mick stood outside his gran's room breathing hard and wondering if this was the right thing to do. On the other side of the door was his own flesh and blood and a sledge full of dark memories he'd never forget. He turned the door handle with a gloved hand and walked in.

The room smelled of lemon sprinkled with sugar.

She lay on a medical bed gazing blankly at the dark window and sucking on a lemon drop, her favourite. Her head turned to look at him, left hand clutching a pair of steel scissors.

"Hello, Gran."

Mick closed the door softly and stood over the bed. Her hand tightened around the steel scissors.

"Gran, it's me, your Micky."

Her slow eyes shifted towards Mick, then the wall clock. She watched the second hand tick-tock for a full ten seconds.

"Nurse will be here at nine."

"I won't stay long. I need to talk."

For a moment she looked confused, sat bolt upright, raised the steel scissors and brought them down again and again on the bed. "Sacrifice the virgins!"

"No, Gran. No."

Her body became limp, and she fell back against the pillow, panting. "Micky," she said between breaths, "your eyes are all puffy. You are too young to let yourself go. What have you been eating?"

"Gran, I came to talk."

"When you get to my age, you can let things slip. Not yet, though."

"Gran!"

"I know you are a man and that takes less effort, but look at you, and take that sneer off your face. What the hell are you wearing?"

She gazed at his ragged blue hoodie, baggy brown trousers and filthy walking boots. Then her eyes drifted to what he held in his left hand.

"Why are you wearing gloves and carrying around that ugly black bag? You are letting the male side down. Don't get like my Bob."

Mick did not want to remember Grandad Bob, his gran's sixth husband. He had eyes that everyone said looked kind, smoked a bent stemmed pipe, had a hacking cough, and would come running into the house to hide from the police. Even as a kid, Micky knew it wasn't tobacco grandad Bob smoked in his pipe.

On Friday night grandad Bob would get drunk, look at you with those kind eyes and smash your face in.

"Your grandad Bob was a real man," she said.

"Strong with his fists. Didn't take crap."

Mick looked at his gloved hands and flexed them. They still hurt where Grandad Bob made him write out betting slips and beat him on his knuckles with an iron rod if he got it wrong. He'd never been able to write right after that. Nowadays his handwriting was nowt but monkey scrawl.

"He was a good thief, too," she said. "We lived like kings with Bob."

When Grandad Bob got a job in a butcher shop, he brought home pigs trotters in brine. Friday, for months, they dined on pigs' feet. Mick shuddered at what happened when the owner of the Butcher shop fired Grandad Bob for theft.

Grandad Bob came home, got drunk and tried to cut Mick's feet off with a meat cleaver. He said pickled boy's feet tasted better than pig trotters. His gran yelled bloody murder, made Mick dig a big hole in the vegetable plot and he never saw Granddad Bob after that.

Mick said, "I wanted to be the first to tell you, Gran, so I came here."

She didn't seem to hear and raised herself so her face was level with his. "Your dad was an angry man, Micky. Always shouting and fighting and stealing from poor folk. He weren't nowt but a bit of stinking filth. Did you hear me? Filth. The type of stain you can't get clean in a soak and wash. Even If you tried there'd be nowt left of him but his lies."

"My dad did an important job," Mick said in a whisper. "He was the captain of a warship."

He'd read that in a book when he was eleven and thought it sounded cool. So he told everyone that's what his dad did, and even half-believed it himself, no matter how much his gran beat him for telling lies.

His gran laughed. "He was a road sweeper."

"Supervisor, Gran. He led his men."

"Don't be daft. He worked the broom just like the rest. Why do you think you have that arched back?"

Mick straightened. It was true he'd always had a bit of a hunch, but that couldn't have come from his dad working the broom, could it?

His gran was still speaking. "They were nowt but a bunch of deadbeat bums and drunks. No one else but the council would hire the layabouts. Every one of those rats had been inside for... nasty crimes."

His gran reached for the bedside cabinet, picked up a small tin, opened the lid and flipped a lemon drop into her gummy mouth. "Never met a person with such a foul temper as your dad. Right nasty he were. He were so revolting even the filth that floats in the toilet after a good curry kept away from him." She sucked hard on the lemon drops, eyes tiny black dots. "Things would have turned out better if Percy had never been born. The world needs fresh air not stink. Pervert Percy. That's what the police called your dad. I told your mum not to shack up with him. Deb, I said, the man reeks of it. Keep away."

She picked up a pair of reading glasses, placed

them on the tip of her nose, looked at Mick so her eyes seemed huge and sniffed.

Mick knew what came next. She always said the words when she tilted her nose up and sniffed like that.

"They smell, you know. Perverts."

Mick didn't want to think about his dad. He didn't want to think about what his dad had done. He didn't want to feel the lick of shame that washed over him every day as a child.

But he couldn't get away from the memory.

There he was, snotty-nosed with tears in his eyes on his dad's birthday in school. The only boy in short pants in his class. He wore Jesus sandals and a pink and white striped shirt with a hand-painted crucifix on the back. The other kids had formed a ring around him, laughing. He remembered their small, pointing fingers and pink tongues. His teeth were jagged and yellow, his face blotched with bruises. And he was in the middle of the ring of kids, wriggling to get free but the teacher's hand held him firm.

"No, you stand right there in the centre of the circle of adoration," she said. "God loves you, you know. And for all the bad that you've done you should be grateful he ain't sent two thunderbolts up your arse." Then she clapped her hands. "Everyone sniff."

And the kids sniffed, long and hard.

"Who can smell it?" she asked.

Everyone raised their hands. Everyone swore

they smelled the stench of pervert Percy oozing from Mick's skin.

"It's biology," the teacher said. "He can't help it. It's deep in his genes."

He had no friends at school. No one wanted to know a boy branded a pervert before he was a man. The teachers gave him a wide berth, watching him through narrowed eyes.

Mick hated school. Hated going to class. Hated the fact that his gran was the teacher. But he loved her nonetheless, the way a child loves its mother, or a dog its abusive owner.

He tried to change the subject. "Are the nurses treating you well?"

Her huge eyes watched him closely for a long moment, then she said, "They don't pay them enough. That's why you have to watch them. The thieving dogs would have the clothes off me back if I didn't keep one eye open when I slept. The male ones are the worst." She eased up on her pillow. "I need a drink. Give me some booze."

Mick searched his black bag for the hip flask and leaned forwards to tilt it to her lips.

"What do you think I am, a savage? Pour it into a glass."

Mick poured out a good measure and watched her drink it in slow gulps.

At last, she reached for the tin and popped another lemon drop into her toothless mouth. "What do you want?"

The smell triggered a memory. He was five or

six years old, standing in a bedroom doorway. The sweet scent of lemon clung to the air in the small room. His mum lay on the bed with his baby sister in her arms. Slowly, his mum turned her head, gazed at him and scowled.

"One more bloody mouth to feed is all we need!"

And now he saw his mum's face more clearly than he had in all the years.

His gran.

Jesus!

He stumbled backwards. That couldn't be so! He now remembered the beatings were to make his memory right. He must not remember his mum's face or that he had a sister. That's what they told him with each whack of the stick. That's what he told them to stop the blows to his head. No. He didn't remember his mum's face. He never knew who she was.

Shaking, he said, "It's the police, Gran. They have found Pam Wells!"

CHAPTER 52

Sloane placed her hand on the door handle for the third time and knew big trouble lay ahead.

It was almost ten o'clock as she stood in the hallway and listened once more to the soft snore of Bren. Her firstborn went to bed last and slept the longest. The familiar rhythmic breaths drifted from the half-open door of the kids' bedroom. When Bren fell asleep, it took an earthquake to wake her.

It's time, Sloane thought as she reached for her handbag and slipped on her coat. The quiet fear of sneaking out of the house for the second night in a row curdled into a solid ball of dread in her gut. She'd got lucky at the canal last night. No one saw her leave or return, and with Jack backing her up, she had a watertight alibi. If anyone asked.

But tonight was different. Tonight she knew about Mick Knowles. How the hell could she sleep with that man on the prowl for her daughter?

A red-hot fury suddenly engulfed Sloane. It came with such force she gasped. Her hand twitched nervously as she pulled out the knife from her handbag. A mother bear has to protect her cubs.

Max appeared, his tail wagging. He looked up with hopeful eyes. When Sloane ignored him, he began to whine.

"Stop it."

Max howled.

"Stop it. Stop it. Stop it."

Max whimpered.

The past few days had been too much. Jack's ring, Jane Ragsdale, that bloody dog and now Mick Knowles. The thought of him groping her daughter throbbed with the raw edge of a throat sore.

Max whined.

Sloane felt tortured, glared at the dog and knew she could not hide behind the lies anymore. It was all too much to carry, she had to talk to someone. Jack! She'd drive over to his flat and tell him it all—the drugs, the ring, Bren and that stupid dog. No holds barred. Let the chips fall where they may.

Max yapped, wagged its tail and continued to look at Sloane with hopeful eyes. She cursed at the hound, stomped through the front door and eased it quietly shut.

CHAPTER 53

Sloane blinked as her eyes adjusted. A chill clung to the street and with it came the smells of the sea. Bold grey clouds clotted the sky and smudged the moonlight into a smear. She heard something moving furtively in the dark. She prepared to run back to the front door, hand in her handbag clutching the knife.

A bark sounded and for a moment she thought it was Max. It came from the dirt yard of a house opposite. A small black dog with a mouth full of teeth and a nasty snarl darted to the fence.

Sloane threw several choice swear words at the hound for startling her, then climbed in her car, started the engine, turned the heat high and glanced back at her flat. A streetlamp bathed it in an eerie glow, the windows dark.

She thought of Jack as she drove. She didn't love him. Not in the way she had loved Tim. But she and Tim were teens when they met and life was in vivid colours back then, not the endless shades of grey she now saw.

Jack has money, she reminded herself, and she quite liked him. That would have to do. Anyway, he worked at such a manic pace she half wondered if he'd live long. A heart attack, she thought, or a stroke which renders him useless. She'd do a spot of research into the life expectancy of vets and urge him to up his life insurance policy. When he croaked, she wanted a million in cash as well as everything he owned.

As she turned onto Hope Street, the moon bloomed through a gap in the clouds. Rundown bedsits littered the street. Boarded windows with patched-up doors guarded by rusted iron railings with pointed tops.

She had always taken this cut through to Jack's flat during the day. It was quicker than taking the main road clogged with cars and trucks. Although at night that wasn't the case but she took the route, anyway. Instinct, she supposed. And caution. By taking the backstreets there was less chance of getting stopped by the police.

The thought of the police made her slow the car to a crawl. There was no way in hell she'd be pulled over for speeding. They would ask what she was doing, where she was going. They might even ask about what she did last night. The ball in her gut tightened.

"Take your time," she said, gazing at the dark buildings.

She'd heard they were going to knock the houses down and replace them with upscale boutiques and luxury flats. Redevelopment, they called it. She liked the idea, then felt a touch of sadness as she remembered the regulars she'd gotten to know by sight. There was the tall thin man in a grey suit who sat on the steps of number fifty-five and drank from cans of cheap ale. The stooped old woman with matted hair and wonky wheeled shopping trolley full to the brim with plastic bags. And the man in the wheelchair with beefy arms and withered legs. He always waved when she drove by. Terrific people, she supposed, but they must find somewhere else to live. You can't stand in the way of progress.

But there were no people about as she continued her crawl. Too early for the drunks and too late for those who worked nine to five. No sound but the rough grumble of her tyres on the road and the soft purr of the engine. There was a smell about the place, too. A sour stench of decay floated through the warm air vents of her car as though rotted flesh carried on a sea breeze. Hope Street seemed more than derelict in the cobalt light of night. It appeared sinister.

The flashing blue lights in her rear mirror took a moment to register. Then came the scream of the siren. It tore through the night with the piercing wail of a gull. A spasm of fear shot along Sloane's spine. She pulled to the curb, too nervous to think. A waft of warm air carried in the stink of the street so intense in its sourness that Sloane thought she might throw up. She grabbed at the heat dial and turned it off. The soft hum of the fan faded to silence. What would the officer ask her? What would she say?

Bloody Hell!

She watched the mirror as the police car slowed and then pulled alongside her. The officer gave a curt wave, then sped off, lights flashing, siren blaring. Whoever they sought this night, it wasn't Sloane.

For a full five minutes, Sloane leaned on the steering wheel, breathing hard and swearing. She simply could not take all the lies. She'd tell Jack everything. Another police car with flashing lights hurried along the road. This time she slumped down in her seat and held her breath as it sped by.

When at last her fear faded, she eased the car away from the curb, more determined than ever to tell Jack the truth. He was into crystals and the woo-woo. The flashing blue police lights were a sign he'd take note of. Sloane didn't believe any of it but took heed of the warning, anyway.

What would happen when Jack learned the truth? She imagined his face when she told him about the oxy. He'd probably think she had been smoking weed or slugged one too many from the gin bottle. Then his soft eyes would go wide and thin lips hang open. But if he was half the man she thought he was, he'd take her in his arms and tell her it would be all right. He was her Prince Charming, and she liked that one thing about the man.

At Shaker Road, she turned onto South Pearl Lane and her thoughts about her Prince Charming took on a Cinderella-like quality. Jack didn't care about Ester's ring, did he?

An optimism bloomed in her chest. All she had to do was speak the truth and Jack would come swimming to her rescue. He'd save her from drowning. That she was a drug addict wouldn't faze him, either. He'd help her fix the problem. And when she told him about Mick Knowles, he'd come up with a plan to deal with the odious man.

A car passed on the other side of the road, windows down, music blaring. Freedom! When was the last time she felt joy? Not since Tim passed. Never with Jack.

And then she was on Jack's street and parked by the curb outside his flat. She climbed out and felt alive at the swish of cold air. There was no moon now, just the harsh glare of the street lights and the distant moan of the sea.

Sloane tilted her head to stare at Jack's flat. No lights. He'd be tucked up in bed after his book, glass of wine, and harmonising chants with his crystals. That was his night-time ritual. What right did she have to pound on his door, bringing with her a boatload of troublesome vibrations?

Reality suddenly broke in causing her mood to dip. It was nothing but the fantastical workings of her mind to think Jack would hear the truth, then wrap his arms around her, tell her things would be fine and he'd fix it all. He might be an animal crazed vet, but he wasn't a fool. He wanted a woman with a ready-made family, not a lying drug addict and scheming gold digger. And if the shoe were on the other foot, she'd tell him to bugger off.

Sloane let loose a volley of curse words. They spat from her lips as vivid as sparks on fireworks night. No. Jack would never know what she'd done. There was no way she'd tell him. Ever. Not before the wedding. Not after. Never. She'd deal with it all herself.

And with that, Sloane climbed back into her car, cursed once more and in a foul mood drove off into the night.

CHAPTER 54

Sloane did not arrive back at her flat until two a.m.

When she parked her car in the exact spot she drove from earlier, her chest heaved in relief. She sat for a few moments with the engine off and looked at Bren's phone. Yes, she would give it back later.

She got out of the car, clicked the lock and tried to forget tonight's sins. No one need know that she'd left the kids alone. No one need know she'd left the house. Except for the black dog with the mouthful of teeth which snarled from a half-lit corner of the neighbour's yard.

"I've got a treat for you," she said, picking up a stone and hurling it at the hound. It missed, but the dog got the message and raced away whimpering.

As she climbed the steps to her flat under a cloud-filled sky, all she wanted was to fall into bed and drift off into a deep sleep. But as she got halfway up, she suddenly had the feeling that someone was watching.

She spun to survey the street. Darkness cloaked the windows of the houses. She tilted her head, eyes slowly going over the neighbours' doorways. Then she walked down the steps, out to the garden gate and looked both ways down the street.

The moon had broken through the low cloud splashing the road in a pale glow. Two white vans were parked opposite and so close she wondered how they would get out in the morning. A movement caught her eye, and she watched as a cat slinked along the street. It disappeared into a garden. Don't be a fool, she told herself. Who'd be watching?

As she made her way back along the pavement and through the gate that led to her flat, she knew something wasn't right. She took the steps two at a time and stopped dead at the front door.

It was open.

She went over the entire evening, from the moment she heard Max whining in the hallway to the instant she... shut the door. Yes, she'd definitely closed it, and now it was open!

A cold chill crept along the nape of her neck. She fought it back refusing to let it flip the switch of fear. There had to be a reasonable explanation. Maybe the door hadn't clicked shut and the wind caught it?

Breathing fast and shallow Sloane considered what to do. Her gut told her to call the police, but then there'd be questions—why wasn't she at home? Where did she go?

Next, she thought about Jack. He'd come over in a heartbeat but would want to know where she'd been all night too. He'd taken her bait, hook line and sinker for Tuesday night, but to feed him a cock and bull story again? No way he'd bite.

She stared at the dark gap between the door, listening. If she hadn't closed it properly, she'd look foolish.

No police.

No Jack.

Not yet.

With one hand in her handbag clutching the knife, she gave the door a gentle push. It swung open on silent hinges. From just outside the threshold, she called Max. He whined, but he did not come. Strange, he was usually at the door with his rear wagging like crazy. Again she called him. Nothing.

With her senses on high alert, Sloane stepped inside and hurried along the hall. She stopped at the kids' bedroom. The door was ajar. Just as she'd left it. She hesitated with her hand on the door handle. The moment she stepped into their room they would be up—asking for water or to go to the toilet or telling her about their dreams, good or bad. Once one child got up, it stirred the others. Soon they would be chatting and squabbling like birds at dawn. And in the morning she'd wake up ragged and have a devil of a job getting them out of bed. So she stood outside the door and listened to their breathing—knew the sound of each child's breaths.

In. Out.

In. Out.

Her girls were safe. No need to disturb them. Let them sleep in peace.

"Max," she whispered. "Max, come."

Max appeared out of the darkness and whined. The stupid thing wanted to go potty when the door had been open half the night. Sloane shooed him along the hallway and out the front door, then shook two white pills into her hand and swallowed.

It didn't take long.

Much better, now.

Walking on tip-toe, she went into the living room and turned on the lights. There was a blanket on the sofa where Bren had laid earlier, and her keys were still on the coffee table. Other than that, the room was as she left it. She went to the kitchen. Everything as it should be. And finally her bedroom —a dark rug covered the bare floorboards. Bed neatly made. Novel resting on the bedside cabinet alongside a glass and jug of water. Nothing out of place.

Yet Sloane continued to feel the strange sensation of a chord tugging at her gut and went back to the hall and stood outside the kids' bedroom. Once again, she listened to the soft sounds of their breathing.

In. Out.

In. Out.

Something was wrong.

An ice-cold finger of dread tumbled down her spine. She couldn't hear Bren's snore. Sloane pushed the door wide, stepped into the room, and stared in horror at the tangled pile of blankets on Bren's empty bed.

CHAPTER 55

Sloane's world fell apart so fast she couldn't believe it, and from where she stood it looked like a bottomless pit.

She closed the kids' bedroom door softly and ran along the hallway to grab her phone from her handbag. As her breaths jerked in sour panic, she called the police.

"Emergency. Which service?"

At the sound of the operator's voice, Sloane jabbed the off button on her phone. There would be questions she wasn't ready to answer. Questions that would land her in jail. She waited thirty seconds for the phone re-boot, then called Jack on speed dial. He seldom visited her flat. She didn't want him to see how tatty it was. With kids came chaos. Better he found that out after the wedding bells rang. But tonight, he was her Prince Charming. He'd ride to the rescue.

"What's up honey?" he asked, answering on the first ring. Despite the late hour, his voice seemed bright, even jolly. "Is Max playing up?"

"Something terrible has happened to Bren," Sloane sobbed. "She's been taken."

"Now slow down Sloane. I'm not following you,

honey. What's going on with Bren?"

"Please come over." Sloane's voice sounded so thin and gassy that it frightened her. "I don't know what to do."

Fifteen minutes later, Jack knocked on the door. Sloane ushered him into the living room. Not wanting to disturb her two younger daughters, she kept the room dark. She also didn't want him looking too closely at her face. Not yet. Not until she'd got her story straight. Jack accepted the darkened room without complaint. He understood once the girls were up, all hell would break loose.

"Where's Max?" Jack said, placing his black vet's bag on the floor.

He always carried it with him, like a police officer carries their badge. Sloane felt a wave of irritation. Why the hell did Dr Doolittle ask about the dog before he asked about her?

"Max has gone for a pee," she said. Deep down at the edges of her panic, Sloane hoped he'd run away. "He'll be back soon."

He nodded and settled into an armchair. "So, what is all this about?"

It took Sloane three tries to tell Jack what she thought had happened to Bren. Even then, he took several minutes and a shot glass of rum to digest her words. When she explained about Mick Knowles, his eyelids opened so wide the eyeballs jutted out.

"But the man's forty-two and Bren's only just turned sweet sixteen!"

His voice was so filled with shock that Sloane

began to cry.

"I think he targeted her because of me," Sloane sobbed. "And now he's taken her from me."

They both fell quiet. A car moved slowly down the street below. Music blared. Sloane wondered whether it was the car she'd seen earlier—the car full of joy. Jack took her hands.

"Now, let's not get all hysterical, honey," he said in his comforting vet voice. "There has to be a rational explanation."

"He's taken her," Sloane said and cried in gushing sobs. "God knows what he is doing to her and where."

Jack jerked to his feet, poured himself a half shot of rum, walked to the window and stared out into the street. Sloane watched his back as he tilted the shot glass to his lips. He downed it in two short gulps, then shook his head as though to clear it from old cobwebs. In that single movement, Sloane knew he'd come to a decision, and her gut told her she wouldn't like it.

Still staring at the street below, Jack said, "Let's play the game of intuition, use our inner self to figure it out."

"Okay," Sloane said, there being little else she could think to say.

"What we do next is critical. This is very important. Please move those red jasper crystals I gave you from your office desk. Put them nearer to the window. They'll give off more energy in the light. That's what we need now—Chakra energy." He turned, rubbing his bracelet, eyes half-closed and speaking in a chant-like voice. "How'd Mick Knowles get in?"

"I don't know."

"The energy in this place is all wrong."

"I know."

Jack gazed around. "Did he break through a window?"

"No," she said, avoiding Jack's glaring eyes. "The door... when I... I... er... got up from bed to get a glass of water... the door was open."

"Don't you keep a jug by your bed?"

"Thank God it was empty, otherwise I'd not have found out until the morning."

"So, he came in through the front door?"

"Yes."

Jack got up and almost ran to the hall to examine the front door. Sloane followed behind, hoping the movement would not disturb the girls. He carefully inspected the door, then he studied the lock and finally ran a hand around the door frame, pressing hard for signs of weakness. When he finished, he stared at Sloane and shook his head. She followed him back to the living room where they sat on the sofa in silence.

"Not a break-in," Jack said at last, voice tinged with suspicion. "That means someone opened the door for him. Unless he had a key?"

"That's crazy," Sloane replied.

"How well did you know Mick Knowles?"

"He was a client, that's all."

"Are you sure?"

"Jack!"

"You didn't give him a key?"

"No."

"Sloane, tell me the truth."

"I have."

"I mean, are you sure he isn't more than just a client?"

"What are you trying to say?"

"You've been acting strange since I proposed. Mick Knowles is your only male client and now he walks into your home without breaking in. I mean, something doesn't smell right is all I'm saying."

"How dare you even think that of me!"

"I want to know what is going on."

"Mick Knowles is a client. Nothing more. I swear."

Jack shook his head. His voice sharpened to a shard of glass. "When you said you felt odd about wearing my Ester's ring, I knew there was more to it than met the eye. You're not one for the woo-woo, like me. You're not a sensitive."

"I love you, Jack."

"Uh-huh."

"I mean it."

"Then give me Ester's ring. Now."

That bloody thing had been a millstone around her neck from the moment she pawned it to Jane Ragsdale. Now that cow was dead, and she still didn't have the ring. A wasted death, she thought with bitterness.

"Oh, Jack, let's not argue." She got close and placed her hands on his chest. "I thought we'd have our ceremony on Saturday after we choose my replacement ring in London. We are still going to London, aren't we?"

Jack ran a hand through his hair but didn't move away. "And you think Mick Knowles has taken Bren?"

"Yes."

"But I don't see any signs of a break-in or struggle."

"Mick Knowles is not right in his head. The way he talked about his wife scared me."

"He was married?"

"Not technically. Years ago he had a girlfriend who he was to wed. He called her his wife."

"You never said that before. What happened to her?"

"She vanished."

"Eh? People don't just vanish."

"Her name was Pam Wells. I think he killed her."

"Jesus, Sloane." Jack's eyes swelled to dinner plates. "I can't believe what I'm hearing."

It was suddenly so quiet Sloane fancied she heard snores coming from the kid's room. Outside a gust of wind rattled the living room windows. It carried with it the snarl of the neighbour's dog. Max hadn't returned yet.

A thump sounded from the hall.

Jack placed a finger to his lips, picked up his

vet's bag and quietly left the room.

CHAPTER 56

This cannot be happening. Sloane paced the living room. Bren was gone and now there were strange noises in her flat.

She wanted to follow Jack but his rigid body language warned her off. She didn't know what made the sound. It came from the hallway but the front door was closed and she'd checked the flat. If anyone were hiding, they had to be in one of the cupboards. But only a midget could hide in such a confined space.

The radiators? They sometimes creaked and groaned. Yes, that was it. She was sure. Should she tell Jack? No. She was his damsel in distress. Best let him do his man thing. So, she sat and waited, thoughts drifting to Tim.

Since he died, she'd been on skid row. In truth, they had been on that row for years. Tim driving a van in the day and delivering pizzas at night. Not enough cash to pay their way. Final demands for payment through the letterbox every day. She, in a job she hated to stem the flow. And still it was not enough. Everything had been on the slide for years. It was only when Tim passed that she paused long enough to notice. That's why she had to grasp onto

Jack with every sinew. He'd haul her from the pit of shit she'd fallen in.

Jack returned a few moments later. He flipped on a floor lamp, sat, and stared at Sloane for a long while.

"Another rum?" Sloane said.

"No one in the hall," he replied, ignoring her question and rubbing a hand over his bracelet. "But I can sense a boatload of negative vibrations, right here in this room. I don't get it."

"You are so brave. My hero."

"Wonder what made that noise?"

"No idea."

"I checked your bedroom."

"Thank you." What else could she say? She didn't like him poking around in there but somehow managed a weak smile. "I feel better now."

"No one hiding under the bed or in the wardrobe," Jack said.

"Thank God for that."

"But I did notice your bedside table."

"What about it?"

"The jug is full of water."

"Really?"

"You said it was empty. That's why you got up, right?"

"Why, yes. I filled it and put it back."

"Before or after you noticed Bren was gone?"

"What difference does it make?"

"Before or after?"

"Before, I think."

"Not after?"

"No. Definitely before."

His eyes narrowed. "I see."

"What is that supposed to mean?"

"I just thought that once you'd filled your jug with water and placed it on your nightstand, the natural thing to do next is to get into bed and go to sleep."

Sloane coughed, then thumped the centre of her chest with her fist. "Excuse me. Something caught in my throat. Oh, yes, I guess I'm a creature of habit. I always check on the girls after I've filled the jug with water. I'm sorry, I should have told you everything before."

"And you've told me everything now?"

"Yes."

"Then we'd better call the police."

"We can't."

"Why not?"

What to say next? Sloane didn't know. The only thing she knew for sure was that she'd never let go of her chance to marry Jack and get into his wallet. If the police came, their questions would mess things up. She smiled at him and then placed her head in her hands. Through the slits between her fingers, she peeped and waited.

Jack placed his warm hands on hers and slowly lowered them so he could see her face. "There is nothing to fear, honey. When the police come, they'll search the flat. They might find a clue to tell us what happened."

"They will wake the girls."

"I'll book a suite for you and the kids. How about the Giles Breeze Hotel?"

"But that place is so expensive, it'll cost you a packet."

"Only the best for my Sloane, and the girls will love it. Have you seen the size of their indoor swimming pool?"

A sudden realisation dawned. With all his cash she wouldn't have to give up her oxy. The man was loaded and, if she were clever, wouldn't miss drug money siphoned from his purse. Yes, she could keep on with her little white pills. They were such a great help to her life, why give them up? That thought washed so much joy through her veins that she wanted to sing. But if the police came with their questions her dam of lies would burst and Jack would find out the truth about everything.

She said, "The police will ask so many questions."

"That's their job."

"I know... I know." She looked at him with pleading eyes. "And my job is to be a good mother. What will they think?"

She brushed her hand across her eyes so Jack would see the tears springing from them.

"Don't worry, honey," he said, wrapping his arms around her. "I'm sure there is some explanation."

"It's not my fault Bren's gone. I've tried to be a good mother, but it is so difficult on my own."

"Don't blame yourself. I've no idea how single mums do it." Jack spoke softly, holding her tight. He kissed her on the lips. "Maybe Bren let him in?"

"She'd never do that."

"Love makes you do odd things."

"Maybe you are right," Sloane replied, thinking. "Bren was so smitten she'd be content in a grass hut in a snake-filled swamp with Mick Knowles. Yes, she must have opened the door and let him in."

Jack, being practical as always, said, "That means she wasn't *taken* but went of her own free will. Check to see if she's packed anything."

He followed her to the hallway. It only took Sloane five minutes, creeping around the kids' room in the dark, to realise Bren had packed no clothes.

She went back to the front door, feeling a twinge of guilt as she watched Jack's expectant face. Didn't she read somewhere that a mother bear might kill a cub to protect the others? Jack's wedding ring was the best way to secure the future. His money would make their life more comfortable.

"Oh my God!" Sloane said. "Bren's favourite clothes are missing, and she's taken her backpack!"

Jack let out a sharp gasp. "That means she left under her own steam. Imagine if we'd gone to the police, we'd have looked like fools." He sucked in a hard breath. "Don't worry, honey, teenagers run away all the time. If she has left to be with Mick Knowles, they will soon run out of money. We'll track him down and find her."

"I... I suppose so."

"I can still sense negative vibrations." He looked at Sloane with sad eyes. "There is something else, isn't there, honey?"

Sloane nodded. "It's Ester's ring. Bren must have taken it. It's gone!"

CHAPTER 57

It was dark when Fenella arrived at the Port St Giles police station on Thursday morning. The cloak of night lingered over the town still stirring from its sleep. Darkness mixed with swirls of fog blown in by the sea so that everything appeared a dull grey. An ominous sign of things to come, she thought as she sat at her desk in her tiny office and sipped from a mug of hot tea.

She had come in early to spend time on the Jane Ragsdale and Pam Wells cases. Jones had compiled a file on each woman, and Dr MacKay had sent over a draft report. The still of the early hour gave her a chance to learn more about their lives; to sense them as they were in life and to understand more about their deaths.

Footsteps sounded from the hallway. Then came the mumble of low voices. For a moment she considered turning her office light off. It attracted visitors like moths to a bulb. She wanted to read in peace and without the flutter of questions by random passers-by or people popping in just to say hello. She decided against it, kept the light on and settled down to read.

It was just before 7 a.m. when she finished Dr

MacKay's report. Jane Ragsdale had eaten a packet of lemon drops before she died. Not what you'd call a square meal. It didn't say what Pam Wells ate last, her body being too decomposed.

As she opened her notebook to jot down her thoughts, a knock came from the door and Superintendent Jeffery strode in. Her body language didn't look good.

"Sallow, those—"

"Working on them now, ma'am," Fenella said, nodding at the stack of papers in her in-box.

She had no idea which forms the boss wanted this time but knew she'd find them somewhere in the tottering pile. Better to say she was on it rather than have the boss rip an inch from her hide. And she'd get round to it, whatever *it* was as soon as she possibly could. But first, she had to get rid of Jeffery so she could think about Dr MacKay's report.

"Very good," Jeffery replied and gave a wolfish smile. "By the way, I've signed you up for a management course."

"I've been on four training programs this year, ma'am. More than anyone else in the station."

"You have not taken this one. The seven pillars of building a joyful team. I'll teach the class. It starts on Friday, eight a.m. sharp."

"Tomorrow, ma'am?"

"We'll get brownie points with Carlisle if we have a strong showing from our senior detectives."

"Friday at eight in the morning, ma'am?"

"You got lucky, Sallow. You are the first I've

invited. I saw your office light on. First come, first served. The room will only hold twenty."

"Can't do this Friday, ma'am," Fenella blustered. "What with the Pam Wells and Jane Ragsdale cases and those forms you've just requested. I'll have to skip this one. I'm sure there will be other eager takers."

Jeffery didn't answer for a while. It was as if she was remembering that they were police officers with crimes to solve. Then she waved a dismissive hand.

"Tell Dexter and Jones to join. They'll boost our minority count. Make sure they sit in the first row with you. We have a photographer taking snaps of it all. And those forms? Carlisle is on my tail to get them in. Have them on my desk before you leave this evening."

She spun and marched from the room, arms swinging at her side.

Fenella stared at the door wondering if Jeffery was out to get her. The boss had cut her team to the bone, and now this training session. It would go down like a lead balloon with Dexter and Jones. Who wants to spend Friday listening to management waffle? And she was still none the wiser about which forms she needed to hand in.

As she settled back into her chair, the tottering in-box pile tipped over. Papers scattered on the desk and fluttered to the floor. She took a slug from the mug and grunted. It was a sign of the way the day was going. Everything a mess with more work than could be done.

She picked up the papers, placed them in her in-box and straightened the stack. Then she tidied her desk so the pens were lined up in a neat row. A trick she'd learned in a management training course. It was supposed to signal to the mind that everything was in order and you are ready to begin. It never seemed to work, though, and she got up to make another mug of tea.

Outside, the fog had begun to lift from the town with the first rays of gold sunshine splashing on the buildings. It looked like a great day to be out and about.

As she sipped, she looked at the stack and calculated she'd be done by five. At last, with a disgruntled sigh, she settled down to a day of dull paperwork.

CHAPTER 58

At 11 a.m., boredom broke through Fenella's ramparts of concentration and stamped out her will to do more.

Her brain cells fizzled under the mind-numbing task. She took a long gulp from her third mug of tea and wondered how Jones and Dexter were getting on. She hoped they would find a nugget for her to chew on soon. Anything to take her numbed mind away from those damn forms.

She walked to the window and looked out into the courtyard. The fog had cleared, leaving a bright sky with no clouds.

She hadn't realised the depth of the disappointment she felt when Dexter and Ria Leigh failed to haul in Mick Knowles. But it was there now. A sharp pang in her chest. The feeling she always got when she wanted a case to be over.

She slowly took another sip of tea. The forensic techs hadn't found any incriminating evidence on his narrowboat. No surgical gowns. No blade. Nothing to stitch a wound. That troubled Fenella. A killer who strikes twice years apart and leaves no clues in their home is a cocky bugger. A psycho who thinks through their crimes and executes them with cold-hearted precision.

Her phone rang.

Jones.

"They've found a set of fresh fingerprints on the Gold Kite that don't match Jane Ragsdale or Mike Knowles," Jones said, excited.

"Got a name?" Fenella asked.

"Not yet, boss."

"Put the rush on to see if there is anything matching them on file," Fenella replied. "I want to know who she or he is? I know it is tedious, but it's the tedious work that pays off. Anything else?"

"I've been on to the phone company for details of Mick Knowles. They say his phone hasn't been used since Tuesday. More to come, but it will take a day or two."

As Fenella hung up, there was a hoot of laughter from just outside her door. She glanced up expecting it to open. A good laugh and a chat were just the boost she needed. It'd give her the energy to keep on with the administrative tasks. The laughter continued along the hallway fading to a soft chuckle.

Her mind drifted back to Mick Knowles. What troubled her the most was the lack of hard evidence against the man. If he was the killer, it meant he took the medical stuff with him—the gowns, blade and stitches. Or he hid them someplace else. Why? To strike again. A pang in her chest grew to a dull thud. They had no clue who she would be.

She placed the forms she'd finished in the outbox and leaned against the desk, thinking once again about Pam Wells and Jane Ragsdale. They were both girlfriends of Mick Knowles. Was he seeing another woman? If so, who?

She pondered the idea for a while and decided it might pass muster as a working theory for the next victim. But without a name, there was nothing she could do but wait.

Another killing would drive the news media crazy. Jeffery would throw a fit. A knot of tension seized her neck. How the hell could she just sit in her office filing forms and waiting for a lass to lose her life at the end of a medical blade?

She sent a text message to Dexter to see if he could dig up a name on the grapevine. Then she remembered Ria Leigh and sent her a message too.

Fenella looked at the remaining pile in her in-box and knew she'd not be done by five. Since they were going to be handed in late, there was no point getting in a huff. She'd do the rest on Friday during the management training class. They called that multitasking, didn't they?

Her mood lifted and again she wondered what Dexter was up to. Her hand drifted to her phone and dialled.

"Guv, was about to call you," he said, picking up on the first ring. "I've had a chat with a few of my contacts about Mick Knowles."

"News?" she said, pleased she'd ditched the dull paperwork and made the call. "Found Micky's hidey-hole, have you?"

"No such luck, Guv. But I have found that he worked as an odd job man at the Navigator Arms, hauling bags of sawdust and the like. I've something else that might be worth a follow up." He paused and Fenella thought she heard him crack his knuckles. "Seems our Micky has a very bad temper. The man flies off the handle at the slightest thing. It has gotten so bad he is seeing an anger management therapist. I lose my rag sometimes but it ain't so bad that I got to see a shrink. Sloane Kern, a widow with three bairns. She rents an office in Hodge Hill. Funny thing is, I hear she only takes on women clients."

"Then why would she take on Mick Knowles?" Fenella asked, wondering at the chance that Sloane Kern might be the third victim.

"That's the question I asked myself, Guv. Ain't got no idea, but it might be worth a prod to see what she's got to say. She was married to a Mr Tim Kern; he died a few years back. I did a bit of digging because I thought the name rang a bell. Sure enough, it did."

"Don't keep me in suspense, what have you got?"

"Mr Kern was another odd jobs man, Guv. He delivered pizzas, drove a van, and turned his hand to anything. Small fry, really. Don't know yet whether he knew Mick Knowles. But Mr Kern wasn't straight with his books and got caught up in a tax evasion sweep."

"Oh aye?"

"He'd been running a second-hand furniture

reselling business on the side. Nowt declared to the taxman. Revenue and Customs don't like it when you do that. Got my hands on some reports and his second set of books. Dry reading. I'll email copies."

"Tell you what," Fenella said, standing, "I'll pop round for a chat with Sloane Kern. It's about time I got out of this office, and it'll be lunchtime by the time I get there."

CHAPTER 59

Fenella drove straight to Hodge Hill.

She sat in her car looking across the half-full carpark and thinking about the questions she'd ask Sloane Kern. They'd tidied the grounds since her last visit. That must have been five years ago, maybe more. The mown lawn edged with blooming mauve hyacinths gave the place an English garden feel. Much easier on the eye than the brown grass and thick mud that stuck in thick clods to your shoes she remembered.

The two-story office building hadn't changed much. Clouded windows, peeling brown panels and a flat roof. It looked like a school plopped down from the 1970s. The type they'd condemned and knocked down years ago everywhere else. The rent had to be cheap and Fenella supposed anger management therapy didn't pay much.

Inside, she walked to the second floor, found the right door, knocked and poked her head inside.

"Sloane Kern?" she asked and was pleased to see the room empty of clients. She'd not called ahead. Best take them by surprise.

And she, too, was surprised by the size of the office. Poky, with an armchair for clients, worn sofa, a small wooden desk with a spider plant, window and nowt else. If she had anger management issues, the claustrophobic room would do her head in. She'd not want to sit in that tatty green armchair with the stuffing oozing out the side. Or stare at the stained brown tile ceiling as she talked about uncontrollable rage.

A thirty-something woman hunkered over the desk, hand on a brown appointment book. "How can I help you?"

"Mrs Sloane Kern?"

"That's me. What do you want?"

Automatically Fenella took in the woman. Hair in need of a comb, face pale, eyes bloated, red lipstick smeared at the corners of her lips as though she'd put it on without the aid of a mirror. But what woman puts on lipstick without checking in a mirror? And that hair? Still pondering that question, she glanced about the room and wondered why there were no clients in and from Sloane Kern's disappointed stare, got the feeling there had been none all morning.

Fenella said, "We've met before, luv."

"Have we?"

"Last Sunday at the Garden of Remembrance, you were kneeling on the grass. I suggested you sit on the bench, told you your hubby would prefer it."

"So you did, and I did sit on the bench," Sloane said. "My Tim was much happier with that."

"I'm Detective Inspector Fenella Sallow." She flashed her warrant card. "Can I have a quick word?"

Maybe the therapy business paid even less than she thought. "I'm rather busy," Sloane said. "Is it important?"

"Just a few questions to help with an inquiry."

"I'm sorry but I can't help."

"I haven't asked any questions yet, luv."

The whites of Sloane Kern's eyes were lined with thin veins the colour of plum wine. Fenella wondered if she'd been at the bottle and sniffed hard but didn't smell alcohol. Not high on booze then. Something else?

She said, "You'll have heard about the woman found in the canal?"

"I haven't kept up with the news. Too busy with my work."

"Everyone's talking about it. Her name was Jane Ragsdale."

Fenella had hoped to see a chink of recognition, but only got a blank stare.

Sloane said, "Is that why you are here?"

"Did you know her?"

"I can't see the relevance of your question."

"I'm investigating the murder of Miss Ragsdale."

"Murder! I thought she drowned."

"So you did hear the news?"

"No... er... your mention of the canal made me think it was a drowning."

"I see."

Fenella kept her gaze on the woman. She didn't believe she'd not heard the news but couldn't figure out why she'd lie. Now she waited for Sloane to speak.

Sloane sat stiffly; arms folded across her chest. "What has this to do with me?"

"Routine inquiry, Mrs Kern."

"Please call me Sloane." She gave a weak smile. "I suppose you want to know if she was a client?"

"That would be a big help."

"My client information is confidential; however Miss Ragsdale is not on my books. I've never met her." Sloane stood. "If you have no further questions."

"Look, you must be pretty busy, so I'll be on my way," Fenella said, also standing. "I'll leave you in peace. Just one question. Is it true you only treat women?"

"That's right, Inspector. But there are a lot of women in Port St Giles, roughly half the population if I'm not mistaken. I did not know Jane Ragsdale. I've never met the woman. I'm sorry, but I can't help you. I wish I could."

"Aye, pet. Happen you're right about that." Fenella moved towards the door. "And that's what I can't understand."

"I'm not with you, Inspector."

"I was wondering why you took on a Mr Mick Knowles as a client if you only serve women."

"I can't comment on that."

"Aye, luv, you can." Fenella smiled. "Mick Knowles is wanted concerning the brutal deaths of two women. I want you to tell me everything you know about him."

Sloane raised a hand to her chin in a slow, controlled movement. "When it comes to men like Mick Knowles, there is no anger management technique I can teach. No self-care tool I can show. There is only the soft clink of the prison door."

"How do you mean?"

"I took him on as a client, but I'm referring him to a psychiatrist. I'm afraid the man is beyond my help." She gave a sad smile. "I'm trained to treat people with anger management issues. Mr Knowles has problems way beyond that. He has issues with women and talked about their deaths in a rather grisly way."

"Oh aye?"

"I really can't say any more."

"Course you can, pet. I'm with the police. You can tell me anything."

"I don't know that it would be ethical. I could get struck off."

"I won't tell anyone if you don't."

"Really, Inspector, this is most unusual. I simply can't go against the code of conduct."

"Well, I suppose I could speak with a magistrate and have them issue you an order. That'd mean the police poking about in your business, and who knows what we'll find. Not that we'd be looking for anything untoward in your books or anywhere else, you understand?"

Sloane stared with unblinking eyes. Her ring finger tapped the appointment book in a solemn beat. "You're a very persuasive woman. I suppose it'd be quicker if we chat. I don't want to hold up your investigation and pushing around bits of paper through the courts isn't good for the trees."

"I'm listening," Fenella said and waited.

"It is all in my files," Sloane began. "But if you don't mind, I'll cut to the chase. Mr Knowles is an angry man whose rage is steeped in women. He talks like a cold-hearted butcher—slicing out tongues and chopping off ring fingers. I believe he went to medical school, so perhaps it is not as disturbing as one might think. Still, I feel he needs psychiatric help."

"I see," Fenella replied. "All that tricky mind stuff is beyond my pay grade. I'd never be able to work it all out."

"It requires training, dedication and a unique insight into the human mind. That's why I chose this line of work. It brings me so much... joy."

"Aye, luv. I think I understand. So why did you take him on as a client if his mind weren't right?"

"The challenge, I suppose. But I bit off more than I can chew. Like you say, he's not right in his head. I won't make that mistake again."

Fenella had the unmistakable feeling that every word was a lie. She changed the subject. "Jane Ragsdale was his girlfriend. Did he not mention her in one of your sessions?"

"No."

"Did Mr Knowles mention a lass by the name of Pam Wells?"

"No."

Fenella didn't believe either reply but couldn't pinpoint why. She said, "My memory's no good these days. I have to drink coffee to jog it along, even in the afternoon. Why don't you take a look in your notes to double check?"

"I don't have any problems with my memory, Inspector. There was no mention of a Pam Wells by Mr Knowles. And I've never heard of Jane Ragsdale. I don't need to check the files. I'm absolutely certain of my facts."

"Honestly, I wish my mind was as bright as that these days. I need coffee and tea and wine too. It all helps the old brain cells get moving." Fenella lowered her voice. "Tell me, how can you be so sure?"

"Mr Knowles only spoke in vague terms about women. He never mentioned names outside of his close family. His gran, dad and grandad Bob come to mind. No other women though."

"You sure?"

"Certain."

"What about his mum, did he talk about her?"

"Well, yes, they always talk about their mum."

"She was a woman, right?"

"Of course."

"Did he talk about any other women?"

"No."

"That clears that up," Fenella said, reaching for the door handle. "I don't suppose Mr Knowles told you where he might run?"

"No, I'm afraid not."

"Thank you for your time." Fenella hesitated for a moment, then turned. "Everything good at home?"

"Yes."

"And the kids?"

"Fine."

"Is there anything else you want to tell me?"

Sloane looked at her for a long while then slowly shook her head. "No. Absolutely nothing."

CHAPTER 60

Sloane had no idea what disaster was going to hit her next, but she sensed another wave coming.

She stood by the window in her office, drinking a mug of tea. Below, the woman detective walked along the path, stopping occasionally to look at the hyacinths. At the carpark, she climbed into an ancient blue Morris Minor. A car they'd stopped machining years ago, driven by the long-dead.

Sloane glanced at her watch and counted off three minutes. Why hadn't the detective started her car? Was she watching her, even now, as she sat in the darkened vehicle? Did they know what she'd done?

Be reasonable. They know nothing.

But she felt sick to the pit of her stomach. She'd lied. Worse, she hadn't reported her daughter, Bren, missing. How could she explain doing a thing like that?

I am a good mum.

Her mum had so many boyfriends Sloane stopped calling them dad when she was five.

Everything I do is for the children. That is more than my mum ever did.

And Bren? She'd only been gone one night, and

teenagers run away all the time. Hadn't she fled her mum's council flat when she first met Tim? When she returned, months later, Bren was in her belly. Her mum hugged her and said she knew she'd be back. Her mum's new man wasn't so keen to see her, but that's boyfriends for you.

Sloane didn't know if it was the oxy, but she was more worried about the police than Bren. She'd taken two pills last night and two more when she awoke in the morning. If the police looked hard in her business, they'd find two sets of books and fiddled numbers. How long would it take them to discover she'd used business expenses to pay for her oxy?

No! Best keep away from the police, for the sake of her girls. If she ended up behind bars, it would crush their mental health. *Protect my girls like a mother bear*. She had to keep up with the lies to shield her cubs.

Did she even brush her hair? She couldn't remember. The morning was a blur and last night was covered in a tired haze of fog. She was about to search her handbag for a mirror when she thought again of Jack. Dr Doolittle would be livid if he found out about her double set of books. She could see his eyes stretched wide and mouth agape. A jolt like that and he'd see right through her. It'd be like the Frankenstein movie where a sudden shot of electricity shocks the monster to life. Once its eyes opened, there was no stopping what it saw.

And last night she felt something shift. A curl

of doubt at the corner of Jack's lips and his gaze riveted on her as though she were some hideous turd stuck to the bottom of his shoe. Did he believe her tale about the ring? She felt a tinge of shame for blaming Bren for taking it. But it was a gift horse. What else could she do? There were times when a mother bear had to sacrifice a cub for the benefit of the family.

She searched her handbag for the small brown bottle, shook out two pills and swallowed them without water. It only took a few moments for the glow to wash over her. But this time it came with a sense of dread. Was Frankenstein waking?

A sudden fear that Jack would call off the wedding seized Sloane. Her web of lies felt like a tightening noose. She rushed to her desk to get her phone. As she hurried back to the window, she pressed speed dial and then waited with growing agitation for Jack to answer.

"It's me," she said in her little girl's voice the moment she heard the click. Jack liked that voice, and she'd found he'd dance to whatever tune she played when she used it. "What time will you pick me up for London tomorrow? I've seen a wonderful ring that—"

"Sorry, can't talk now."

The line went dead.

Sloane felt fire rushing to her cheeks and stared at the phone for a full sixty seconds, wondering whether to call him back. No way would she let her claws slip from him. She almost had the man by the throat and when the wedding bells rang, she'd have him by the balls too. Jack Parkes would not wriggle free.

Still undecided on whether to call him back, she had an idea. Why not get married in a registry office? A low-profile ceremony where they signed a bit of paper was all that was really needed. They could book it for next week! It was not the flowing white gown, aisle strewn with rose petals and ringing church bells she wanted, but it would have to do.

He'll see right through that now.

Sloane's temper boiled at that thought. She cursed Jack for not proposing sooner. If he'd asked last winter, they would have had a spring wedding. White gown, church bells, the works. She'd be his wife now and would never have taken Mick Knowles on as a client, and Bren would still be at home. This mess was all Jack's fault. She'd make sure he bought a bigger house in posh Westpond now, just to spite him. And she'd make him take out a larger life insurance policy. Two million pounds wasn't greedy after all she'd been through.

It wasn't just the money Sloane wanted, though. There was prestige in being the wife of a vet. She'd be expected to attend dinner functions and sit on important committees. No more, for her, the spoilt and sour-faced clients with rage issues. No more the grovelling around in the gutter to bring new faces through her business door. At last, she'd be a full-time mum for her daughters.

The rattle of a car engine broke into her thoughts. That bloody detective! Sloane watched as the Morris Minor pulled away, spitting out a belch of black fumes. It won't be long before the cow is back, she thought, blood boiling with rage.

CHAPTER 61

Instead of going back to the station, Fenella went to Mustard's Chippy to buy a bag of haddock and chips. She waited in line and thought about Sloane Kern. By the time the assistant wrapped her order, she'd not come to a firm conclusion.

She ate in her car, hoping the stodge would fuel her through the rest of the day. And fish was good for the brain. Nan had packed her lunch—more slices of cold lamb wedged between thick-cut bread, but she didn't want that today. If Dexter were here, he'd have had the lamb sandwiches and begged half her fish and chips.

She popped the last crisp bit of fish into her mouth and wiped her hands on a napkin. She wished she'd ordered a battered sausage as well but the line now streamed out of the door. A mix of school children, workers and homemakers waiting patiently to be served.

The only thing Fenella knew for sure was that Sloane Kern knew more about Mick Knowles than she let on. As to why she'd not told everything remained a mystery. And Fenella didn't like mysteries or loose ends or people who didn't tell her the full story.

She sent a text message to Jones to have a quiet look into Sloane Kern's financials. Then she opened her handbag to jot her thoughts in a notebook, saw the wrapped lamb sandwich and called Dexter.

"Find out anything from Sloane Kern, Guv?" he asked as soon as she picked up.

"Nowt but that she is hiding something."

"Wonder if Mick Knowles might be more than a client, Guv. Wouldn't be the first time a professional lass has fallen for a bad boy."

"Aye, but I think there is something else. Can you have a nose around? We know she has three kids. Check with the schools. See if anything odd shows up. I'm certain we'll be speaking with her again, and next time I want to be more prepared."

Fenella hung up and thought about going back to the station, as there was nothing much else she could do but wait. That stack of forms needed to be signed and filed. If she worked quickly, she might make a dent in it before nightfall.

She lowered the window to let out the smell of the fried food. The early start at the station had not given her time to sink her teeth into the Pam Wells and Jane Ragsdale cases. Their boyfriend, Mick Knowles, bothered her on many levels, not least their inability to find the man. And now there was a link to Sloane Kern.

She tapped her phone and began to read the reports sent by Dexter. Tim Kern bought posh furniture for cash from rich folk in Westpond and resold them at a profit to dealers in Whitehaven and

Carlisle. Nothing recorded in his official books. All the details in his secret books. Items he couldn't sell he donated to charity.

Tim Kern's second set of books must have been transcribed from the original because they were typed rather than handwritten. She poured over the names and addresses. Her mind swirled. She flipped randomly through the pages on her screen until she saw something of interest. She paused, pinched the screen to make the text larger, going more slowly, and now with her reading glasses perched at the tip of her nose:

Mrs Millard,5 Town Lane. Mr Eaves, 14 Layburn Court. Mrs Tattersall, 72 Davids Lane. Mrs Padavona,66 Trinity Crescent. Mrs Blunden, 86 Brackley Road...

She lost track of the time reading and rereading the reports until the haddock and chips began to make her sleepy and she decided to visit the Navigator Arms. What had happened to the man with the devil's wisp beard? Another mystery. And she fancied a half pint of draught ale.

CHAPTER 62

Ria Leigh always got what she wanted, and she knew today when she asked, it would only be a matter of time before she scored another win.

She made herself comfortable in the green armchair, sniffed the stale air, and then stared for a moment at the brown-stained ceiling tiles.

"You seem confused," Ria said.

"Today isn't your regular appointment day." Sloane held a mug of tea in her right hand and put it to her lips but did not sip. "Are you here on... police business?"

"I thought I'd pop in to have a quiet chat. In confidence."

"I've already spoken to the police. They came by to ask about a client."

"Who?"

"I really can't say... well, since you are with the police, I suppose you'll find out anyway. They wanted to know about Mick Knowles."

"I thought you only took on female clients."

"He was a mistake."

"Who did you speak with?"

"Inspector Sallow." Sloane hesitated. "I don't know what she really wanted. She has a way of asking questions which are more than they first seem. But I think it was to learn more about Mr Knowles. I couldn't help her. Is that why you are here?"

"No," Ria said. "That's not why I am here."

Sloane fell quiet for a moment. Something shifted in her face. A shadow which when it passed made her seem aged. She placed her mug on the desk and toyed with the handle. "Are you having issues with rage?"

"No," Ria replied. "I feel good today. Very good."

Sloane looked confused. There were tear stains where her makeup had run, and that red lipstick might be okay on a clown's face.

The woman is near breaking point.

This was going to be even easier than Ria dreamed. Still, she'd take her time. Play with the woman a little. It'd be like when she was a child and found that large spider under her bed. The black bug was just like the creature in her nightmares. But she wasn't asleep, tied to her bed unable to close her eyes. She was awake and could move.

She'd trapped it in her hand.

Grinning, she lowered her face to look at its wriggling form and told it that its life would soon end. She poked the edge of her fingernail into its bulging eyes and twisted until liquid squirted out. Then, one by one, with two fingers, she tore off the long dangly legs.

Time to apply the pressure.

"What do you want?" Sloane asked again.

The crow's feet at the corner of her eyes wrinkled, cheeks sunken in. It was clear she hadn't looked in a mirror for a while. Ria saw the small vein pulsating on her right temple, and counted to thirty, letting the silence linger, so that when she spoke the quiet shattered like broken glass.

"Isn't it obvious why I am here?" Ria made a plucking motion with two fingers of her left hand. "We have things to discuss."

"I'm afraid I'm not with you," Sloane said.

Ria reached into her handbag and retrieved a clear plastic bag filled with white pills.

"Maybe this will help jog your brain cells," she said, waving the bag.

"I don't know what that—"

"I hope you were not going to say you've no idea what these are. That would be a lie, wouldn't it, Sloane?" Ria paused and held Sloane Kern's frightened gaze. "Why don't you have a sip of tea, ease the dryness in your throat?"

"It's quite cold, thank you." Sloane glanced down at the mug, hand tightening on the handle. "Dead cold."

Ria adjusted her position and waved the bag of pills as though she were tempting a donkey with a carrot. "These little white treats are oxy, but you know that since you are a user and your supplier was Jane Ragsdale."

"You've got no proof of that," Sloane snarled, eyes suddenly small and hard. "None whatsoever."

"You deny taking oxy?"

Sloane gulped slowly from her mug. In an even slower motion, she stood. "I used oxy to help me get through a difficult time after my husband died. And, yes, Jane Ragsdale was my supplier. But I've ended my addiction. I told Jane that the last time she came here. I'll never touch drugs again."

Ria gave a slow clap. "My God, you are very good. Very good indeed. If I didn't have proof, even I'd believe you."

Again Ria reached into her handbag, pulled out a tablet computer, stood and walked to the desk. She was ready to pluck the final leg from her still spider. And, just like when she was a child watching the legless creature die, she felt a deep sense of God-like power.

"Go on," Ria said, handing the tablet to Sloane. "Take a good look."

Sloane stared at the glowing screen; mouth slightly open. Slowly, she sat down.

The photographs were taken at night, so at first, it was difficult to see what they showed. As Sloane scrolled through the images, her eyes widened in horror. When she finished, she stared at Ria in dazed shock.

"I took them Tuesday night," Ria said. "That's you on the aft on the Gold Kite. That's you tugging at the door. That's you breaking in. And that's you going inside."

Motionless, Sloane stared at the room. The worn sofa, scruffy armchair with her patient Ria, lips twisted into a sneer or was it a grin? She dropped her head, squeezed her eyes shut, clenched the mug handle between her fingers, blowing out a series of short breaths. Her fingerprints were everywhere on the Gold Kite. Everywhere!

Ria cackled with laughter. This was more fun than she expected, and Sloane's face, well, she'd never have imagined her pale sweat-soaked face would get that contorted.

More fun than pulling legs off a spider.

Again Ria laughed, this time with a sneer. "Got yourself in a spot of bother a while back, didn't you? Swung at a medic, fingerprints taken." The sneer became smug, triumphant. "Your fingerprints are all over that boat. It would only take a little bird to point the police in your direction. And since I am the police, we can do away with the little bird, can't we?"

"I can explain," Sloane said in a rush. "You see, I couldn't sleep and went for a walk. I mean, at night sometimes I sleepwalk—"

"Shut up!"

Sloane gasped, face as pale as baker's dough. But she did as she was commanded, her lips a straight line.

Ria brimmed with joy; it was all going to plan. A few minutes more and she'd have what she wanted, but first she had to twist the knife even farther. Just like she'd done with that spider under her bed.

With her father's scalpel, she'd sliced it in three to make sure it was dead. Leave nothing to chance. That was her way. That's how she'd won Civic Officer of the year three times in a row. That's how she'd win it for the fourth.

"If I were a police officer," Ria began, "I'd find it curious that you were on Jane Ragsdale's boat the night she died and didn't tell anyone. Oh, but wait, I am a police officer. How many years do you think a judge will give a cold-blooded killer?"

"Listen, you've got it all wrong. I—"

"No, you listen. Hundreds of small-time drug dealers have crossed my path. Liars, thieves, and fools every last one. All losers on a downwards slide and don't even know it. Not Jane Ragsdale, she had class."

"She was low-life scum," Sloane shouted, face red with rage. "A cockroach and a thief."

This was going better than expected. It felt so good to see the anger therapist overtaken by rage. Like that spider trying to run from her palm with no legs. Oh joy!

Now Ria took her time and lowered her voice. "You are not a bad person for saying that. I know you help people. Most who come to you are in desperate need. Week in, week out, they come for your advice. And you do it as a single mother with three daughters to care for. That takes a big heart. All you want to do is give. I understand."

Sloane nodded as tears flowed. "I did it for my girls. It's all for them. So many women need hope. That's why I chose anger management. I do it for them. For the women without hope. For those just like us. I'm doing my bit to do good in the world, but somehow it's all going wrong."

"I understand, I really do," Ria said. "Tell me, why should one little indiscretion get in the way of your life's mission? So, why not bend the truth a little, eh?"

Sloane looked up; eyes suddenly clear. "What do you mean?"

"Only you and I know what you did."

"Then you are not here to arrest me?"

"I wouldn't do that. Nor will I tell anyone about your nighttime activities. If a piece of scum like Jane Ragsdale gets rubbed out, too bad. Helps keep the place clean and tidy. I like you Sloane. I really do, and want to help. Tell you what. I'll make sure her death ends up in a cold case file along with hundreds that will never be solved." Ria picked up the tablet computer, slipped it back into her handbag, and clicked it shut. "Case closed, Sloane. Case closed."

Silence, besides the long exhale of Sloane's breath. Ria placed her hand on her handbag to check it was firmly shut. A soft click confirmed its full closure. It took several moments more for her to realise Sloane's exhale contained a simple question. A question Ria knew she would ask.

"What do you want?"

Ria's lips twitched into a grim smile as a sudden memory hit. There she was squatting on the bathroom floor of her flat with her mum sprawled out on the cold tiles, covered in vomit, the sour reek unbearable. She had seen so many dead bodies in her time as a cop that one more didn't cause her to flinch. Not even the cold corpse of her mum.

Before she called for an ambulance to cart the body away, instinct jerked her to her feet. Taking her time, she tip-toed around her dead mum to the medicine cabinet. With a glance in its mirror and a quick tidy of her hair, she opened the door. The bottle with the small white pills squatted on the second shelf. Oxy, although the label said aspirin.

One by one, Ria shook the pills into a small plastic bag. The pills she'd confiscated from small-time dealers in her patch. The pills she'd sold to her mother. And the leftover pills which she later sold to drug users in search of an oxy high. The cash paid the bills and now, the carefully accumulated wealth paid the deposit on her new house. And this year, her drug-free section of Whitehaven would yield her Civic Officer of the year. Number four. Nothing wasted. Careful and precise. That was the Ria Leigh way.

"I want you to go into business with me," Ria said. She was tired of the small-time drug dealers in Whitehaven and wanted to move to a better class of clients. "You supply the patrons. I'll supply the pills. You'll get twenty-five per cent of the take."

Ria liked low-hanging fruit, and it seemed to her that the ripest fruit existed in such large numbers in Port St Giles that she had to gorge on their sweetness. And what better way than through a therapy business where middle-class neurotic women come for help?

"Do we have a deal?" Ria said, staring at Sloane

the same way she'd stared at that legless spider.

CHAPTER 63

Fenella strode across the carpark of the Navigator's Arms under a blue sky and warming sun. It was Thursday and given she'd be in training all day Friday, she thought a half pint of ale would go down a real treat. She'd have a word with Alf and Stacy Bird at the same time. Did they have any new thoughts about what happened to the man with the devil's wisp beard? She didn't have a clue but thought they did.

She stopped on a grass verge to take in the front of the building. Small frosted glass windows blocked out prying eyes. The red slate roof could be seen for miles. Afternoon drinkers sat on the benches shaded under large yellow umbrellas. The men wore jackets and flat caps, the women light coats and headscarves. Locals.

Fenella thought she recognised the woman in the tight green headscarf. She stared hard but couldn't figure out from where. Like the Mona Lisa's secret smile, she thought as the woman looked at her and let out a loud laugh. She wondered what the men and women did that allowed them to spend their afternoon in a pub supping ale.

A note written in large block letters was posted

on the door:

Closing Early Today for Private Social Farm Club Event.

She tilted her head to scan the front of the pub for CCTV cameras, an instinct she'd picked up years back when she was in uniform. None.

A dog barked. Fenella turned to look at the canal. A middle-aged woman stood at the rear of a narrowboat. At her side a plump dog watched. The woman waved. Fenella waved back. If she spent her days floating up and down the canal at two miles an hour, it would drive her potty. She'd not want to spend her days in a pub, either. Solving crimes with Dexter was the life she loved. And young Jones was coming on a real treat. She wouldn't change places for the world.

She watched the rear of the boat as it chugged around a gentle bend. Then her gaze fell to the drinkers on the benches and she felt a sudden thirst. Yes, she was definitely in the mood for a half pint of ale. She'd jog it off along with the haddock and chips when she went for her evening run on the beach near her cottage on Cleaton Bluff.

And she'd shame Eduardo into going with her. He claimed his weight-loss diet had stalled. But when Fenella and Nan forced him on the bathroom scales, they were shocked to see it had reversed. He'd gained ten pounds in the last week. She smiled. He'd have no choice but to join her. Then she remembered those damn forms and sighed. No run on the beach this evening. She'd not get home till late.

Out of the corner of her eye, black figures flittered. Fenella spun around so she faced the pub. The men and women on the benches continued to sup their ale. She tilted her head. On the roof, a flock of crows landed and began to scream.

She counted the birds. Six. That meant bad luck or something. If Dexter were here, he'd tell her the meaning, his granddad was into folklore. The birds continued to scream.

With one eye on the crows, Fenella walked along the side of the pub. She wanted to take a look at the back of the building and followed a low fence which marked off the beer garden. It ended abruptly, replaced by a hedge which grew close to the brick sides of the pub. Keeping in the gap between the hedge and the wall, Fenella picked her way along the uneven ground until she came to a small potholed courtyard.

Against one wall lay a broken wood-burning stove, three bicycles with warped wheels and a stack of rusted cages made from chicken wire. She stepped into the centre of the courtyard and looked at the rear of the pub. No windows, but there was a short double door made of slatted wood and rotted at the bottom. It was probably first hung in the days when horses delivered the ale, she thought. To the left and right of the door were two spotlights with motion detectors. And a little higher up, perhaps eight feet from ground level, a single CCTV camera operated by Scroop Security.

It was as Fenella, hands on hips, took this all

in that Stacy Bird appeared. She tottered into the courtyard in high heels. Bleached black rooted hair, and the same low-cut top the colour of raisins she wore when they'd first met.

"Can I help you?" Stacy Bird said, flashing a set of pearly white teeth which were not her own. She wore pink lipstick and her eyelids were shaded light blue. An exotic bird except for the set of her face which looked more like tropical thunder.

"Thought I'd take a look around the back," Fenella said.

"We like our patrons to use the front."

"I'm not a patron, luv. I'm with the police."

"I know who you are, Inspector Sallow. I haven't forgotten that you dragged me and my Alf down the station." She spoke with an oily confidence, false teeth click-clicking. "Our solicitor will be in touch with your superior. We will file a formal complaint—false imprisonment. What crime did we commit, eh?"

They both knew the police had nothing on them. They'd taken over the pub after Pam Wells had died and neither Stacy nor Alf Bird had known Jane Ragsdale.

Fenella said, "We found a body in your pub and wanted to have a quiet word. The police station is a good place for that, pet. Much better than chatting at the bar where all the drinkers can overhear. You are not accused of anything."

Stacy stared with small, cold eyes. "What do you want?"

"Had any thoughts about the man with the devil's wisp beard?"

Best to be direct. She'd not have long to get her questions in. Stacy Bird was the type that blew up in a torrent of cursing or else stomped off in a tottering huff.

"We've had it up to here with you lot poking about." Stacy's mouth opened so wide the teeth jutted out. "Police officers snooping about the place is bad for business. How can we run a pub with you lot on the prowl?"

"I didn't mean to get you angry, luv. It must have been an accident or something. Humour me this one question, will you?"

Fenella couldn't take her eyes off Stacy's mouth with its pearly white false teeth. She wished she knew who her dentist was so she could warn her friends not to go near the place.

She said, "What have you figured out about the devil's wisp?"

"I can't help you on that score. I'm not even sure I saw him."

"Aye, pet, you did. He jumped right over the counter while you were pulling pints. A short bloke, dressed in black. You couldn't have missed him."

"Devil wisp beard, you say?" Stacy batted her eyelashes in a way that made it clear she wasn't about to help. "What colour were this bloke's whiskers?"

Fenella frowned, pointed at the double doors. "Where do they go?"

Stacy shrugged. "They lead to the room where we store the casks of ale. They are not used these days."

"Why not?"

"This entrance was built when the pub first opened. Ale and coal were delivered by horse and cart back then. They had to roll the casks through those doors one at a time, and there is a pit with a chute for coal. It's a tight squeeze with the modern barrels, and we don't use coal much these days." Her tone became vaguely mocking. "I suppose you must remember those horse and cart days when folk gathered around a coal fire for warmth."

"Aye, luv, they were golden."

There was no way the woman's jabs would get under Fenella's skin. Not with those false teeth. And, yes, she'd let her hair go grey, but she didn't feel much different from when she was thirty. She would have called an end to the chat if not for what Stacy said next.

"Ever seen a ghost, Inspector?"

"Half the people I know are like the living dead. I am too until I've had my coffee."

Stacy smiled. "They say that doorway is haunted. I've never used it, though. I never want to disturb the dead. Who knows when a ghost will get very upset?"

"Spooks don't commit crime, so I'm good with them, luv. Now, about those doors?"

"We have a delivery hatch at the front. I think it was added sometime in the 1980s. I can get the exact date if you like."

Fenella doubted there was much more to hear or see, thought she'd wasted her time and decided to nip inside to grab a quick half pint to ease her parched throat. Still, she didn't like that cocky tone in Stacy Bird's voice, and her words about not disturbing the dead rang an alarm soft in her head.

She said, "Aye well, mind opening the doors, so I can have a look?"

Stacy Bird shook her head. "Nah. The only way you go through that entrance is with signed paperwork. Now, I'd like you to leave our property. You are not welcome on these premises."

CHAPTER 64

Fenella got back to her car feeling tired, thirsty and annoyed. She scanned her emails on her phone, listened to voicemail, and then read the text messages. Dexter and Ria Leigh reported the same thing—no word on the whereabouts of Mick Knowles. No new details on Pam Wells or Jane Ragsdale, either. No name of a third woman. Nothing from Jones.

She dialled the station to find out whether there had been any reported sightings of Mick Knowles. Another blank. Nothing to chew on. It felt like she'd come to a dead end.

An urge for that half-pint of ale gripped her. It would slide down her dry throat a treat. She gazed across the carpark to the frosted windows of the Navigator Arms. The crows were gone from the roof, but Stacy Bird stood in the doorway, watching.

"I'll pass on the ale," Fenella said to the empty car. Best thing, she supposed, given all the forms she had to see to.

She was about to start the car when she noticed the woman in the tight green headscarf on a bench, half shaded by a large yellow umbrella. Her cane leaned on the table. The woman took a long gulp from her pint and laughed so loud it carried like the scream of the crows. For some reason, the woman turned towards Fenella's car, raised her glass and flashed a gap-toothed grin. Another bark of laughter cackled across the carpark as she drained the pint and called Stacy Bird over to fetch her another.

"She'll need that cane after all that booze," Fenella said sourly. If this were any other day, she'd be at the bar with a glass of ale herself. "Looks like she's going to drink that damn pub dry!"

As the car engine turned over, her mobile phone rang—Superintendent Jeffery. Fenella looked at the dashboard clock and realised it was time to get back to the office to slog through the pile of forms in her in-box. She picked up the phone.

"I've news, Sallow," Jeffery said in her waspish voice.

Nowt good came from Jeffery's mouth when her voice buzzed like bees. And when the boss had news, it was always bad. Fenella pressed the phone to her ear and waited.

"Are you in your office?" Jeffery asked. "Why don't you come up here for a quick chat? We'll have a whiteboard session."

Whiteboarding with the boss was best avoided. It led to more work on your plate.

"I'm on the road right now," Fenella said, thankful she didn't cut the engine. She let it roar for several moments. "Might be an hour or two before I'm back at the station, ma'am."

"Never mind about the whiteboard," Jeffery replied. "Listen, about that management training course you signed up for with Dexter and Jones. We spoke about it this morning?"

"Oh aye, the seven pillars of building a joyful team, " Fenella said, trying to think of something to say to get out of it and drawing a blank. "Has it been called off?"

"There will be a video crew to film the talk as well as our police photographer. Nice, eh?"

Oh crap! Now Fenella would have to sit up straight and look alert all day. She'd warn Dexter to keep those damn peanuts in his pocket and tell Jones not to ask questions as it slowed things down when Jeffery went off on a rant. Then she remembered the paperwork. How the hell would she do it under the prying gaze of video cameras? She'd have to work late at the station tonight. Do an all-nighter.

Jeffery said, "Alas, I'll have to leave at noon because I've got a jolly with Chief Inspector Rae in Carlisle."

"Sorry to hear that, ma'am." Fenella did her best to hide her joy. "Part two next month, or will the morning do?"

"Neither. I've put you down to teach the afternoon sessions. Fifteen minutes for lunch, then hard at it until five. Any subject you like Sallow but keep in with my theme of the seven pillars of building a joyful team."

Fenella cut the engine. Why didn't she run like the plague when Jeffery came knocking on her office door? Only a fool makes a management presentation on a Friday afternoon after a hard gruelling week at work to an audience who doesn't what to be there. No way in hell was she getting saddled with that!

"Sorry ma'am," Fenella said, thinking fast. "But I've nowt prepared. And with all those forms you need to be done by today there'll not be—"

"Come now, Sallow. Why don't you present a summary of those management courses you've taken this year? Four, wasn't it? You have the notes, right? It'll take you ten minutes to throw something together. Whatever you decide, keep it fresh."

Jeffery hung up before Fenella replied. There would be no time to work on the Pam Wells and Jane Ragsdale cases now. There was nowt for it but to return to her tiny office.

As she reached for the key to restart the engine, a sharp knock came from the passenger side window. She turned to see a gap-toothed grin staring in. She lowered the window, curious to discover what the woman in the tight green headscarf wanted.

"Me names Mrs Edna Brown, me ducky." Her breath was heavy with ale. "I'd like to know what you lot are doing about all that killing."

The name rang a bell, but Fenella couldn't quite place it. "I'm Inspector—"

"I know who you are." Edna stepped away from the car and leaned on her cane, eyes glittering. "You closed the pub and found nowt. And you've got nowt on poor Jane Ragsdale's death. Why are you dragging your feet on the matter?"

Edna turned and pointed to the benches filled with drinkers. Stacy Bird was gone. In her place Alf Bird watched. A few boozers raised their drinks. A plump man in a white butcher's apron let out a cheer and tinkled the bell on his bicycle which leaned against the table. Edna gave a slow bow. It seemed she had an audience and was enjoying her part in the show. She waved her cane in a swashbuckling flourish. "See them folk? They want to know what you lot are doing. If Jane's death wasn't an accident why haven't you caught the killer?"

Fenella said, "Mrs Brown, I'm—"

"Edna to you and everyone who knows me."

Mrs Edna Brown was a gossip. Fenella liked the woman for that. They'd tell you things that other people wouldn't, and in this case, she needed anything she could get. But even a gossip takes time to warm to you before they sing. So Fenella took her time and chose her words with care.

"Well, Edna," she began and smiled. "I'm the world's worst at names and faces. I mix them up all the time. Were you friends with Jane Ragsdale?"

"Honestly, me ducky, I wouldn't say we were friends, but I knew the lass right enough. I took an interest in her comings and goings. Not that I'm nosy or one to gossip, but we have to look out for each other, we women, don't we?"

"Aye, happen you are right about that," Fenella replied thinking of what to say to prod the woman so her mouth opened and she spilt the beans on Jane Ragsdale. She decided to go straight for the kill. "Tell me about Miss Ragsdale?"

"I'll not gossip about anyone." Edna sniffed. "And now Jane is dead, it wouldn't be right to talk about her, would it?"

"I'm the police, luv. What you tell me is confidential."

"I couldn't say a word against the lass," she slurred. But by the quirk at the corners of her lips and the brightness of her eyes, it was clear she couldn't wait. "I really couldn't."

That's when Fenella remembered where she'd heard of Mrs Edna Brown. She thought for a moment and it all came back. Dexter had mentioned Mrs Edna Brown was Jane's landlady. The landlady Jane bizarrely expected to pay her money to live in Mrs Brown's flat. The same landlady who kicked Jane out and with whom Dexter smoothed things over.

Now Fenella had to hear it all. Not that she was being nosy. It was part of her job to pry. Still, she had to be careful. Prod Edna wrong and she'd clam up.

"It's been bothering me that we've not been able to contact any of Jane's friends," Fenella said. Asking about friends was a sure-fire way to find out about someone. "It doesn't make sense for such a young lass. When I was young I had so many friends I lost count. Not Jane, though. It breaks my heart."

"Break your heart!" Edna's face flushed so brightly she looked like she'd caught the sun. "Inspector, Jane wasn't good enough for Micky."

"Now, Edna, what on earth would make you say a thing like that about a dead lass?"

"Jane were a right one. The lass were ruthless and could spin a cock and bull story better than a spider spins its web. Told me she had a magic wand that would make all my dreams come true if only I paid her a monthly allowance until she found it. That was after she moved into my bedsit and refused to pay rent."

"Did you report it to the police?" Fenella already knew the answer and wanted to keep Edna's tongue wagging.

"Oh aye. I spoke with one of your detectives. A nice chap goes by the name of Dexter." She raised a spindly hand to adjust her headscarf and gave a gapped tooth smile. "He knows how to sweet talk a woman."

A narrowboat moved slowly along the canal, its engine's grumble rising above the voices and chink of glasses of those sitting outside the pub.

A cockerel crowed.

Fenella turned back towards the pub, trying to figure out from where the sound came. People were keeping more birds these days and growing organic food. One of her neighbours had bought a flock of Kashmiri goats, transported from Great Orme in Wales.

She drew a blank on the bird. "Anything else you want to tell me about Jane?"

"I hear she were dealing drugs."

"Are we talking marijuana?"

"I don't know nowt about those things, but I hear it was pills."

"Who told you Jane was a drug dealer?"

Edna shrugged. "I don't know. Word gets around we women."

There was something odd in the way Edna spoke about Jane Ragsdale. Fenella couldn't quite grasp what the oddness was. "How'd you get on with Mick Knowles?"

"Micky?" Edna staggered back a step, regained her balance and raised her cane. "It's me old knees that makes me trotters wobbly."

Fenella thought it was the ale but didn't say anything.

Edna said, "When he were a tenant, he were nowt but a gentleman."

"He rented a room from you?" Fenella kept her voice level, trying to hide her excitement.

"Years ago now, when he were in medical school. Paid on time. Never late. You should have seen his room. Charts of the human body on the wall. It were an education for me, it were, looking at those charts. Extensor digitorum."

"Eh?"

"That muscle extends the finger." Edna raised her left hand and curved her gaunt fingers. "I recalls it all even now after all these years. Micky even had a full-sized skeleton he bought second hand from a charity shop. It were almost perfect, except one of the fingers were missing."

"Which one?"

"I don't rightly recall." She glanced at her left hand. When she looked up, she was smiling. "Might have been the ring finger."

"You're sure?"

"Like I say, it were a long time ago, me ducky. What Micky needed was a more mature woman. A woman of experience. A lass who could take him in hand and mother him. Jane Ragsdale couldn't do that." Edna adjusted her headscarf once more, her cheeks flushed bright red. "I wrote to him when he were put away, you know."

"Really?"

"Oh aye. Even visited him in prison. It weren't his fault, me ducky. But he took the blame for everything. So I visited him. I think he appreciated contact with an older woman. Gave him a sense of peace." Her face became a frown. "Jane were nowt but a spoilt baby who lived in the land of fairies. In the end, I reckon it were the drugs that did her in. Never liked the lass. Not really."

"But you like Micky?"

"The lad's a straight shooter and has got a good way with the lasses. Nowt in him a woman with a clear head won't like. Like I say, what he needs is a mother who'll take care of his every need. An older woman who knows how life goes."

"We are looking for him," Fenella said slowly, eyes never leaving Edna's face. "Any idea where he might be?"

Edna looked at her ring finger then flashed a gap-toothed grin. "You're the police, me ducky.

Figure it out."

CHAPTER 65

Fenella sat in her car and watched as Mrs Edna Brown made her way back to the pub benches. Her cane tapped the ground with a pistol crack. Two black-headed gulls appeared high in the sky, beaks open wide and screaming. The high-pitched cries were like words in a strange foreign tongue, unintelligible to the ear, but clear in their warning shrieks.

A headache began to brew in her skull. She glanced at the tiny clouds which had suddenly appeared in the sky. They scudded and clustered, colour changing from bright white to dull grey.

Fenella had a sudden and intense memory. It was summer. A hot one and she'd been in uniform two or three years. As she neared the end of her regular beat, she noticed the broken padlock on an abandoned fishmonger store. The place had closed down months before, padlock firm and secure. Now it was busted in two, dangling limply to one side.

It was daytime, she was curious and wanted to look inside. She'd heard rumours on the grapevine the shop had been sold to a luxury property developer. She pushed open the door, stepping into the tomb-like gloom.

The stink of days-old fish and scraps of spoiled meat clogged her nose and seared deep into her brain cells. A sweet and rotting stench that made her lungs gasp and gut heave. To one side of a dust-smeared shop counter, she saw red high-heeled shoes. They were attached to putrefied legs. She'd never seen so many flies.

The press swarmed like a colony of ants over the story. Fenella never discovered the woman's name. They never caught the killer.

She suffered deep scars from the nightmares which lasted for months. Back then the help available for what a police officer saw was next to none. Nowt but a mug of sweet tea, a pat on the back and, if that didn't work, a stern talking to. Fenella had licked her wounds in private and healed with the help of time. But she'd made up her mind about one thing. One day she'd rise through the ranks to become a detective and work to solve the most heinous cases. And, come hell or high water she'd always get their name.

She sent a text message to Dexter, Ria Leigh and Jones:

Focus on Mick Knowles' known girlfriends. Discover who they are and where they live. Names to me as soon as you can.

A sharp tension seized her neck. A warning ache like joint pain in those sensitive to rain. She sensed a thunderstorm brewing. If she didn't act fast, there would be torrential rain—another body without a name and a colony of news ants crawling all over the story. Her fingers moved with speed over the phone's keyboard:

Won't get those forms to you today, ma'am. They'll be on your desk next Friday.

She got out of the car, took one last look at the pub and headed towards the towpath. She wanted to revisit the place where they'd hauled Jane Ragsdale's body from the canal. Then she'd follow the path to the Gold Kite. This case came first. The paperwork could take a bleedin' hike.

CHAPTER 66

The first inkling that something was wrong came at the place where they pulled Jane Ragsdale from the canal.

Fenella was slightly out of breath at the speed of her walk. In truth, it was more of a run. She wanted to get a head start and see if anything popped out. When a detective revisits the scene of a crime, they sometimes see things they'd missed. A key piece of evidence which cracks the case wide open.

All signs of police activity were gone except a ragged strip of blue and white tape wrapped around the charred stump of a tree. It had died years back after a lightning strike.

Dexter was standing by the canal's edge, staring into the cold still water. He must be thinking along the same lines as me, Fenella thought. He turned, as though expecting her arrival.

"Afternoon, Guv."

"Thought I'd take another look too," Fenella replied. "You never know what might jump out at you."

"Been looking for a while now and caught nowt, not even a tiddler."

He spoke in a low voice, his face scrunched tight. There was something other than the case on his mind. She'd wait, but if he didn't spit it out soon, she'd have to pry.

"Seen the news media sites, Guv?" He didn't wait for an answer and showed his phone. "Big bloody picture of that wardrobe we found Pam Wells in. It is on the front page of the local newspapers, too. Don't know how they do it." He sucked in a ragged breath. "They've put out a call for witnesses to come forward, so it ain't all bad. But it won't be long until they link it to Jane Ragsdale and the can of worms is opened."

"Let's hope we have a few days before they find that out," Fenella replied. The clock had started and she feared it now ticked at double time.

"Twenty-four hours max," Dexter replied.

"Aye, happen you're right."

For several moments they stood in silence, staring into the hidden depths of the canal. From somewhere came the shrill crow of a cockerel despite the late afternoon hour.

Dexter said, "Ain't no one on my contacts list seen sight nor sound of Mick Knowles. Best I can guess is that he's left the county, maybe headed to London to lie low in the crowds."

"Aye, happen that might be the case," Fenella said, slowly. "Something is bugging me, but I don't know what. Have Jones get the details of Mick Knowles' time in prison. Maybe there is something in it that will help point to where he has gone?"

They stood for several more minutes watching the slow waters of the canal. Under the warming rays of the afternoon sun, a narrowboat chugged by. Fenella recognised the woman at the rear. She'd seen her earlier and gave a friendly wave. The woman waved back, but the fat dog at her side gave a nasty snarl. Poor thing must be fed up going backwards and forwards with nowhere in mind, Fenella thought. She wanted to snarl as well. Nothing had jumped out at them as the dark, cold water rippled. And she still didn't know what was on Dexter's mind.

She turned to head towards the Gold Kite, with Dexter at her side. The crime scene, now a slice of water no different from the rest, receding behind them. As they walked, a great black cloud slid across the sky, darkening the sun.

"You going to tell me what's got you down?" Fenella asked after they'd taken several steps.

That was best practice she'd learned in one of the management courses. They called it active listening. The fresh-faced instructor, who looked no older than twelve, said, "When a member of your team shares a concern, listen without questions to learn."

But she thought they'd got that bit wrong as the nervous lad was reading from his notes. First, you have to probe them with questions to find out what is on their mind.

"Nowt but the case, Guv," Dexter replied. "I'd like to get my hands on the bugger who's been chopping off the ring fingers and tearing out the tongues of lasses."

"You and me both," Fenella replied, sensing she must wait a little longer to get at what was on his mind.

They walked on in silence. From somewhere came the soft chug of a narrowboat engine, and from even closer the soft whine of a dog. A black-headed gull hovered overhead and screamed. They'd worked together for so long that they both knew each other's thoughts.

"We don't have much time," Dexter said.

He didn't say before what. They both knew.

"Aye, perhaps less time than we think."

A plump man in a white butcher's apron sped past them on a bicycle. He tinkled the bell as he went. Fenella recognised him. She'd seen him drinking ale at the Navigator Arms.

"That bugger had a skinful of beer and now he's off back to work," she said. "Thursday afternoon and all! I sometimes think we're in the wrong profession."

An exaggeration, of course. She loved working for the police. Poking around in people's business gave her a jolt of joy. Uncovering secrets to solve crimes thrilled her even more. She'd not give it up for a butcher's apron and a jar of lunchtime ale.

She was still thinking about this when Dexter said, "Guv, been toying with a problem, which I can't get off my mind."

"Oh aye," she said and waited.

"Have a pain in me side, Guv. "Internet says it might be me kidneys. Not to worry, though. I've got two of the buggers. If one is bad, the other will take the strain."

"Will they have to whip the bad one out?"

"That's what I don't know."

"Go see your doctor."

"Aye. I hope he don't want to look inside. I don't like them drugs and the thought of a masked figure in a green gown coming at me with a knife. Well, it's terrifying."

"Surgeons know what they are doing."

"Aye, and so did them that built the Titanic, didn't stop it sinking though, did it?"

Dexter rubbed a hand over his chin and then cracked his knuckles.

"There is more," she said.

"Eh?"

"There is more on your mind. What is it?"

"It's to do with my Priscilla."

The way he said her name sent a spasm of dread coursing along Fenella's spine. Priscilla and Dexter's relationship had been on and off for as long as she could recall. They'd break up. Dexter, losing himself to the job and even more to booze. Priscilla, swept up in the glamour of singing in nightclubs, which glittered but oozed with slime. Then something would happen to throw them back together. They'd broken up so many times and got back together again that Fenella had lost count.

Dexter was speaking. "It's this concert at the

Tarns Dub Music Festival, Guv. Turns out to be a bigger deal than I thought. Can't say I realised how much cause I'm not into the music scene. Sure, I sing a little in the shower and listen to my favourites on my phone, but I don't know the business like my Priscilla."

He stopped and for some reason, they also stopped their walk. A narrowboat appeared from around a bend. Its soft chug-chug carried across the water. The sharp yap of a dog came from behind the trees, followed by a long persistent whine. Now Fenella waited, sensing she'd soon get to the core of what was on his mind.

Dexter said, "I'm not sure how to tell you this, Guv. But I think it is best to say it straight. My Priscilla's dream has come true. She's been offered a two-year contract as a backing singer. It'll mean travelling the world to sing at upscale gigs." He paused for a half-beat. "And moving to New York City."

For a moment, Fenella thought she'd misheard. She opened her mouth, but Dexter spoke first.

"She wants me to leave the force and travel with her. Says she won't go without me."

CHAPTER 67

The news sent Fenella into a shocked silence. When at last she spoke, it was with only one word. "When?"

"Priscilla's contract starts next weekend when she sings at Tarns Dub," Dexter replied. "Straight to New York City for rehearsals the following week."

There was so much more Fenella wanted to know, but her mind hadn't cleared of the shock, so she stood stunned, mute, tugging at a lock of her grey hair. It was the sad whine of a dog coming from beyond the trees that broke the tense silence and caused them both to turn.

"That don't sound good, Guv," Dexter said, scanning the foliage. "The poor thing sounds like it is in pain."

"Over there," Fenella said, pointing at a gap between the trees. "Come on, let's take a peep."

She took off at a trot towards a narrow dirt trail which snaked between the trees to a broken section of railing and eased through the gap. The sad whine turned into a high-pitched woof. Fenella knew dogs. Knew its bark came from fear and anxiety.

She trotted along a dirt track without encountering anyone and emerged into a quiet clearing, hidden from the canal by trees. Ahead of her, chained by a length of rope to a tree trunk, she saw him.

A scrawny, misshapen, bandy-legged, potbellied dog no bigger than an overfed cook's cat. Its clouded eyes watched her, rear end wriggling in a tailless wag.

"Hello there," Fenella said, recognising the dog was harmless and friendly.

"I'd like to know who chained him here, Guv." Dexter glanced around. "No food. Not even a bowl of water! Don't know what they are playing at, the poor thing will starve."

"Not the actions of a dog lover, that's for sure," Fenella said, hands on hips.

"Ain't nowt worse in my book than folk who mistreat animals," Dexter replied. "I'd throw the bugger in a snake pit and leave them to their fate."

Fenella reached into her handbag, pulled out the wax paper which contained Nan's lamb sandwiches and offered a piece to the dog. He nibbled it from her hand, then gobbled it down and licked his lips.

"Knew I'd find a use for this," she said. "Lamb and bread twice this week is too much for my stomach."

"Ain't had me lunch yet," Dexter said, eyeing the waxed paper. "Nowt but a half bag of peanuts. Guv, I hear dogs get sick if you feed them human food. Best save some back, eh? For those with stomachs that can digest it."

Fenella ignored Dexter, offered the dog another morsel, rubbed his ear and placed a hand on its collar.

"No dog tag," she said. "But someone has written something on the collar. In a black marker pen... looks like Wayne."

At the name, the dog's rump moved backwards and forwards so fast Fenella thought it would dig a hole in the ground.

"Not a bad name for a dog, that, Guv. Used to know a bloke of the same name. Looked a bit like this hound, too, now I comes to think about it."

Fenella grinned but felt a touch of sadness. She'd miss Dexter's sense of humour and humility if he flew across the pond to New York City. Some detectives thought saving animals was below them. They only wanted to solve murders, fraud and robberies. Animal welfare was low on their list. They'd push it to a uniform to deal with. Not Dexter, though. Nor Fenella. They saw eye to eye on the important things in police life. She'd miss that too and wanted to cry.

Instead of tears, she took in with pride of friendship details she had taken for granted. His nose for the truth. Sense of justice. The fact that she'd never worked with an officer who'd stood so reliably at her side.

She sniffed and gazed at the dog. "Well, Wayne, living in the woods is against the town's bylaws. We'll have to find you a new home, eh? Somewhere nice and warm with a fireplace you can curl up in front of and a postman to chase."

"Postwoman these days too, Guv," Dexter said with a sly grin. "We don't want our Wayne getting no sexist notions."

Fenella was about to give a witty reply when she spotted a dilapidated wooden shack. Not the shack itself, but the bloom of black smoke which seeped from the doorway. No flames, though. Just a smouldering smog which rose and twirled, vanishing into the cloudy sky.

She took off at a full run, hoping there was no one inside. It took less than twenty seconds to reach the shack. With her bare hands, she yanked at the rotted door. When it screeched open on a rusted hinge. The odour of the past seeped out. A cloying reek of rusted tools, oil and the heavy smell of smoke.

Inside, through the feeble light, a small pile of twigs smouldered. They were too damp to cause a blaze, just thick choking fumes.

"Kids," Dexter said. "Bleedin' teenagers who should be in school."

"I don't think it was kids," Fenella replied.

She pointed at a pile of plastic bags heaped up against the far wall. Underneath, a figure in a medical gown lay slumped on the ground.

CHAPTER 68

Fenella knew the person was dead.

They had that rigid look that occurs when rigour mortis sets in. Her heart sank to her boots as she stooped down to examine the body. *If there was a chance to save them.* But another wave of shock washed over her at what she saw.

"Gawd help us, Guv," Dexter said in a gasp. "The ring finger and tongue are gone!"

Fenella called for backup after that.

The day had slid so low it felt like she'd reached rock bottom. Another death. An almost exact copy of what she'd seen with Pam Wells and Jane Ragsdale. From her vantage point, she couldn't tell if the victim's torso had been slashed and stitched. But that they wore only a medical gown was all the evidence she needed. She'd leave it to Dr MacKay to examine the body for that clue.

As she stood with her hands on hips scanning the scene, a flash of pink caught her eye. In the opposite corner to the body, wadded up into a ball, was a pink scrap of paper. With gloved hands she picked it up, flattened it and read.

I'M SORRY YOU WILL BE NEXT.

"The bugger's got you in his sights, Guv."

"How'd he know I'd find it?"

"He called you on your phone, didn't he?"

"Or she."

"They must be watching."

Dexter walked to the door and peered out. "That dog will bark if anyone approaches... or whine for food. Wayne's a greedy bugger."

Fenella took a photo with her phone and dropped the note into an evidence bag. "I've never seen scrawl like it," she said. "The person who wrote it must have had their eyes closed and penned it with their left hand."

Officers arrived in minutes. Sirens at first, then the pulsating beat of blue flashing lights. Within half an hour two dozen people were at the site. They moved around and talked in low voices. Everyone knew this was victim number three. No one knew when the killing would stop.

Dexter was talking to two uniformed officers as they stretched crime scene tape between the trees. And Fenella stood in the midst of it, looking grim. At the stinging realisation that she'd not been able to save the third victim, her mood sunk to dark depths. She didn't know what to think or say as she watched the white-suited crime scene techs move in.

"What's going on here?"

Fenella spun to see Lisa Levon, the head crime scene tech. Despite the stench of smoke and death, Lisa looked as beautiful as ever. Like a film star stepping onto a Hollywood stage with her auburn hair, raven eyes, and twenty-year-old face even though she was closer to forty. And indeed, the crime scene was her domain.

"Not what I was hoping for," Fenella said, voice raspy. "Not what I was hoping for at all."

Lisa said, "It's another medical nasty you've got for my team, eh?" She lowered her voice. "Victim's ring finger?"

"Gone."

"Tongue?"

"Same."

"Oh my God," Lisa said in a whisper so no one would overhear. "After we hauled that woman's body from the canal, I hoped the killing was done."

"So did I, pet. But it seems our killer has some vengeful score to settle. You find anything, I want to be the first to know."

Four crime scene techs saw Lisa and came to stand nearby. She made a shooing motion with her hands. They scattered like seeds blown in the wind at her command.

She turned to Fenella. "People think forensic science is like magic, but if the killer left no clues, there will be nothing for us to find."

"I know," Fenella replied, feeling hopeless. "All I need is a nugget to latch onto. Right now we are suffering from a drought when it comes to that."

She watched Lisa Levon as she headed towards the shack, then she squeezed her eyes close to retch the image of the body from her head. When she opened them, the light had changed. Duller now, with the scent of rain.

Dexter strode over. "Doubt we'll find a witness to this one, Guv. This trail isn't much used and the shack can't be seen from the towpath." He ran a hand along the back of his neck. "Can't get my mind around what's happened, here, though. This bleedin' ring finger and tongue business blows my mind. And now with this body... well, I'm baffled. Ain't got a clue what to think."

The body they'd found half-hidden by plastic bags and wearing nowt but a medical gown wasn't that of a woman. It was a man. A man they wanted to question about the deaths of Pam Wells and Jane Ragsdale. The body in the shack was Mr Mick Knowles.

CHAPTER 69

It was three-forty when Fenella eased into a chair in Logan's Bakery, her mood foul and frustrated.

She sat in a dim corner in the empty shop, far from the window which looked out onto the street where mothers hurried with their small children from school. They had the evening meal to see to, homework to be monitored, kids put to bed and then later a spot of telly and a glass of wine. Routine and order. No bloodied bodies or mysterious killers trying to evade the police. That was her job, so they slept well at night and enjoyed peaceful dreams.

The hand of Mick Knowles with the bloodied finger chopped off played again and again in her head. And his pale face, dark mouth open and tongue torn out flashed like lightning across her mind.

Some crimes must never be forgiven.

Jones arrived at the table clutching a tray on which balanced iced buns and four mugs of flat white coffee. Fenella wanted to discuss the news about Mick Knowles, and she wanted to do it away from the station. A few people came in to buy baked goods for their supper, though no one sat at the tables. Too late in the day. Patrons were in a rush to get home. A safe place to discuss secrets and for her team to share what they knew.

"Thanks for the grub, Guv," Dexter said, coffee mug in one hand, iced bun in the other. He turned to Jones. "Ain't nowt like Logan's grub to feed hunger, lad. Get one of them iced bun's down ya."

"I'm on a low-carb diet," Jones replied. "All that dough and sugar will fog my brain and make me want to sleep."

"Go on, take a bite," Ria Leigh said, although she'd not picked up a bun. She'd joined the team to share with them all that she knew. "That small thing won't do any harm."

Jones flashed a Hollywood smile, picked up a bun and nibbled. Fenella didn't miss the way they looked at each other. Were PC Beth Finn and Jones still an item? Or had the pair broken up? Either way, she couldn't see Jones and Ria making a good match. There will be sparks, she thought. "I want to nail the person who killed Mick Knowles. I want them sent down for the murder of Pam Wells and Jane Ragsdale as well. Ideas?"

Dexter shook his head. "We've been fishing in the wrong spot, Guv. Ain't caught nowt but weeds. This one's a bugger to figure out, right now I don't have a clue."

"Anyone else?" Fenella said, hoping for something, but fearing they all felt the same as Dexter. "Ideas, anyone?"

"It boggles the brain and baffles the mind,"

Jones said and then fell silent.

Fenella waited.

"Is it possible," Ria began, speaking slowly to get their full attention, "that Mick Knowles killed himself?"

"A final act of violence to end it all?" Jones nodded, agreeing it might be a workable theory. He flashed Ria a pearly white smile, flexing his arms a little so his biceps bulged. "We studied a case like that in detective school. Now, what was it called?"

"Nah," Fenella said before he recalled the details. Jones reminded her of a peacock flashing its feathers to attract a mate. She thought about bringing up PC Beth Finn to rile him but decided to stay on task. "Mick Knowles might have chopped off his finger, but I can't see him tearing out his tongue."

"And don't forget the stitches, Guv." Dexter crammed the iced bun into his mouth and chewed thoughtfully for several seconds. "We didn't look but as eggs is eggs, they were there under that damn medical gown. Ain't no man on Earth who'd slash his gut and stitch it up before he did away with himself."

Jones said, "But—"

"But nowt, lad," Dexter replied before Jones finished his sentence. "Mick Knowles doing himself in ain't gonna work."

Ria said, "I know Jane Ragsdale was dealing drugs, oxy mainly, but I was never able to get enough evidence to prove it." She picked up her mug, took a sip and put it down with forced precision.

"Jane lived with Mick on the Gold Kite. Two and two make four if you get my drift. Might have been a hit job. They were both in it together and paid the price. Sad, but that is how it goes with drug dealers."

"Go on," Fenella said, interested. "You think it was a hit job?"

"I reckon a rival gang knocked them both off. A crew from Carlisle." The corners of Ria's mouth quirked upwards as if forcing back a smile. "I say you kick this case to the regional crime squad; drug dealing is our domain. And, since I work in that group, I'd be happy to take the lead and keep you informed every step of the way."

"A collaboration?" Jones said.

"That's right." Ria's lips curved and she flashed a million-dollar smile. "And you guys will be right at the heart of it. Once the case is cleared up, you'll get a fair share of the credit, too."

"If it wasn't for Pam Wells, I might agree," Fenella replied. "No. This has nowt to do with drugs. I think it is something else."

"Like what?" Ria said, face a cold blank, eyebrows furrowed.

"That's what I'm going to find out," Fenella replied.

Yes, there were drugs in Port St Giles, and dealers too. But drug gangs running around bumping each other off? No way. Anyway, Micky Knowles was a lone wolf, drug gangs hunted in packs.

"I think you should consider handing it to

regional," Ria said. A hint of the guttural came out in her words, as though something bitter had stuck in her throat. "That'll leave you free to focus on other things."

"Nah," Fenella replied. This was her case. She'd run it her way. If that irked Ria, too bad. "Jones, compile a list of Micky's known associates. Include any family that you can find, so we can have a word."

Jones dropped the bun on a plate, pushed it away, pulled out his laptop and began to type.

Dexter said, "Lad, if you don't want the rest of that iced bun, mind if I have it?"

It was in Dexter's mouth before Jones looked up from the keyboard.

The door to the shop opened and a woman with a child in a pushchair strolled in. She gave a wave to the owner, Barry Logan, and joined the line waiting to be served.

Fenella stood. She needed to stretch her legs and the atmosphere with Ria seemed off. She said, "I'll get in another round. Who wants a top-up of coffee?"

She took the tray and mugs, glanced at Ria's sour expression, and joined the small line of walk-in customers. It moved slower than normal, although the shop was no busier than usual. She supposed it was because Barry Logan, the owner, served the customers. He was one for a natter and that slowed things down.

At last, at the front, she said, "Four more iced buns and refills on the coffees."

"Sorry about the wait, Fenella," Barry replied with a broad smile that made you want to stop and chat. "Short staffed today."

"Oh aye," Fenella said, still wondering about Ria's attitude.

"Two of my girls are out sick and the other has gone AWOL."

"Absent without leave, eh?" Fenella said. "You running this place like a military operation now, Barry?"

"That's how I bring in the dough." Barry laughed. "But Bren Kern's not one to miss work. Regular as clockwork, so I called her mum who said she'd left town. That's teenagers for you. This one is on the house. It might not be much but I like to do my bit to help the police."

"Guv!" Dexter was at the counter and waving his phone. "Call from Dr MacKay."

They hurried back to the table and put the phone on speaker. Even though there was no one around to overhear they kept the volume low.

"What you got?" Fenella asked.

"I've had a quick look at Mr Knowles," Dr MacKay replied. "A more detailed examination will come later. My best guess is that he was killed late last night or early this morning. I'd say between midnight and one thirty. This is a strange one."

"Refills of coffee and a round of iced buns," said Barry Logan placing a tray on the table and flashing his broad smile. "Thought I'd bring it over. I've thrown in a couple iced fingers and there's a steak and kidney pie for you each to take home for your tea."

He gave a salute, spun on his heels and hurried back to the counter where a mother with a toddler waited.

Dexter eyed Jones. "I best take care of your pie, lad, all that pastry isn't good for a young fellow. Too much carb."

"Where are you?" This was Dr MacKay.

"Logan's," Fenella replied. "It's empty. That was Barry bringing us supper."

"Give him my regards and remind him he owes me a bottle of Glenmorangie unless he wants to double down on his bet." Dr MacKay paused and from the speakerphone came a sound like the scratch of a fountain pen. "When I opened Jane Ragsdale to have a look inside, her kidneys were gone."

"Both of them?" This was Dexter.

"Same for Mick Knowles," Dr MacKay replied. "They'd been snipped like grapes from a vine. Years back I recall a case of a surgeon who removed a patient's kidney when he was supposed to be working on the spine. He stumbled into the operation room as drunk as a skunk. Same for the rest of the team. They'd partied late and hard."

"Gawd help us," Dexter said, jumping to his feet and clutching at his side. "Bloody hell!"

"Terrible mess," Dr MacKay said. "Lawsuits, questions in the House of Commons and police all over the hospital. Don't know what they were looking for. You don't get a kidney back once it's gone, do you?"

"So, what do you think we are dealing with here?" Fenella asked, unable to hide the shock in her voice and feeling a twinge of pain in her side which she took as sympathy for Dexter's plight.

Dr MacKay said, "Pig's kidneys with mustard sauce goes down a treat with a nice red wine. Shiraz is a good choice. But human kidneys! Have you considered the possibility that we are dealing with a man-eating psychopath?"

CHAPTER 70

Fenella stared at the bakery shop window as rays of the sun sprayed across the busy street. There were more people now and more cars on the road. It was the start of the evening rush to get home to a nice, warm house. Everything was in motion, including her mind.

Dexter sipped from his mug, then prodded his side as though testing whether his kidneys were all in order. Ria Leigh crossed her arms, eyes half-closed. She's either thinking hard or had a tough night, Fenella thought. Maybe both. And Jones pecked away on his laptop, his only sound the occasional grunt.

Fenella probed the deep recesses of her mind for anything that might link Pam Wells and Jane Ragsdale other than Mick Knowles. She drew a frustrating blank. What was she missing? Now the scents of fresh bread and baked pies and roasted coffee curdled in her stomach. They seemed too intense and yeasty and full of worm-laden earth. It was hard to imagine when she first walked into the shop, she'd thought the smell delicious.

Tapping Dexter on the shoulder, Fenella said, "Tell me what you know about Mrs Edna Brown?"

"Who's Edna Brown?" The question came from Ria.

"Wears a green headscarf," Fenella said. "Gapped tooth grin. Looks like she's retired. Strong arms, stout legs. Late sixties, I think."

"Back in the day she were a nurse, Guv," Dexter said, still prodding at his side. "When I first met her, years back, I thought she were a bit odd. Not quite right in the head. I suppose that is why she attracted Jane Ragsdale to her place. Birds of a feather and all that."

"Do you suppose," Fenella began, thinking fast, "Pam Wells might have rented one of her bedsits?"

"Ain't got a clue, Guv."

Barry Logan had drifted across from the counter and hovered close to their table.

"You talking about Edna?"

"Oh aye," Fenella said, knowing the man was a gossip. "You know her?"

"Pleasant woman, been shopping in my store for years. Don't think she got over being jilted at the altar. Not nice to dress up all in white and have the groom run off with your best friend and chief bridesmaid as the church bells ring. It happens, but it ain't right. Oh look at me, I feel like a gossip."

He gazed around with glittering eyes and seemed satisfied when he saw he had their full attention.

"When her dad died, she left nursing. Not much of a loss. I hear she was vicious with a needle and partial to a jar of ale. Not a good mix for a kid's nurse. She taught for a while in the town high school, English. Twelve years, I think. Hard work, teens, I was surprised she lasted that long. Edna's a tough old bird."

He stopped and once again glanced about.

"Go on," Fenella said softly, "We're listening."

Barry puckered his lips and continued. "When she left the high school, she bought one of those old Victorian houses on Hodge Hill with her dad's inheritance. It used to be a posh area back in the day, all green parks and trees. A bit run down now, though. She converted the house to bedsits and rented them out."

"Did she remarry?" Fenella asked.

"Oh no, although she calls herself Mrs Brown after the man who ran off with her friend. Edna used to say she was too busy running the bedsits to date anyone." He chuckled. "Said her tenants were her husband. I guess she is too old to wed now. Shame to let life pass you by like that."

Again he stopped and glanced around. He still had their attention, smiled and continued.

"She likes to visit the town cemetery. Don't know why. Her dad was buried in Leeds. That's where her family are originally from. She is the only one who lives in Cumbria. I've always thought it strange, but people are odd, aren't they?"

He wandered back to the counter with the smoothness by which he appeared.

Fenella considered for a moment, then said, "Jones, find out where Mrs Edna Brown was last night, will you? And the night Jane Ragsdale died. Find out if she knew Pam Wells. I'd like to know whether the lass was a resident in her place. And when she lets you in have a poke about if you can swing it." She made a shooing motion with her hands. "Get going. Mrs Brown was half drunk when I spoke with her earlier. If she sobers, her lips will be less inclined to flap."

"You'll have to excuse me as well," Ria said, getting to her feet. "I've got to drive to Carlisle for a debriefing. I hope you don't mind if I leave now."

Without waiting for a response, Ria stood and hurried from the café on the heels of Jones.

"Now here's a question I've been thinking about but can't get straight in my head," Fenella said to Dexter. "It's about that pub."

"The Navigator Arms, Guv?"

"Aye. Have you seen the front of the place? Lots of benches and umbrellas for locals to enjoy a pint and plate of food. Everything is as it should be at first sight. But something is missing."

"Missing, Guv?"

"I went to the back of the pub. There is a double set of doors, the type they rolled barrels of ale through in the old days. According to Stacy Bird, they haven't been used in years."

"Aye, Guv, lots of pubs brick up the old doorways. Don't suppose we'll go back to the days of horse and cart."

"What's strange is that there are no CCTV cameras at the front of the pub. But there is one at the back, right above those double doors. What is that camera there for?"

"Don't sound right, Guv. Wonder what it's protecting?"

"Exactly," Fenella replied. "I'd like to get my hands on that CCTV footage for last Friday when we had lunch in that pub. But I don't think Alf or Stacy Bird will hand over the tapes without a court order. She wouldn't open the doors when I asked, said they'd been closed for years. Still, I'd like to have a poke around and see what's inside."

"What's the name of the security camera service, Guv?"

"Scroop security."

"That's run by Seth Scroop. He's an old contact." Dexter picked up his mobile phone and dialled.

It took only three minutes.

"Seth can't give us the Navigator Arms tape, Guv. It is against the terms of their contract. But if we stop by his office, we are welcome to take a look."

CHAPTER 71

Scroop Security was located on an industrial estate on Hodge Hill. It stood between a storage unit and a bicycle repair shop. A flat-roofed concrete low-rise pug of a building with a solid metal door and bricked-up windows. One of those buildings which at first glance had seen better days. At second glance, one wasn't so certain.

Fenella parked her Morris Minor in front of the bicycle shop. It had a patrons-only sign in large block red letters in the window. There were no other spaces available. As they climbed from the car, a man in a beret and heavy foreign accent rushed out of the store.

"You no park there," he screamed. "Only for buying in my shop."

Fenella flashed her warrant card. "Police."

The man looked at it with a squinty eye, turned on his heels, speaking words in a foreign tongue that sounded like curses.

"Like the bugger was lying in wait," Dexter said with a grin.

"Aye," Fenella replied. "Let's hope we are not long else he'll be writing to Town Hall to complain about the abuse of police power."

At the door she pressed the bell, noting the lack of CCTV cameras and the sign to one side of the door hand-painted in a black scrawl:

Scroop Security. 24-hour surveillance your wallet can afford.

"What do you want?" came a female voice through a hidden speaker.

"To have a chat with Mr Scroop," Fenella replied.

"Got an appointment?"

"We spoke to him on the phone a short while ago, luv. I'm Detective Sallow, and this handsome man on my left is Detective Dexter."

A buzz, and then the door clicked open. They entered a hallway lit by a single low-wattage bulb. It smelled of microwaved food, stale tobacco smoke and cheap ale. Patches of paint, gunship grey, curled from the brick wall. They walked through a metal door and found themselves in a tiny square reception area with a desk and nothing else.

The woman behind the desk's brow furrowed in concentration as she applied a blush of blue nail polish. A cigarette dangled from the corner of her neon red lips. She didn't appear to have noticed they'd arrived.

Fenella waited for two heartbeats then said, "Hello, we are the detectives you buzzed in."

"Dexter!" The woman jumped up, scurried around the table and gave Dexter a huge hug. "Seth should have told me you were coming. My God, my hair must look a right state."

"How you been keeping, lass?" he said in a soft voice.

"Better now I've seen you," she replied and squeezed her arms around him.

Dexter was as bad as Jones when it came to women, Fenella thought. He was grizzled and rough but had a way of weaving a spell and seemed to know every lass in town. No wonder his bleedin' side hurts. It's all that hugging from the opposite sex.

"We are here to see Mr Scroop." Fenella pointed at a door behind the desk. "Through there is he?"

She didn't wait, strode to the door, flung it open and stepped inside.

It took a moment for her eyes to adjust to the gloom of the windowless room. A shelf ran the length of one wall. On it sat a stack of obsolete VHS tape cartridges and an oversized spider plant next to a yellowed poster of Captain Kirk from Star Trek. Underneath the shelf, a bank of video screens glowed with grainy scenes. Images of storefronts, the inside of a laundrette and the back door of the Navigator Arms.

Seth Scroop sat with his feet on his desk reading a yellowed computing magazine and eating a slice of curled pizza. Scattered around the desk were the empty pizza box, a dozen empty fast-food cartons, a coffee mug stained brown at the lip, and a blue saucer used as an ashtray filled with cigarette butts. Two huge monitors emitted a blueish tinge. The buzz of a fly came from overhead. It landed on a video screen and crawled in a wide arc.

"Hope this won't take long," he said looking up from the magazine, teeth brown nubs. "I'm reading about the history of the internet and I'm up to 2003."

Fenella said, "Right historian, aren't you?"

"It passes the time." He took a bite of the pizza and scowled at Dexter. "Brought any cans of ale with you?"

"Next time," Dexter replied looking shifty.

"I'll hold you to that."

Seth looked at the crust of pizza, sniffed and threw it at the fly as it continued to crawl on a video screen.

"Got it!" He turned to Dexter, grinning. "And don't forget it's your turn to buy the curry. Chicken Tikka Masala, extra hot."

Fenella glanced around and sighed, wondering what she was doing in this dingy grime pit. The suffocating air, the low hum of the monitors and the slob with his feet on the desk reading an outdated computer magazine added to her doubts.

She said, "Does your team watch these screens twenty-four seven?"

Seth dropped the magazine on the desk and picked at the cheese stuck to the pizza box. It stretched, a thin yellow line of goo, brown nubs snapping at it until it twanged.

"It's not much of a team, just me and the wife," he said, licking the remains of cheese strands from his lips. "That's the wife on reception. I've no idea how people think we can watch these screens day and night on what they pay for the service. It's not a lucrative business. We run things on a shoestring. I look at the screens when I can."

Fenella pointed at the monitor displaying the rear doors of the Navigator Arms. "Ever seen those doors used?"

"Nope. Never."

"What about your wife?"

"She doesn't look at the screens, prefers to stay in reception where she can chat with her friends on the phone and paint her nails."

Fenella had hoped for another response, hoped Seth or his wife had seen something being carried in or out. Even if the doors were used on the hour, every hour, she doubted he or his wife would have noticed. Still, you never know what might come of your questions so she said, "Why do they have the camera aimed on the rear doors?"

Seth shrugged. "Pirates, I suppose. Who else would nick from a pub?"

Fenella had a sinking feeling. She sighed. "The Navigator Arms, last Friday lunchtime, do you have the tape?"

"Lined up and ready to fire," he said and waved them to his side of the desk.

That wasn't the response she expected, but welcomed it with open arms and rushed forward, heartbeat picking up in anticipation. Dexter followed.

On the opposite side of the desk, they stared at the Scroop Security logo as it floated across the screen.

"We didn't come here to watch your screensaver, nice as it is," Fenella said.

"I got the CCTV deal for the pub when the new landlord took over," Seth replied. "Alf and Stacy Bird signed a five-year contract. That is pure gold in my line of work. I'd be toast if they found out I showed you their feed without the legal stuff."

Dexter coughed. "That little matter we discussed last week, I'll have it sorted for you, Mr Scroop. And Chicken Tikka Masala, you say?"

"Extra hot, with a dozen bottles of that fancy Loweswater Gold ale."

"Righto," Dexter replied.

Seth grinned then clicked his mouse. "I've lined up the images from about eleven a.m. to three p.m. Playback at quadruple speed. There is only one camera and the picture quality is not the greatest."

They watched for several minutes. Grainy images of the rear doors flickered in the changing light. Not much else happened, except the tick of the timer at the bottom of the screen.

"Now you see why I read these old computer magazines," Seth said. "A man can't stare at a screen with nothing going on. Even with all these monitors, we'll go for months where the most exciting event is the rain. What are you looking for?"

"When I see it, I'll let you know," Fenella replied.

The light continued to change on the images, marking the passage of time. Fenella glanced at the timer. It clicked to the time she and her team ended their meal in the pub. A shadow appeared in the corner of the screen. It lengthened until a deep shade covered the doorway.

Seth stood, yawned and stretched. He ambled to the bank of video screens, stooped down, picked up the pizza crust, sniffed and chewed. Then he shuffled back to the desk. That's when they saw it. The doors opened, and a shadow flittered out. Only an instant at quadruple speed. Blink and they'd have missed it.

"Stop and rewind," Fenella shouted.

Seth turned back the video. Fenella and Dexter's eyes remained glued to the screen, their excitement mounting. Backwards and forwards, he played the images, slowing them down at the critical moment. Finally, Fenella's lips quirked into a satisfied smirk.

CHAPTER 72

As the rush hour peaked, Fenella arrived at the Navigator Arms. The sun shone through a dimpled sky, scattering orange light across the trees. From the west, a bank of black-tinged clouds began their slow roll inland. The air smelled of storm.

Two patrol cars and a minivan swept into the carpark behind her Morris Minor. The warrant came through within the hour, fast-tracked by Superintendent Jeffery. Fenella sold it to the boss as a sure thing but knew her hunch was far from certain.

On a wooden bench, a wizened man in a flat cap and jacket with patched elbows watched. He drank from a pint glass of stout and ate pickled onions from a jar. There was no one else outside the pub. That's odd, Fenella thought as she and Dexter climbed out of her car. The frosted glass windows of the pub were dark.

As the officers began to exit the van, the wizened man scampered to the front doors of the pub and flung them open. Without stepping inside he yelled, "Pigs. Run!"

"They've got a bleedin' watchdog," Fenella said to Dexter.

The man scampered back to the bench, snatched up his pint glass, grasped the jar of pickled onions and headed towards the towpath.

"Pigs save ya self!" he yelled as he ran.

His cries roused the patrons inside the bar. They rose like a great swarm of gnats and fled against the tide of the arriving police.

"We have a search warrant," Fenella declared, stepping inside the dim bar.

"This is ridiculous," Stacy Bird screamed, three tables from the door and blocking her path. "We are having a private meeting."

She picked up two empty beer bottles, and in a violent rage, hurled them at Fenella. Both missiles sailed over her head. But Dexter let out two pained yells as they hit him in the side.

Three uniformed officers surrounded Stacy Bird, with Dexter in the lead.

"Now let's not be having any more bother," he said, in a tone more growl than voice.

"I'll have you for this," Stacy yelled, as they put her in cuffs and led her away.

Fenella strode deep into the pub and scanned the scattering crowd, almost all men. The smell of the farmyard filled the air. Tables and benches had been shifted to one side and sawdust spread across the floor. On top of the sawdust, grass sods formed a rough square. Wooden benches, barrels and boxes enclosed the tight space. Fenella had seen this before. Her stomach churned in disgust—a cockfighting pit.

She studied the bird lying in the corner, neck twisted, eyes gone, the blood on the sods of grass not yet brown. It was an Old English Game chicken —a black-breasted cockerel with the wattles, combs, and earlobes cut off. A fighting cock who'd fought and lost.

Alf Bird, behind the counter, looked as if he'd seen a ghost. Bent double like a scythe, he ran with the crowd. Fenella turned on her heels, catching up with him at the door. She grabbed his shoulder.

"You're nicked," she yelled.

He wasn't an athletic man and was wobbly on his legs. He half-turned and swung his fat elbow. It should have connected with her jaw, but she ducked, kicking out the tip of her shoe into his right calf. He bellowed, stumbled to one side, and it was over. Two uniforms had him by the arms while another slapped cuffs on his wrists.

"Now," Fenella said, panting hard, "you are going to be a nice chap and cooperate with us, aren't you, Mr Bird?"

He swore, strained to wriggle free, and got a whack on the shins from a truncheon for his troubles. Again he bellowed, but this time with the wail of a child caught doing wrong.

"Want us to charge him, ma'am," a uniformed officer said.

Fenella recognised him—PC Jon Phoebe. He wore size fourteen boots and had a scowl like an upset gorilla. They'd worked from the same station for donkey's years and she knew his wife well.

"You've got no right to treat me like this," Alf Bird hissed.

"Assaulting a detective is a serious offence," PC Phoebe replied. His face contorted into a foul sneer. "Want to try your fancy elbow strike on me?"

Alf Bird's eyes dropped to the floor, and he whimpered. "I want to speak with my solicitor."

"Of course you can, sunshine," Fenella replied. "After a ride in this nice officer's motor car. And be a good boy else he has my permission to tan your hide. Take him away."

CHAPTER 73

The rain fell silently at first, in sheets of soft drizzle. There was no wind, only snarling black clouds which blotted out the sun and smeared the sky with night before it was time. There will be a downpour soon, Fenella thought as she stood in the doorway of the Navigator Arms.

As she was about to dash to her car, her phone buzzed. A message from Jones:

No joy with Mrs Edna Brown. She is not at her house. Knocked on every bedsit door. No one knows where she is. Might be shopping? Waiting in the car outside her house.

She was about to type an answer when a hand lightly touched her arm. She turned to see a fierce face with brutal eyes, dressed in black with a thick brown book under her arm and a newspaper neatly folded inside.

"Inspector Sallow, my name is Sister Fran Burge."

The soft American accent surprised Fenella, but then she recalled the face. She'd first seen the woman in the pub which she'd just stepped from. That was last Friday. The day the devil's wisp disappeared before her eyes. Now she had a name to the face and knew instinctively why the woman was here.

"Last Friday, you were looking for Micky Knowles in that pub," she said, noticing the woman's ring finger was missing.

"My heavens, you make it sound like I'm a regular boozer. But there were important reasons for me to be there."

"And that is what you want to talk with me about, Sister Burge?"

"It is."

Fenella glanced up at the darkening sky as a sheet of quiet drizzle continued to fall. It would pelt it down at any moment. Part of her wanted to get back to the station to throw the book personally at Alf and Stacy Bird. Heavy rain would slow her drive back to a crawl. But she was curious. "How'd you know I was here?"

"Word travels on the grapevine."

Fenella wondered if the news had got to the nun's ear that Mick Knowles was dead. She thought about the Birds. Let them stew in a cell. Anyway, she was intrigued by the soft accent, Iowa or Dakota? She could tell by the slight twang to the vowels the nun had lived in England for years.

She said, "Let's go inside, eh? Get out of the rain."

They sat at a round table with stained beer mats and half-finished pints of ale. Sister Burge placed the brown book on the table and leaned her elbows on it. Officers moved about and a police photographer's camera flashed in short bursts.

"Iowa?" Fenella said once they'd settled down.

"Sioux City. I worked on a farm and lost my finger, but that was a long time ago."

"Never been to Iowa. I've always wanted to visit Iowa City, though."

Sister Burge's fierce face softened into a smile. "That's clear over there, as we say back home, and the opposite side of the state."

A sudden boom of thunder roared across the treetops shaking loose from the blackened sky giant pellets of icy rain. They smashed against the frosted windows and clattered on the pub door.

"I know Mick Knowles is dead," Sister Burge said.

"How?"

"Word gets around."

"Tell me about him."

"He was a kind man at heart who led a challenging life, which I suppose, in the end, lead him downwards." She paused, glassy-eyed. "How did he die?"

"I can't say yet." Fenella gave a sad smile. "But it wasn't at his own hand."

Fenella paused as another burst of thunder rattled the windows. There is no point rushing out to face that, she thought. There'd be more about Mick Knowles if she stayed for a longer chat. He was no saint, but it would help paint a picture of his life and death.

Sister Burge said, "I met Mick when he was in

prison, liked the man, and when he got out, I offered him a job. He was a model inmate, with a memory for detail. Photographic. Never forgot what he saw. Much of it he didn't like to talk about, but when he did, it played back with vivid colours." There was a pause, and she shifted in her seat. "Listen, he had challenges with women since his girlfriend, Pam Wells, died. I don't think he ever got over her, seemed to live in the past, suffered from a sort of Peter Pan syndrome."

"How'd you mean?" Fenella asked.

"Although he was middle-aged, he acted like a teen and went out with a string of young women. They all had a likeness to Pam Wells, I think. Well, except Jane Ragsdale. He met her and was even more unhappy."

"I see," Fenella said and waited.

"He even got banned from visiting his grandmother. She lives in Grange Hall Care Home. I felt sorry for him. He found it difficult to control his rage and said he'd been wrongly imprisoned. Claimed to have been fitted up by a police officer of all things!"

"This officer, what was their name?"

"He liked to make things up, Inspector." Sister Burge shook her head slowly. "One time he told me he thought he knew what happened to his first girlfriend, Pam Wells. I got used to it, ignored his outbursts, and we got along fine."

"And what did he say happened to Miss Wells?"

"He didn't say they'd find her body in a

wardrobe." Sister Burge looked at Fenella. "You know, I don't think he talked about the details, just that he had figured out who took her."

Fenella took several moments to process all that had been said, then she asked the only logical question. "I don't suppose he gave a name?"

"Oh yes. He'd rattle off names ten to the dozen, most from the front pages of the morning newspaper. I took no notice after a while."

Fenella turned to see Dexter standing at the entrance. She gave him the thumbs up, and he vanished. He'd see to those doors at the back of the pub, explore the room behind and tell her what they found. He'd not mind a splash of rain either. She'd like to have a poke about herself but couldn't be in two places at once.

Sister Burge was speaking. "I'm no psychiatrist, but it seemed to me Mick Knowles had a touch of Tourette syndrome." She paused. "Coprolalia to be exact—involuntary outbursts of obscene words, derogatory remarks, and socially inappropriate behaviour. I often wondered if he'd suffered brain damage as a child, but he wouldn't speak about it. He said he was brought up by his gran, who loved him, but I got no more than that. I prayed for him and those adults responsible for the damage."

"Brain damage, eh?" Fenella said, wondering how in the world he was referred to Sloane Kern for anger management therapy. The bloke needed more than that.

Sister Burge said, "The real world was so

painful he preferred to live on a boat, drift anyplace he wanted. Float away in his dreams. That he got into medical school was his pride and joy. Alas, with his condition, it didn't work out. But he still carried a black bag with his medical kit and certificates around with him. He was different. I didn't judge him, just loved him as God commanded. I wish I could have done more."

"We always wish that, luv. That you listened and gave him work is a miracle to me."

Fenella wanted to dig deeper into Mick's life, but she changed her mind. "What did he do for you?"

"Occasional work lugging furniture donations. I sell them to second-hand furniture stores; all the money goes to the convent. I gave Micky the things I couldn't sell and paid him in cash for his work. He'd fix up those items to make a little extra. For a while he had a small business going, then he had one of his incidents."

"How'd you mean?"

"He'd draw in on himself, become moody, and you wouldn't see him for months. You can't run a business like that. Last Friday, I was looking for him to help me carry some furniture we received from Carlisle. Alas, it was not to be."

Fenella couldn't imagine Sister Burge hurrying to the pub just to tell her that. The woman had a no-nonsense attitude and wasn't one for chit-chat. If she sought her out, it was because she had news. She decided to be direct, the best way with a woman like that.

"That's not what you came here to tell me, is it, Sister Burge?"

Sister Burge opened the brown book and unfolded the newspaper so the front page was visible.

"I saw the wardrobe in today's newspaper and thought I recognised it." She tapped a finger on the colour first page image. "That item came with a load of furniture that was so ugly, I didn't even try to sell it and gave it straight to Micky. He dumped the items here in the cellar. I doubt he even got around to opening the doors. Yes, Pam Wells was his girlfriend but I don't believe he killed her. Micky had feelings of rage and violence, but he wouldn't hurt a fly."

She opened the brown book and flipped through the pages.

"Micky was obsessive, used to study these order books like he was reading for a history test. He'd spot errors and I'd correct them. How many handymen can do that?" She found the page she was looking for and glanced up. "I keep exact records, Inspector. I can tell you where every donated item came from and to who we sold it."

Fenella sat up straight. "That wardrobe?"

"Look, there is the date, and here is the address. It came from a Mr Tim Kern."

CHAPTER 74

Fenella drove straight to Sloane Kern's flat with Dexter and two uniformed officers—PC Crowther and PC Woods, who'd wriggled out of his Tarns Dub duties. The rain had stopped but the wind whistled in chill blasts from the beach. She stood for a moment on the glistening pavement, breathing the smells of the sea and looking up and down the street as dusk crept across the houses.

She always felt a little sad when she visited this part of Port St Giles. It had once been a tree-lined lane, pink and white blossoms in the spring and green and leafy in the summer. But the council had cut down the trees to reduce their costs. Only rotted stumps remained of Nature's glory and many houses had been left to run to ruin or converted into dingy bedsits and flats.

They found the right house and walked through a fenced courtyard. A small black dog, mouth full of teeth, snarled as they went by. Fenella turned and threw a chunk of her lamb sandwich. It wolfed it down, sat and wagged its tail for more. She fed it the rest of the food from the wax paper, then told PC Crowther to go to the back in case anyone darted from the house. PC Woods waited by the gate.

With Dexter at her side, she approached the door, rang the bell, and when there came no answer, slammed the knocker hard three times. She felt a thrill of excitement as she waited for the door to open.

Not long now before she had answers.

Not long until all the secrets were exposed.

The door opened.

It was Mrs Edna Brown. The woman in the tight green headscarf. Standing in the doorway as though she owned the place.

"All right, me duckies." She leaned on her cane, staring at the detectives. "Not you lot again. What do you want? I've just settled the girls down to sleep."

That Fenella was surprised to see Mrs Edna Brown in the doorway of Sloane Kern's flat didn't show in her voice. She said, "Can we come in?"

Edna seemed in two minds. She tapped her cane on the tile floor three times, thin spindly hand grasping it tightly, muttering as though casting a spell. Then she craned her neck out of the door and looked both ways. She must have seen a neighbour's curtain twitch for she slowly stepped aside.

"Be quiet and quick," Edna whispered. "I want to watch Coronation Street in peace."

Fenella watched the show too and was curious to know what would happen in this episode. It promised to reveal the real father of a plump brown baby with chicken skin and Bambi eyes. Edna steered them to the living room, where a large television played commercials at a low volume.

"Please take a seat," she said and sat in an armchair opposite the flickering box. Next to her, on a coffee table, were three bottles of ale and a large packet of roast chicken crisps. "Sloane's dog's run off. I'm keeping an eye out for it. I likes dogs. You can trust them and they don't spread gossip."

Fenella tapped a message to Jones to tell him she'd found Edna. He replied with a short text message:

Sloane Kern's financials are not great. She is in heavy debt. Anger management therapy is not a business I'd go into. On my way, boss.

She marvelled at how fast the young typed; it took her an age to peck out a single letter. She sat next to Dexter on the sofa, facing the door.

"Been waiting to see what happens all day," Edna said, watching the screen with hypnotic intensity. "I think I know who the dad is, but I ain't totally sure. Sloane's not here if that's who you were looking for."

"Righto, we'll get to Sloane in a moment," Fenella said, "Since we've got you, can you tell me what you are doing here?"

"What do you mean, got me?"

"A turn of phrase."

Edna sniffed and picked up a bottle of ale, but put it back on the coffee table, eyes still on the flickering screen. "You'll not stay long then, ducky."

"A few questions and we'll be on our way."

"I'm babysitting tonight." Edna's thin spindly hand clutched the remote to lower the volume.

"Sloane asked, and I like to help when I can."

"Are you her regular sitter?"

"Aye, me ducky. But I wouldn't say it was all that regular, just when Sloane calls me. First time in a month or so, tonight. Gives me something different to do. I get along with the kids and Sloane don't mind if I have a jar or two of ale."

"Mind if I look in on them?" This was Dexter.

"Has Sloane complained about me or something?"

"No luv," Fenella replied.

"Well, it feels like a police raid."

"You invited us in."

"Listen, ducky. I used to be a nurse. I know how to take care of little ones. If anyone has a complaint, they should come straight—"

"So, you don't mind if I take a peek in at the kids?" Dexter said, interrupting before it turned into a rant. "They'll not know I'm there."

She didn't say yes, but she didn't say no, either. Dexter slipped from the room. He came back moments later, gave the thumbs up, and once again left the room.

Fenella said, "Mind telling me where you were yesterday evening?"

"What time?"

"Say between eleven p.m. and two in the morning."

"I'm no spring chicken, me ducky. Don't dance the night away no more. I were at home doing me knitting then went to bed around ten. Didn't wake up until me usual time, around seven."

"Can anyone confirm that?"

"I live alone."

"What about Monday night?"

"Same routine."

"Did you know Pam Wells?"

"Everyone knew Pam, me ducky. A real talker. She'd talk and talk so much that if you had a heart attack and died, she wouldn't notice until the medics lifted you on a stretcher. Even then, she'd finish her story." She paused to take a breath. "I knew her dad too and was gutted when she vanished. Even more so when she turned up in the cellar of me favourite watering hole. And to think I've been eating and drinking on her grave!"

An advert came on for instant noodles with young people dancing around a microwaved pot. They munched as though it were gourmet food served up from an Egon Ronay starred restaurant.

Fenella said, "Do you drink at the Navigator's Arms in the evening?"

"Never. Rough crowd. I prefers the daylight folk. A tipple and a natter at lunchtime to get me through the day." She glanced at the coffee table with its bottles of ale. "One of me little treats, along with me babysitting beer."

None of the bottles had been opened yet. She's saving them for Coronation Street, Fenella thought. "Do you own a mobile phone?"

"What would I be doing with one of those, eh?" Edna gave her a challenging look. "If people wants to call me, they must do it on me landline, and that's that. That's what Sloane does. Leaves me a message and tells me what time to come round to keep an eye on the little nippers."

It all seemed to fit, and Edna answered the questions without hesitation or stalling for time to think. And she didn't own a mobile phone, so it wasn't her who made the call to Fenella on the beach. Unless she owned a burner, and she was a damn talented actor. But one thing bothered Fenella.

"I heard Bren Kern has gone missing and wanted to check up on her," she said. "Do you know where she went?"

"Well, she ain't here." Edna straightened and seemed oddly uneasy. "Her mum told me she'd gone to London."

"And you don't believe her?"

"That's what she said," Edna replied, holding Fenella's gaze. "That's what I'm telling you."

But London seemed too neat an explanation, and Barry Logan said Bren was as regular as clockwork. Since when do clocks stop and run away to the capital city? Still, Fenella didn't understand why Sloane hadn't mentioned that her teen was gone when she visited her office in Hodge Hill. That's the first thing she'd do if her kids went missing, and she'd had five.

The commercials ended and the opening melody of Coronation Street began, but Edna's gaze remained on Fenella.

"Why would Bren go to London?" Fenella

asked.

Edna shrugged. "I've no idea, but that's what teenagers do, me ducky. When I was her age, I took the boat to Belgium just to see what was there. But I was always a wild thing."

"And Bren isn't?"

Edna pressed a button on the remote control. The television screen went blank.

"Why don't you tell me what this is about, me ducky?"

Fenella considered. "Do you know where Mrs Kern is?"

"She went to see her boyfriend, Jack Parkes."

"So, she is in a relationship?"

"Birds of a feather those two. Sloane's husband, Tim, died a few years back. Same for Jack. He was married to Ester Padavona. Hard on her mum, Giorgia. She had a big house in Westpond where they all lived. When Ester passed, she sold the house and moved to Grange Hall Care Home."

"Giorgia Padavona," Fenella said. "Lovely name. Quite distinct for around these parts."

"Italian, but Ester was Port St Giles born and bred." Edna adjusted her headscarf. "Jack and Giorgia don't get along. Both are strong-willed. After Ester died, Jack moved into his own flat. Sloane met Jack at the gym. He is in great shape for a man in his late forties."

"So, tonight Sloane is at the gym with Jack?"

"Oh no, Jack is not a fitness instructor. He is a vet and tends to work late at his veterinary clinic a few days a week. Sloane went to see him. I don't know when she'll be back." She frowned. "Has something happened to Bren?"

"No."

"I don't believe it. I've been around long enough to know if a detective shows up on your doorstep it is bad news. And Sloane was in a right state when she called me to babysit. The last time I saw her that bad was when Tim died. Bren's dead, isn't she?"

"I don't know," Fenella said, truthfully. "But I want to clarify a few things with Mrs Kern. Do you have the address of Mr Parkes' office?"

Edna gave her the address.

"They've been seeing each other for a few years. Sometimes she stays over. It's serious, me ducky. She talked about getting married soon. A big flash wedding."

A sense of excitement washed over Fenella—a fox on the scent of a hare. Dexter cracked his knuckles.

Edna tightened her green headscarf. "Bren told me she were seeing an older man, me ducky. I don't like to gossip, but I think it were Mick Knowles. She showed me a letter with handwriting like monkey scrawl."

"How can you be sure?" Fenella asked.

"I recognised it. Taught English for a few years in the high school, years ago, now. Micky was in my class when he were a lad. Never seen handwriting like it. It were like someone beat his hand with a stick as he wrote. I called it monkey scrawl, but only to myself. Important that kids learn to read and write, and he were a sad lad back then."

Fenella pulled out her phone, scrawled for a moment then handed it to Edna.

"Recognise that?"

It was a photograph of the pink note she'd found in the wooden shack. Edna stared for a heartbeat.

"Aye," she said, eyeing Fenella. "That's the handwriting of Micky Knowles. See what I mean about Monkey scrawl?"

Dexter appeared in the doorway; hands encased in latex. It wasn't the gloves that caused Fenella's heartbeat to race. It was the bundle of medical gowns, surgical blades, and masks he held by his fingertips.

"Found them in Sloane's bedroom, Guv." He lowered his voice. "In her wardrobe, hidden under a pile of kinky underwear."

CHAPTER 75

Fenella felt uneasy on the drive to Jack Parkes' veterinary office. Thick black clouds hung close to the street, brushing the rooftops in fog. She had called in the crime scene techs, a family liaison officer, and left Jones, who'd arrived, in charge of the scene at Sloane Kern's flat. There were a lot of unanswered questions. The most important of which was where is Bren Kern? And that's what made her gut churn.

She told herself there was no hurry. It was normal for Sloane to spend time with Jack while he finished up. A normal evening, like any other visit to her lover's workplace. How would she know the police were on the way?

Dexter slowed the car to a crawl as a billow of fog engulfed the road. The streetlamps became dots of blur, an orange constellation of stars visible in the dark but offering no guiding light.

"Can't go no faster else we'll end up in a ditch, Guv."

They inched forward, every rumble of the tyres on the road tightening the bands of dread around Fenella's stomach. Was Bren dead? As a mother of five, that thought terrified her.

As the car paused at an intersection, she looked along the lamppost lined lane. Swirls of fog mingled with night. It was too dark to see more than a few feet ahead. Too dark to know how it would all end.

"Do you think Sloane will still be at the vet's office, Guv? Or should we head to her boyfriend's flat first?"

"Keep going. Let's put one foot in front of the other and hope it goes somewhere." She thought for a moment. "It can't do any harm to have a patrol car keep a watch on his home."

"Or she might be on her way back to her flat," Dexter said. "Might have argued. It happens, you know?"

They continued in silence.

"Nearly there, Guv."

He swung the car into a dark driveway and parked in the shimmering shadows of a tall oak tree. Fenella jumped from the car as it came to a stop, with Dexter three paces behind. They ran through the dancing swirls of fog past iron railings and a stone wall covered in ivy and moss. At the gate, the building was dark.

"Think we are too late," Dexter said, letting out a gasp of breath. "They've closed up shop and gone home."

"Look," Fenella said, pointing at a dim light at the back of the building, away from the main reception. With the dark and the fog, it was easily missed. Any other night it'd have shone as bright as a star. "Let's take a look, eh?"

"Spooky in all this fog," Dexter muttered. "Like one of those horror movies your Eduardo loves to watch."

Fenella glanced again at the swirls of fog and the dim light from the side room. There were monsters for sure. In human form. When they reared their ugly heads, she caught them and put them away.

"Come on," she said. "Let's do a bit of monster hunting."

They crept along the side of the building, keeping close to the brick and their footsteps light. Within a few steps, they had a clear view of the curtainless window.

"Two people inside, Guv. A man and a woman."

"That's her. That's Sloane and the bloke must be Jack."

They watched for a moment. Jack bent over a limp dog on a table, whispered into its ear and carefully lifted it and disappeared from view.

Their gaze shifted to Sloane. She seemed stiff, with her arms folded. They were close enough to make out the scowl on her face. Whatever had happened that night, it wasn't good. Fenella recognised the body language of a woman who'd argued. A woman who'd yelled. A woman who'd lost her rag. And she felt a deep sense of sorrow at secretly watching, at having to knock on the door and tell Sloane what they knew.

"Come on, let's knock and see what she's got to say," Fenella said, "Then we'll take her in. Call back up, will you? Sloane Kern looks like she wants to swing for someone."

CHAPTER 76

Jack Parkes' mouth dropped wide when Fenella showed him her warrant card and asked for a quiet word with Sloane Kern. When he saw Dexter, she thought he'd pass out.

"Something's happened?" Jack said, staring in dazed shock. "I can feel your vibrations. Are the girls all right? Yes, of course, come in."

They entered through a side door which led to the room that they'd seen Jack and Sloane in. There was a scented candle on a counter. Its flame cast an orange glow. Sandalwood with hints of rose. A Jade obelisk stood to one side of a clear lighted bowl filled with colourful pebbles. Low in the background, piped through a hidden speaker, bamboo chimes played. A soothing place to treat a sick pet.

Cat crates and a dog kennel lined one wall. Fenella recognised the dog inside. It was the animal Jack had carried from the table. It lay in a basket curled into a ball, asleep.

"Honey, can you come in here," Jack said, his voice strained. "Some people want to ask you a few questions."

Fenella noticed he said *people* rather than *police* and knew that was to soften the blow. If two detectives showed up on a dark foggy night at the door of her cottage, she'd scream bloody murder. She sensed Jack Parkes was a man who'd grown up on politeness and came from a long-lost era.

Sloane Kern came out a few moments later, even more dishevelled than when Fenella saw her earlier. There were tear stains on her cheeks, a blush to her neck, and her eyes glistened with sadness and fear.

"Inspector Sallow, what a surprise," she said in a mock cheerful voice.

Must be the same voice she used with her patients. Much too high-pitched to be genuine. It would not make her want to share her deepest and angriest secrets.

"I'll get some chairs," Jack said, returning moments later with four black plastic folding chairs. He placed them facing each other, two by two like the seats in a railway carriage. Fenella sat and waved Sloane to the opposite chair. Dexter and Jack remained standing.

"I'd like to speak with Sloane alone," Fenella said. When he didn't respond, she sighed. "Mr Parkes, I am investigating a serious matter involving the deaths of three people. There are sensitive questions I wish to ask Sloane, and she may not wish to have you present."

"I see," Jack replied. "Yes, there is a trace of negative vibrations in the air. Bad energy. I will do as you request." He paused and puffed out his chest. "No. I'm Sloane's boyfriend. Whatever you have to say, you can say it in front of me. Have you found Bren?"

"Ex-girlfriend," Sloane said. "I'm your ex now."

"Now, honey, I'm still—"

"Still what?" she yelled. "You've tossed me aside as though I'm a scrap of rubbish. I love you, Jack, but I'm not good enough to be your wife."

Jack ran a hand through his hair. "It's just that we aren't... look there are so many things... Ester's ring, Bren and now the police. I'm sorry, but the energy from the crystals isn't there for us right now."

"Then go," Sloane yelled. "Leave me to speak with the detectives."

Jack took a step towards the door, body stooped as though suddenly aged. "Is that what you want?"

Sloane stared at him; eyes blazing. There was a theatrical element to her gaze, almost calculating. Automatically Fenella kept silent, watching, waiting for Sloane's reply. It came as a whisper so soft she almost missed it.

"No," Sloane said, in a little girl's voice. "I want you to stay."

Fenella was in two minds. On the one hand, she wanted to speak with Sloane Kern alone and then speak with Jack. On the other, their sour relationship might yield more concrete answers.

Softly, softly, catchee monkey.

"Take a seat, Mr Parkes," Fenella said. She'd interview them formally at the station later. Right now she wanted to sieve the wheat from the chaff.

Jack sat, rested his hands on his knees and leaned slightly forwards so his back arched. Like a game contestant eager to punch on the buzzer and deliver the right answer. Dexter took out a notebook and pen and sat next to Fenella.

She turned to Sloane. "How many children do you have?"

"Three. Girls."

"Hard work, eh?"

Sloane glanced at Jack. "I'm a single mum and try to do my best."

Fenella let that hang in the air and heard Jack's heavy breaths. "Bren is the oldest?"

"That's right."

"Why didn't you tell me she was missing?"

"She's a teenager. She can do as she likes."

"Oh, so she leaves home often, does she? Goes out at night and doesn't come back?"

"Like I say, she is a teenager. They do what the hell they like. I've two younger ones to keep an eye on. Teens do random things, and like I say, I'm a single mum, I can't do everything."

"Aye, pet, I understand."

Some of Fenella's best friends raised kids on their own. But she got the impression Sloane Kern used her single mum status like a monkey clinging to a fig tree. To fill its belly as fast as possible with the sweet, tasty fruit.

Fenella said, "I was under the impression that Bren was one of life's regular, stable types. She works at Logan's Bakery and the owner says she is as reliable as clockwork."

"I'm sorry, Inspector," Sloane replied. "But sometimes teenagers disappoint. They run off."

Jack's eyes were troubled. He tapped his fingers on his thighs. He kept glancing at Sloane as she spoke.

Sloane continued. "When I was Bren's age, I ran away with my boyfriend. London is not so far if that is where she has gone. She'll be back. I'm not worried."

Fenella said, "A lass was brutally killed by the canal and I want the killer behind bars so the bugger doesn't do it again. And you are not worried for Bren? I just want the truth, luv."

"Then you should be out looking for the killer," Sloane replied. "Why are you here?"

That Sloane Kern showed no concern for her missing daughter worried Fenella. What mum wouldn't be troubled if their teen went missing? She had to throw a jab to get the woman to open her mouth. Rile her, so she felt off balance.

She thought for a moment, then said, "Mick Knowles was seeing Bren."

Sloane's lips became a straight line. She did not speak.

"Mick Knowles is dead," Fenella said, throwing out another jab. "An innocent man murdered!"

"The man was in his forties and had no business messing with teenage girls," Sloane replied. "He got what he deserved."

"We found his body in nowt but a medical

gown with his finger chopped off and tongue torn out. Did he deserve that?"

Jack let out a gasp, jerked to his feet then walked to a sink on the far wall and poured water into a bowl, and in another, he shook dry dog food. He walked to the dog kennel, stooped and placed both items into the cage. The dog didn't stir. When he returned to his chair, his forehead was pimpled with sweat.

"I think you should tell them the truth," he said, voice soft.

"Shut up!" Sloane snapped.

Jack rubbed his crystal bracelet and looked down at his shoes.

Fenella assessed Sloane's body language. She'd get nowt more, so she changed direction. "Did you know Jane Ragsdale?"

"You asked me that earlier today, and my answer is the same," Sloane replied. "No."

"That's the woman that was killed," Jack said, voice almost a whisper. "Drowned in the canal, didn't she?"

The room became so quiet the soft snores of the slumbering dog rumbled like thunder. Jack stared at Fenella as a sense of understanding grew.

"An accident," he repeated as though willing it to be true. "The woman slipped and fell in. Was she drunk?"

"I need to know your whereabouts on Monday night," Fenella said to Sloane.

"Is that the night Jane Ragsdale drowned?" Jack

asked.

Sloane said, "I spent the evening here with Jack."

Jack rubbed the back of his neck with one hand and shifted in his seat.

"Who babysat the girls?" Fenella asked.

"Mrs Edna... well, it was a spontaneous date, wasn't it, Jack?"

He nodded, wide-eyed, but did not speak.

Fenella took it all in. "So, you left the girls alone at home?"

Sloane went quiet for a moment. "Bren is good with the other two, and I didn't think I'd be out all night."

"That clears that up then," Fenella replied. She looked at Dexter. "Did you get that down?"

"Aye, Guv. Spontaneous date. Got it."

"So, you watched the telly?" Fenella's question was aimed at Jack.

"Yes, we often watch the telly on Monday night."

The way he said the word *telly* just wasn't right. He was a *television* man, Fenella thought. He might even still call it a *television set*. Either way, she didn't think he'd spend his free time watching reruns of Coronation Street. Soaps were for people who loved gossip.

She said, "What did you watch?"

"What did I watch?" he asked as though confused about why she'd ask a man like him what came on the telly.

"Yes, Mr Parkes. What did you watch?" She realised in her eagerness to catch him in a lie she was shouting. "On the telly. BBC or ITV? There's an easy one for you."

He cleared his throat. "It was a blur, really."

"A blur?"

"Well, you know how it is. One can't concentrate on these modern television set shows. It goes in one ear and out the other. All flash and bang and vivid colours. I never remember half the things I watch."

"You'll have to do better than that, Mr Parkes."

"I... I don't know..." He closed his eyes. "Yes... young people were dancing around a bowl of hot noodles. I don't know the name of the show, sorry."

Fenella turned to Sloane. "Where were you last night?"

"Last night?"

"Aye, Wednesday night. Did you go out?"

"Yes."

"Where?"

"To Jack's flat. I stayed all night."

"Is that so, Mr Parkes?" Fenella asked, turning to look him square in the eyes.

When he didn't answer, she said, "Let me remind you that I am investigating three murders and a missing child."

"She's sixteen," Sloane said, face impassive.

"A bairn," Fenella replied and turned to Jack. "Were you with Sloane last night?"

"Well... er... yes."

"What type of television set do you own, Mr Parkes?"

"Oh!" Jack's body began to shake. "A big one."

"Flat screen or cathode-ray tube?"

They didn't make nowt but flatscreen's these days. A little test to see if he'd pass.

"Cathode... no... flatscreen... yes, that's it... all I know is that it is huge. Takes up one wall. Massive."

"I see," Fenella replied. "So, when I send Detective Dexter to look around your home later tonight, he'll find a massive television?"

"I... er..."

"It's in the repair shop," Sloane said. "It broke down, didn't it, Jack?"

He did not reply, just stared, pale faced, shaking.

"Thanks for clearing that up," Fenella said. "And the name of the repair shop?"

Silence.

Fenella smiled, took out her mobile phone, scrolled for a brief moment and handed it to Sloane.

"Take a good look. Ever seen those before?"

"No," Sloane said. "Never."

"Funny, that. Seeing as we found those medical gowns, surgical blades and masks in your flat."

CHAPTER 77

There was silence for several moments. From hidden speakers came the soft chimes of bamboo. Then the faint breaths of Sloane's heaving chest.

Fenella waited.

Sloane stirred in her chair. It came as a great slow trance-like sway. Slowly, she moved her hand to cover her mouth.

No sound came out.

"Oh my God, Sloane, what have we done?" Jack couldn't look at Sloane now and stared straight ahead. He kneaded the crystal beads which jangled on his wrist. "We have to tell them the truth."

"Yes, I'd like to hear that, luv?" Fenella said and waited.

The *twang-twang-tinkle* of bamboo chimes filled the room. Jack closed his eyes and let out sharp meditative breaths. When his eyelids rose, tears rolled down his cheeks.

"I lied," he said. "Sloane wasn't with me all last night. I showed up at her flat after two to help her search for Bren. She wasn't with me Monday night, either. I don't know where she was. I asked but she wouldn't say." He turned to Sloane. "Where were you, honey?"

Silence, except for the snores of the sleeping dog and the scratch of Dexter's pen. And again came the soft *twang-twang-tinkle* of bamboo.

"I'm sorry you will be next." Fenella smiled. "That's what we found near Mick's body. A note on a pink sheet of paper. At first, I thought it was a warning message for the police to keep away. You see, I had a phone call that told me to never disturb the dead. So, I suppose it was natural to think the note was written by the killer. But it wasn't, was it?"

Sloane suddenly found her voice. "Whatever you find in my flat, I want it on record that I didn't kill Mick Knowles or anyone else."

"I don't think we'll find anything else in your flat, pet. You see, after speaking with your babysitter, Mrs Edna Brown, I realised that Mick Knowles didn't want to hurt Bren. He wanted to warn her. What I found was an unfinished love note from him to your daughter."

Sloane's cheeks blushed red. "What the hell would that pervert want to warn my Bren about?"

"I think he knew the killer," Fenella replied, gaze fixed on Sloane's pale face. "Why did you take him on as a patient?"

"I... er... regret it, now. I'm so sorry."

"So am I, pet."

There were times when Fenella's job made her cry. Being a detective was neither glamour nor glitz. It cost lives to save lives. The lives of those who'd died so she could dig up the truth. That was the terrible reality of her profession, and she wished with all her heart it wasn't so. What kept her going were the saves—the lives she saved of people she would never meet and who would never know how lucky they were. The unknown future victims of a caught killer.

She turned to Jack Parkes with his trembling hands and pale dough face and wondered how life could be so unfair.

"Your first wife was Ester Padavona?"

"Padavona was her maiden name. She took on my surname, Parkes."

"What happened to her?"

"She died."

"I'm sorry, pet. It can't have been easy."

"I focused on my work. It helped."

"How is business?"

"Okay, for a vet. Not a lot of money in it, but at least my business is in the black."

"Did you know Pam Wells?"

"No."

"Jane Ragsdale?"

"No."

"Mick Knowles?"

"Sloane told me about him, but I've never met the man."

"Aye, that's what I thought." Fenella sighed. It had been a long day and she was tired, but the last piece of the puzzle had fallen into place. "Why did you do it, Mr Parkes?"

"Have you gone mad?" He stood, shaky on his legs. "I had nothing to do with those deaths. I don't even know the people who died."

"Sit down, sunshine," Fenella said.

He was well built with muscles, and she didn't like him looming over her. If he dashed for the door, he'd have a head start. With the dark fog and his knowledge of the place, he'd have a good chance of getting away.

Jack remained rooted to the spot. Paralysed. Dexter cracked his knuckles. In the distance came the wail of a police siren. Jack sat.

"That wardrobe where we found Pam Wells," she began feeling more at ease, "we traced it to a Mr Tim Kern. Sloane's late husband. Turns out he got himself in a spot of bother with the tax folk in London. They had him under surveillance. Can't say I'm keen on taxes, but they pay my wages."

"But what has this got to do with me?" Jack asked in irritation.

"You were married to Ester Padavona?"

"Of course. That's what I just said. She was my wife and took on my last name. Mrs Ester Parkes."

Fenella smiled. "Then you will know that her mum, Giorgia, moved to Grange Hall Care Home after Ester died. Giorgia sold her Westpond house. The house you and Ester shared with her."

"So what?" Jack said, a hint of caution in his tone.

"Tim Kern collected furniture from your mother-in-law's house in Westpond. We have the records. Big houses in Westpond, lots of rooms that an old lady would never visit."

"No!" Jack's voice came out as a dry gasp.

Fenella ignored the outburst.

"Tax folk also keep excellent records. So did Tim, in his second set of books. He visited Giorgia and collected chairs, tables, and a wardrobe. The very wardrobe that contained Pam Wells. I suppose you put Pam's body there for safekeeping while you figured out how to get rid of it. Must have been a shock when you found out your late wife's mum gave it away."

Pausing, she recalled Jack's earlier tenderness as he cared for the dog. Now, there was only darkness in the man's eyes.

She continued. "Three lives taken for nowt but greed. Easier when you don't know their names, I suppose. But you did know their names. You knew Pam Wells was Mick Knowles' sweetheart, and you knew he'd been in prison after she died. Thought you'd make a game of it, kill his new lass, Jane Ragsdale, and laugh when we put him inside while you cashed in on her kidneys. What I don't know is whether Pam Wells was a random attack."

"Lies!" Jack yelled, rubbing hard on his bracelet. "I did not know Pam Wells and you've got no proof I did."

"Aye, happen you're right about that. But you did know Jane Ragsdale and Mick Knowles. You'd have heard of Micky and knew about him and Pam Wells. It's all over the internet. You might even have seen Pam's dad's posts. Either way, you decided to make a game of it. Kill Jane and hope the dumb police would think it was Micky. He was a failed medical student, after all. Then you decided to have more fun and kill Micky. Why? I think he worked out you killed Pam Wells and Jane Ragsdale but ran rather than tell the police for fear he'd end up back behind bars. He'd figured out your greedy scheme. Planned to sell their kidneys for a nice profit, didn't you? That was your motive. Greed."

"No, no, you've got it wrong," Jack said. "That's not what you're supposed to think. You have it mixed up."

Fenella tutted, shaking her head, eyes blazing. "Had fun, did you? Chopping off their ring finger and tearing out their tongues before you killed them. And why not have a bit of a laugh at the dumb police with a phone call while you are at it? Took them years to find Pam Wells. They'd never find you even if you called them on a mobile phone; you are too smart, eh?"

"It's not true," Jack said. "I swear."

"Don't lie to me. I've got your number, sunshine. Quite a lush life you are living for a vet. Fancy car, posh flat in Westpond. Cost a packet that lifestyle. I asked myself how can he afford all of that posh?"

For the space of a single inhale of breath, Jack's eyes darted between the detectives, pupils' pinpricks of ice. Another gasp as his mouth opened.

"Sloane did it. Are you too thick-headed to see that?"

"No!" Sloane answered.

"They found the medical gowns in your wardrobe, honey," Jack replied. "That's evidence, isn't it?"

"Aye, pet," Fenella said. "But I never told you where we found them. How'd you know they were in her wardrobe? You put them there."

Fear leapt into his eyes, but he didn't speak.

Fenella wanted more now. A confession. "You needed a little extra money to pay for the wedding, eh? Fancy ring, big stones, church do. The works for Jack's new wife. Why not pay for it with her teen's kidneys? One less mouth to feed and a quick way to earn a little extra cash. A win-win for the poor struggling vet who can't make a go of his business."

She held her breath and waited.

Jack's nostrils flared. "I'm gifted with animals. That's why people bring their pets to me. All creatures great and small, I love them all. But it costs money and most can't pay. Why shouldn't I enjoy the best life has to offer given all the good I do?"

"Killing folk for their body parts is murder, sunshine," Fenella replied.

"I'm engaged in a noble cause!"

"I don't have time for cold-blooded murderers, Mr Parkes."

Jack's face twisted in fury and he let out heavy breaths. "Do you know how much a human kidney goes for?"

"I don't care. What I want is for you to tell me why you did it, in your own words."

"Those that died were bottom feeders," Jack

was shouting now. "Scum. So what if their lives were cut short? Think of the lives that were saved. Their deaths enhanced my life and the lives of the animals I serve. They gave so I could do good."

Through a window Fenella watched the officers arrive, then her gaze settled on the sleeping dog, chest heaving as he let out soft snores. She exhaled. There was one final piece of the puzzle.

She said, "Where's Bren?"

He didn't answer.

"You bastard," Sloane screamed. "Bren had her whole life ahead of her. Where's my daughter?"

Slowly, Jack rose to his feet. With Dexter at his side, he walked to the door, took his tweed jacket from the hook, and put it on.

"It would have been a big ring for you, honey," he said. "And a large house in Westpond, too, but the energy just wasn't right."

The door opened. Two uniformed officers hurried in.

"This way," Dexter said, taking Jack by the arm and leading him through the door as Sloane Kern sprung to her feet, screaming in savage rage.

CHAPTER 78

It was close to eleven o'clock that night when Fenella eased open the door and stepped into the hospital room.

Bren Kern lay on the bed with a tube in her nose and wires attached to her arms. The dim room smelled of antiseptic. An electronic device let out soft beeps. They'd found her in an outbuilding of Jack Parkes' veterinary clinic. She'd been drugged, her clothes stripped, and she wore a beige medical gown.

Jack Parkes claimed he planned to show some mercy with this killing. The tongue and ring finger were to be removed while Bren was unconscious. A small mercy which he hoped would go down well with a jury. Fenella suspected it would send him down all right, for a very long time indeed.

She walked quietly to the edge of the bed. Bren's chest heaved with slow, rhythmic breaths. Her face seemed so pale under the dim ceiling lights, skin taut, almost translucent.

"Bren, you are safe now," Fenella said.

Nothing but the rise and fall of Bren's chest.

"My name is Fenella." She sat on the chair next to the bed. "A very long time ago I made a promise to a child. She was fifteen, almost the same age as you."

She paused and listened to Bren's soft breath and the beep of electronic devices. It was very quiet in the room, nothing like the chaos which surrounded the lass when they first brought her in.

"Her name was Colleen. Colleen Rae. You might have read about what happened to her in the newspapers." There were times when the mention of Colleen Rae's name made Fenella's belly cramp. They never found her body, and her killer, Mr Shred, was on the run. "She was fifteen. Aye, I know there is a world of difference between fifteen and sixteen in the law, but both are still kids in my eyes, so let's not argue about that."

From outside the door came the sound of footsteps. They hurried, slapping on the floor with the crack of tap-dancing shoes. Another emergency for the medical crew to deal with. Another life they rushed to save.

"You see, that fifteen-year-old girl died," Fenella said. "And I promised I'd never let another bairn come to harm on my watch. Not an easy one to keep that. Not when you are a policewoman."

She watched Bren's face, hoping some of her words went in. She continued. "On Saturday, I'm going to pop in for a chat with Sister Burge. You don't know her, but she's taken on your puppy, Max, and an older dog called Wayne. Kind of her, eh? Then I'm off to dance the night away at the Tarns Dub Music Festival. Lucky me!"

A soft knock sounded on the door. Dexter

strode in.

"Thought I'd have a check to see how she is doing before I turn in, Guv."

He stood in silence, watching Bren Kern as she lay frail and pale on the hospital bed. His face was red and his eyes were large and glistening.

Fenella leaned close and whispered in Bren's ear. "When you are well, I will take your statement, pet. Tell me what happened so I can make sure Jack Parkes never gets out. Like I say, the name's Fenella. Ask for me when you wake up."

She stood and turned to Dexter. "The doctor says she'll be fine physically."

"Aye, Guv," Dexter replied. "Reckon the doc is right."

Bren stirred. Fenella's whole body went cold as she watched the girl's lips move. She let out a soft moan but didn't open her eyes. Then she became still.

Dexter's face scrunched up. "That Jack Parkes was a real bugger. The forensic team found a burner phone hidden on his bookshelf. We'll have confirmation it was the phone used to call you by Monday."

Fenella said, "I don't suppose we'll need it. The man is singing like a wren now he is behind bars. Every little helps, though." She gestured toward the door. "Let's leave our Bren in peace, eh? She'll need her strength for the days to come."

Even if she recovered physically, Fenella knew that nothing would ever be the same again for Bren

Kern. They left the room as the medical device let out another rhythmic beep.

CHAPTER 79

The thin woman with the bleached blonde hair and wide chin leaned back in the green armchair and stared for a long moment at the brown stained tiles on the ceiling. "Sloane, these sessions are so helpful. I can't tell you how much better I feel after our talks."

On an ordinary day, Sloane would have smiled, even thanked her client for such kind remarks. But she'd barely got a wink of sleep, spent hours at the police station then the hospital at the bedside of Bren. She'd stumbled into her office five minutes ahead of her first patient, tired but clear-headed.

"It is as though you have a magic wand," the woman said. "I mean, the way you have me think about my rage it is… well, so comforting."

Any normal person would have taken a few days off. Sloane couldn't afford to do that. Not now the wedding with Jack Parkes was off the table. It seemed the man's lifestyle was a sham paid for by… unspeakable acts. The police had only scratched the surface of his depravity. She knew it went deeper. For God's sake, he was willing to sacrifice her child. More revelations would come with time. She wondered about his first wife, Ester; knew in her heart he'd killed her. No crystals required. He'd admit to it in the end. He'd admit to everything and relish telling his story. That was Jack Parkes for you.

"The thing is," the woman said, "when I leave here, your magic seems to... go puff."

"Sorry?" Sloane said, only now hearing the words. "What goes puff?"

"Your magic." The woman rested a slim hand on her broad chin. "I mean, in here I am as calm as a pond. It's when I'm out there that the problem begins. I wish I could carry you around on my shoulder and have you whisper your soothing anger management techniques in my ear whenever I am close to losing it."

The woman laughed. The cackle of crows, fighting at dawn.

Sloane, aware of her lack of interest, smiled. It made them think you were engaged in what they had to say. And she needed every client to think that now she didn't have Jack. Her mind drifted to the bills which swept like an avalanche over her life.

"Alas, I don't think I will fit on your shoulder, despite my latest diet," Sloane replied in her mock cheerful voice.

The woman grinned. A set of pearly white teeth. "When I get totally blotto the anger goes, but that's not practical, is it?" Again the woman laughed. Again came the cackle of crows. "They'd smell it when I showed up at the Women's Institute. And I can't go about whiffing of booze when I have the vicar over for tea. Do you have any suggestions, then?"

Sloane leaned her elbows on the desk and cradled her chin. "How bad does it get?"

"Terrible. Sometimes I feel ready to explode."

"I see."

"That I might punch someone." The woman made a fist and swung it in a wild haymaker. "The vicar, right on the bloody nose."

"That's bad."

"But when I come here, I'm like a pond."

"That's what you said."

"So, what can I do?"

Sloane nodded and felt a knot in her chest. "I have a little something that is only for my regular patients who need an extra boost."

Her hand slid to the desk drawer. It opened silently. She pulled out a small bag of white pills. Twenty-five percent with Ria Leigh was better than nothing with Jack Parkes. Her business was her cub now. She had to protect it like a mother bear.

Sloane said, "There is an additional charge, but I'm sure we can work out an arrangement."

"Oh yes," the woman said. "They are exactly what I need."

"Very good," Sloane replied with a wide smile. "Now, let's talk price."

Sloane Kern had got away with her double set of books for years. Now with police protection in the form of Ria Leigh, she'd get away with drug dealing. How the hell would she ever be caught?

CHAPTER 80

The following Monday, Fenella arrived at the office while the town of Port St Giles was bathed in dark. There was a pile of forms to deal with and her ears still ached from the loud music at the Tarns Dub Music Festival.

When Priscilla came on stage, she'd cheered with Dexter, Jones and Nan until her ears hurt. She didn't think a backing singer had ever been welcomed with such a roar. And the music was perfect, not Aretha, some band she'd never heard of which mixed classic soul with an up-tempo modern beat.

After a long sip of tea from her mug, Fenella began to shuffle through the stack of forms, main lights off, desk lamp on. No moths. She was ten minutes into the pile when a knock sounded on the door. It opened an instant later as Dexter strolled in.

He wore his usual crumpled suit that could do with a steam and iron, but it was his expression that put Fenella on high alert. He'd made up his mind about what he was going to do. Travel the world with Priscilla, seeing sights and sounds he'd only ever get to experience through the telly and pages of a glossy magazine, or stay in Port St Giles and plod on. What would she do? It didn't matter.

Dexter said, "Morning, Guv."

"Bit early for you," she replied.

"Thought I'd get in ahead of the crowd and have a quiet chat with you."

"Oh, aye. What about?" As if she didn't know.

"The pain's gone." Dexter rubbed his side. "Thought I'd have to see the doc."

"Go anyway."

"Aye, that's what my Priscilla says." He squinted. "Been thinking."

"I hear it is good for the brain cells."

Dexter laughed. "Talking of grey matter, at least we know what happened to the man with the devil's wisp beard." He cracked his knuckles. "And who'd have thought the bugger could have crawled down a coal chute and escaped through those half-pint barrel doors?"

"We got him on CCTV," Fenella pointed out. "Run's damn fast for a short bloke."

"Pity the picture was so blurry, Guv. If Seth Scroop had invested in a better camera, we'd have had a nice shot of the bloke. As it is, he looks more like a ghost. It was him all right, though."

They'd found the hatch behind the cracked mirror on the cellar wall. Not big enough for a full-grown man to squeeze through, but a child-sized man was a different kettle of fish. Fenella sensed it wouldn't be the last time she crossed paths with the devil's wisp. Next time she'd be ready.

"Took a bit of a chance with that warrant,

didn't you, Guv?"

"Aye, but I knew Alf and Stacy Bird were up to no good, and with that poultry smell in the cellar, it didn't take much to piece it together."

Another knock at the door. Fenella glanced at the wall clock; it wasn't yet seven.

Jones came in with a small cup of coffee in his hand. "Boss, thought I'd find you here."

"You are not the only one," Fenella replied. "Why don't you flip the switch so we can have ceiling lights? No point in us all standing around in the glow of the desk lamp. We are not moths."

Jones flipped the switch, bathing the room in white light.

"I found something else about Mick Knowles," Jones said, his chest slightly puffed out. "The arresting officer was Ria Leigh."

"Is that a fact?" Fenella stood and began to pace. "So, little Miss Wonder was the one who fingered our Micky, eh? And he was sent down for what, five years?"

"That's right, boss," Jones replied. He flashed a dazzling smile. "That woman is something special, isn't she? Oh, and that third set of fingerprints on the Gold Kite. I don't suppose we'll need them now, but they belong to Sloane Kern. Seems she got into a bit of bother a while back. Swung for a doctor. No charges, but her fingerprints were on file."

"Oh Aye," Fenella said, thinking. "I'll look into that."

She didn't get very long to think about the

matter as the door flew open. Superintendent Jeffery marched in, arms swinging at her side.

Dexter and Jones headed for the door. Fenella wanted to follow.

Jeffery said, "Ah! Just the people I'm looking for. I knew if I came in early, I'd catch the busy bees in their hive."

Jeffery laughed, nodding her head as though encouraging everyone to join in. It took a moment for her to realise her merry solo cackle sounded rather thin in the confined walls of the small room. She cleared her throat. "I've news," she said, looking about, head still nodding. "Good news."

Dexter let out a groan. With the skill of a ventriloquist, it sounded as though it came from Jones.

"What was that, Detective Constable Jones?" Jeffery asked.

Dexter grinned. Jones looked horrified and made a series of muttering sounds that eventually morphed into words. "Coffee went down the wrong way, ma'am." Jones thudded his chest. "Much better now."

Jeffery's lips curved down at the corners. She turned to Fenella. "Your team is a detective down."

"Been that way for months, ma'am," Fenella replied.

"Well, no more. We have a replacement. Detective Sergeant Ria Leigh has applied for a transfer."

"But she's regional," Dexter said. "Why would

she want to work local?"

"It is quite natural," Jeffery replied. "Officers are fleeing the regional crime squad like flies. It's all down to leadership. Poor leadership on their part and a recognition of the well-run ship I have here. This is a major win for me... us. A major win."

"When is she coming?" Jones asked, unable to hide the joy in his voice. "A couple of months, I suppose?"

Jeffery flashed a wolfish smile. "I've already been on the phone to Chief Inspector Rae about her move. I've short-circuited the usual procedures. Detective Leigh will begin work with us in a month. She'll retain some responsibilities in Whitehaven but will be located here. Jones, I'd like you to help her settle into the station. I've some thoughts about how best to do that. Join me in my office now."

And with that, Jeffery spun on her heels and marched from the room with Jones running behind.

Dexter closed the door and trudged to the desk. He eased into the chair, rubbed his chin and looked at Fenella.

"You've decided about New York City?" she said, swallowing the lump in her throat.

"Aye, Guv. I have."

The Detective Inspector Fenella Sallow series continues with Hollowed Bones.

AFTERWORD

If you have enjoyed this story, please consider leaving a short review. Reviews help readers like you discover books they will enjoy, and help indie authors like me improve our stories.

Details of my other novels can be found in the store where you obtained this book.

Until next time,

N.C. Lewis

PS. Be the first to hear about new releases by joining my **Readers Newsletter or visit** https://bit.ly/NCLewis.

Printed in Great Britain
by Amazon